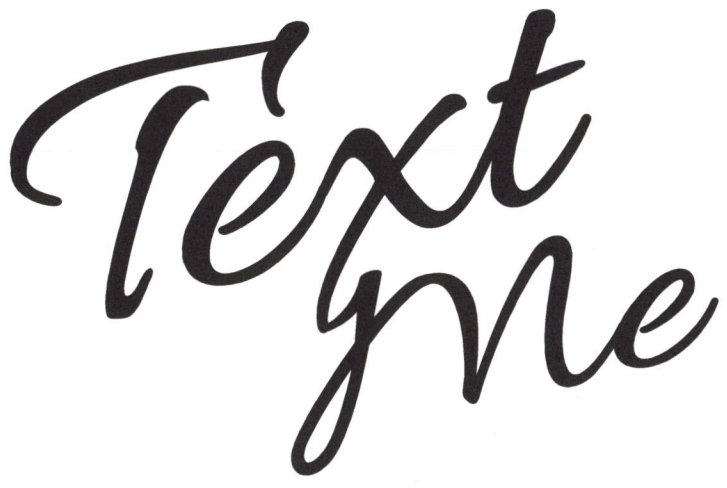

Text me

Shelley K. Wall
author of *The Designated Drivers' Club*
and *Bring It On*

CRIMSON
ROMANCE
F+W Media, Inc.

Copyright © 2014 by Shelley K. Wall.
All rights reserved.

This book, or parts thereof, may not be reproduced in any form without permission from the publisher; exceptions are made for brief excerpts used in published reviews.

Published by
Crimson Romance
an imprint of F+W Media, Inc.
10151 Carver Road, Suite 200
Blue Ash, OH 45242. U.S.A.
www.crimsonromance.com

ISBN 10: 1-4405-8384-6
ISBN 13: 978-1-4405-8384-1
eISBN 10: 1-4405-8385-4
eISBN 13: 978-1-4405-8385-8

This is a work of fiction. Names, characters, corporations, institutions, organizations, events, or locales in this novel are either the product of the author's imagination or, if real, used fictitiously. The resemblance of any character to actual persons (living or dead) is entirely coincidental.

Cover art © 123RF/Andriy Popov

To my husband, Stan, for supporting all my dreams and desires throughout our years together. You are my inspiration, my kick-in-the-ass, and the source of my laughter and joy. I look forward to the next years.

And to my children, Tyler, Kyle, and Grace—never fear change or failure, fear only inaction. Those who do as much as they can in life will leave this world knowing great satisfaction. And perhaps a little exhaustion.

Acknowledgments

Thank you to all at Crimson Romance for seeing a spark in this series and helping bring it to publication. Thank you to good friends, Cindy and Megan, for helping me read, edit, and revise. Thank you to Dawn Dowdle of Blue Ridge Literary Agency for taking an interest in me personally and helping to develop my craft. I have learned a great deal from you.

Lastly, and most importantly, thank you to every reader who has purchased a book with my name on it and taken the time to delve in and read. You have my sincere appreciation if you also post a review. Without you, I would not be able to continue pursuing the projects of my dreams. I wish you great success in all your aspirations and goals.

Happy reading.

Chapter One

Carter Coben arrived home after a grueling day at work and dropped his keys on the counter. He reached for a beer, then remembered his neighbor's dog, and grabbed a bottle of water instead. A quick glance at his watch showed enough time to get Ruckus to the park before dinner. Carter had no idea why he'd volunteered to help walk the dog while Maddie recovered from surgery. Maybe because there wasn't another tenant nearby who'd think to offer?

He retrieved the keys, stepped back out of his apartment, and trudged to Maddie's place. He rapped the keys against the door and announced himself before turning one of them in the lock, knowing she wouldn't—couldn't—answer.

"Hey, Maddie, it's me."

Crash. The tinkle of glass breaking surprised him only mildly. Without much exercise, the beast was bound to break something.

Drool flew from the massive boxer/mastiff mix's mouth and plastered the hallway as he surged toward Carter.

"Jesus, Carter, watch out! He's wound tighter than a drum today," Maddie called from the next room. Her high-pitched squeak of a voice always startled Carter, mainly because the voice didn't match her appearance. She wasn't a small woman. Her German ancestry shone through in the tall and equally hefty stature. Which probably explained the size of the dog.

"Hey, Ruckus." The dog pinned him to the wall, and he rubbed between his floppy ears, staggering under the weight of his paws on his chest. "You ready to go outside, boy?"

Another string of drool threatened to land on his pants. Pushing the animal away, he peeked in on Maddie briefly before leashing Ruckus and heading to the park.

Half an hour later, Carter's patience was shot. If Ruckus didn't hurry up and get busy, he was giving up. The mutt had already watered every piece of grass in the park and only needed to take a dump. Normally the digestive reluctance wouldn't bother Carter, but he was *not* skipping his dinner plans with his girlfriend, Amanda. He sat on a rock and flipped his smartphone open to the message onscreen.

> App installed, do you want to open now?

It had been a crazy idea to try Justchat now. It was a crazy idea suggested by his friend Roger, which should have been reason enough to trash it, but the idea of chatting with someone anonymously sounded—easy. God knows he needed easy at the moment.

"Sure, why not?" He clicked and made up a login and password. The lengthy questionnaire that followed almost drove him to exit. Why should they need his life history for anonymous chatting? When he finally received a "Congratulations and happy chatting!" message, there was a tiny disclaimer at the bottom of the screen that probably should have been attached to the first question.

> We try to pair our members with people of similar interests and locale. Feel free to skip any questions you wish but answering helps us find better chatting friendships for you.

He stared at the open dialogue box. What would be a good way to start? Should he quote someone? Hell, no. The only quotes in his head were too obscene to get a response from anyone worth talking with. Politics or religion? Nah, that could get ugly. He shrugged and began clicking away on the letters.

> For years, I've wondered if there's really anyone out there worth meeting. I mean, I see people once in a while … and I think they're interesting. Then they're gone and the moment escapes me. My life is filled with escaped moments that I never seem to grasp until I've missed them. Does anyone else feel that way?

It was a little dumb but fit his mood. He really should think hard about what he'd written since he planned to jump into a long-term commitment in a couple hours. Sure, most people wouldn't consider season tickets a commitment, but for him, it meant consistency. Going to the same event with the same person regularly. Over and over again. Hmmm.

He dragged his fingers through his hair and caught a quick glimpse of *the running chick*. He laughed.

Now he remembered why he'd volunteered to walk Ruckus. Her. He'd seen her run in the park every night after work. Sometimes he'd been out for a few miles himself. Others he had just been with Maddie as she focused on her struggles with Ruckus and the boot on her foot. The girl always smiled and waved, even said "hi" to Maddie, and petted the mutt. Never a word his way, though.

He had wanted to meet her ages ago—before Amanda. And he wasn't above using the damn dog to do so. She passed and the air stirred. Maybe he wasn't all that wrapped up in Amanda after all. He couldn't decide. Most runners bounced or plodded. Not this girl. In her running pants and tight jacket, the only description that came to mind was *glide*. Yeah, she glided across the ground in an effortless stride that was so smooth it mesmerized. She giggled at her phone as she passed.

Carter's phone dinged a response and he glanced at the screen. A message from *She Hearts Dogs*. How appropriate considering his legs were almost completely wrapped in a leash at the moment.

I know what you mean! For me, it's like I never know what to say before it's too late and the opportunity is gone. Then you want to kick yourself for not coming up with something really witty or interesting and not completely moronic.

Yes, that's exactly what it felt like. Ruckus yanked on the end of the leash and charged after the runner. Carter lifted his legs just as the leather tore loose from his fingers. "Shit." He'd been busy reading the message and hadn't bothered to grip the leash. The dog was bounding straight toward—

The bloodcurdling scream surprised everyone in the park except him. He saw it coming. That was what happened when you wore earphones, turned your music up high while texting, and got attacked by an overly-friendly beast from behind.

When he'd noticed her before, this wasn't exactly the type of meeting Carter had intended. She lay on the ground, blinking at the sky and Ruckus, while struggling to right herself.

The drool didn't help. What the hell was he thinking when he let go of the leash? Oh, right. He wasn't. He himself was drooling. Only Ruckus's slobber was close to landing right on her face. The tendril of spit strung lower and lower.

"Ruckus! Come." The dog turned his way just as Carter lunged and grabbed his collar. *Whew.* The slime dripped to the grass and he yanked him off. "I'm so sorry. He pulled the leash from my fingers before I could stop him. Are you all right? Did he hurt you?"

Running Chick sat up and squinted, blinded by the setting sun at his back. She gulped in air and opened her mouth to speak but said nothing. She sucked in air again and held up a finger.

Carter thrust his bottle of water down. "Here. Drink. It'll help you get your wind back. Can you stand?"

When she took the bottle, he opened his fingers to assist her. She remained silent. Hmmm. He'd never been within fifteen feet of Running Chick before. He and Jackson had made jokes she was probably ugly up close. Actually, Jackson made all the jokes. Missing teeth. Hairy moles. Cross-eyed.

Wrong. Wrong. Wrong.

Seriously wrong, in fact, and somehow that was a surprise. It was hard not to notice when she sucked in another gulp of air, forced a smile, and handed back the water. She was better than he'd thought. Sooo much better. Carter blinked and averted his eyes to the dog. *You have a girlfriend, remember?*

"I'm fine. Just got the wind knocked out of me. Don't worry about it." Great. Even her voice was nice. Unlike Maddie's, it sort of rolled out of her mouth. Nothing obnoxious about it. "You wanted to play, didn't you, Ruckus? Ol' Maddie knew what she was doing when she named you, huh? You sure know how to cause one." She leaned down and patted the dog then brushed leaves from her back. Should he tell her about the two mud spots on her butt?

Probably not.

"Isn't that the truth. You sure you don't need some help?" Should he be totally embarrassed or thrilled? It had taken four months to get this intro. Since before Amanda—the girlfriend he was about to take to dinner to celebrate their three months together. Maybe he should have thought of the dog before.

He glanced at the time. "Oh crap. I need to get going, sorry. Can I help you get anywhere? Walk you home, bandage your knee, uh, strangle the dog?" *Check for broken bones?* He shook that thought out of his head.

She laughed. "No. Seriously. I'm okay. Go. Get to your date." She waved him off and jogged away before he could say another word.

Text Me

• • •

Two hours later, Carter pulled at the collar of his shirt and tried to ignore the jitters in his fingers. He was about to make the first long-term commitment of his life and it scared the shit out of him. Was it normal to be concerned? He thumbed a quick text while he waited for Amanda to show.

> Hope ur right about tickets.

Between Carter's workload and his friend Jackson's busy travel schedule, he hadn't seen the man in a couple weeks and texting was their only communication. Hell, he hardly had time to see Amanda. Work always intruded, and he was damn good at his job. Industrial Project Management hadn't been the path he intended but it worked out fine and he was a kick-ass professional. His new boss apparently agreed because he was scheduled to go on four trips to Thailand over the course of the following year. Four trips for what amounted to a four million dollar project. A good feather in his cap, and hopefully a big bonus in his bank account. Thank God the job change had worked out. Getting fired over a crazy woman's temper tantrum wasn't easy to digest, especially when he'd never had a chance to resolve her mistaken assumption.

He needed the money sorely. When his dad died, he'd taken over much of the finances for his mom. Based on what he'd seen the past months, she was in dire straits, not to mention bad health. He'd tried to convince her to sell the house and stay with him for a while, but she refused.

He dropped his phone face up on the table and peered out the Starbucks window at the people walking by, none of whom were Amanda. It had been a dreary day, but meeting her was sure to brighten it. Actually, the entire week had been dismal, for March in Texas.

Ding.

He glanced down as a message appeared.

If she not like, u can take me.

He smirked and keyed a response as the door flew open and Amanda breezed in. She was beautiful, and it always caught him off guard. Too beautiful for him, if he were honest. He never quite understood what caught her eye, and he hardly blamed her when she often seemed disinterested. Which was happening more often lately—maybe that was the way things went in a committed relationship. Everything was going well for the moment, and he was simply glad to be with her. It was hard to believe he'd lasted more than a few dates. He'd come a long way on the trust scale and he was proud that he'd given it a chance.

He stood, pecked her cheek—mainly because she turned just before he reached her lips—and smiled. "Happy three month anniversary."

Amanda smiled and went through the order line before dropping into her seat. The gift sat on the table between them in a white envelope tied with a red ribbon. He had never been much for wrapping things but added the dash of color as a last minute whim. He was proud of the results of his effort.

Her eyes twinkled as she stared at the slim package. In fact, he was pretty sure there was a drop of water gathering in the corner of her eyelid. *Aw, she's getting all sentimental.*

Good, he was on a roll. Wait until she saw them.

"You bought a gift?" Her eyebrows dipped and her voice was stark, entirely void of the elation he'd expected … the first indication something didn't fit.

"Of course. We're going to celebrate. I made reservations for dinner at Sotby's down the street." Carter kept his voice cheerful but, deep down, his gut had started to turn. She seemed ... apprehensive.

The crowds clip-clopped past on the sidewalk, but at his table, time stood still. Music blared overhead, crooning at them to "cha-a-ange the world." Ironic, if he thought about it too much.

Her face solemn, Amanda slipped a finger under the ribbon and drew it off before opening the gift. She didn't pull the tickets out; she just slid the envelope open and peered inside. A shiver went down Carter's spine.

Someone behind the counter announced the arrival of a cinnamon mocha latte. Amanda dropped the envelope, rose from the booth, and retrieved her drink. She slowly doused the beverage with condiments before stirring it with a stick and returning. Coffee steam wafted toward him.

Ding.

Carter glanced at the phone.

> She seen them yet? What she say?

"You bought me baseball tickets?" She plopped back in her seat. Across from him. He should have noticed that earlier. Not next to him in the booth.

"Yeah, season tickets. We can go to all the games. It'll be fun."

"Season baseball tickets together." There was no smile, no gazing in his eyes in response to his incredible thoughtfulness and commitment. Yes, commitment. Season tickets meant he intended to take her to *all* the games. That was commitment, right?

Ding.

This time her eyes also went to his phone and the message.

> Well?

"To the Astros," Carter explained.

"Yeah, I saw that." She took a sip of the latte.

"You don't like them. I thought you said you love baseball. You watched all those games like a true fan," Carter said as she pushed the envelope toward him and shook her head. Had he really misread her that badly? Should he have listened to his idiot friend?

"It's not that. It's just—I can't do this, Carter. I mean, I like you—"

Ding.

She frowned at his phone display.

Come on, tell me.

Carter chose not to respond to the message. "But…" There was a *but* phrase coming next so he offered the word. Silently he cursed Jackson for the stupid ticket idea.

"This just isn't working for me. I'm sorry."

Ding.

Before he could see the screen, she plucked the phone from the table and flung it to the floor, where the screen shattered like a broken mirror. He didn't even get a chance to read the message. Then she rose and left. That was it?

His mouth dropped open and he stared after her. *Why?*

Carter scraped the pieces of his phone from the floor and dropped them in his pocket. He snatched up the envelope and ran behind her.

"You're breaking up with me because of the tickets?" The light turned and she stepped into the street.

She walked faster and flung an answer over her shoulder. "No, I'm breaking up with you because I met someone else."

Oh. Carter stopped and stared. She raced away then turned the next corner and disappeared. He pulled the mass of electronic debris from his pocket and cursed. His phone agreement still had six months left, and the only way he'd be able to replace it was—if it were destroyed. Now *that* was a commitment, a long-term phone agreement. Which he hadn't been all that satisfied with anyway.

"I was kind of hoping I could get an upgrade." He stuck his hands in his pockets and headed down the street to the phone store. An odd calmness settled across his shoulders. Why was he numb to the rejection? He had no idea. Maybe Jackson was right—commitment just wasn't his thing.

Chapter Two

Still in her running gear, Abigail Jeffries flicked the switch to light up the sign over the new store door. She stepped outside and turned to give appropriate admiration. Her own shop, with a lighted sign over the door, and tomorrow it was open! She wanted to hug herself but instead dropped hands to her hips and nodded at the words "Jeffries Florist." Bright red had been a good choice. The lights certainly got attention. God knows the drab brick needed a boost. She wished she could call home and share the excitement.

"You're going to catch a cold if you keep standing out here admiring that sign." Her friend and top employee-slash-partner, Caroline, peeked her head out the door then retreated.

"I can't believe it's mine. Ours." Abby closeted the touch of bittersweet victory and followed her in before twisting the door lock.

Caroline shrugged. "It is. And so is the life-long debt associated with it."

"Not life-long. Just a ten-year loan. We'll pay it off in no time." She silently thanked the decision to cash in her company investment plan when she'd left her old job managing new store openings for her family's retail business. Her parents still hadn't gotten over the betrayal to their business heritage. She was the only one that hadn't followed the flock. Still, after the big blow-up meeting, her heart wasn't in it. The money cut her loan down significantly. Of course, it was also the only thing standing between her and destitution if the store failed.

Losing everything was a little scary but losing her mind to that job had seemed worse. Abby shuddered, thinking about the meeting that had led to her decision. It had been a harried week at the office. Her dad had delegated one of their biggest new projects, the opening of ten new stores, to her. She wasn't ready and she knew it. Still, he'd assured her she would get whatever support she needed from the real estate development contractors.

Yeah, right. What a group of dirtbags *they* were.

At the initial meeting, she'd started off by introducing herself. She was so nervous she'd forgotten to let them do the same and later had to ask each man's first name.

Halfway into the details, one of them kept interrupting. She tried to rein the group back in but he just kept asking her personal questions and it was—creepy. Why did the guy care whether she was old enough to run a project of this type? Why did he keep alluding to her "boyfriend" or "husband"? Was he fishing? Then he made the casual remark that they'd be going out for drinks after work and wanted her to meet them.

She'd ignored the questions up to that point, but that one came off as if—the guy was hitting on her. Right in front of the entire team, on a conference call, no less. The hair on the back of her neck had risen. "No, I will *not* meet you for drinks, nor does it make one iota of difference if my "boyfriend" or "husband" is concerned about the time on this project since I currently have neither. *However*, right now what I actually *do need* is a real estate contractor that I can trust to do this project without taking this to a personal level. Someone that isn't always chasing skirts or trying to sleep with the boss, secretary, or house-cleaning crew. That obviously *isn't* you so this meeting is over."

A strained silence filled the space between each side of the call. Abby had waited for a response and right about the time she'd given up, one of the other voices spoke. "So, you're one of the power-hungry bitches that rips a man's heart out personally *and* professionally. What next? You send him packing or you just disappear? Isn't that the way your type does things?"

What the hell? Who had the balls to say *that*? She hit the end button on the conference phone and steamed away from the meeting. Her brother, father, and one of the staff sat with their mouths agape, watching her leave.

When her dad tried to talk her into making nice with them in order to get the project back on track, she refused. Instead, she packed up her office and left. She'd planned to do it for some time. That meeting just nailed the coffin in her corporate career.

It wasn't until later that she'd learned the company fired the guy who'd made the last statement. They apologized to her dad. Maybe they would have done so with her, too, but she was already gone.

Badeep deep.

Abby's phone signaled a text message from the depths of her purse, lodged under the sales area. She reached behind the ornate filigreed wood of the counter and pulled the phone up to view the message.

> She broke up, idiot. Tickets shit idea.

"What is it?" Caroline asked.

Abby shook her head. "Someone apparently has the wrong number." She held up the screen for her to read.

"So, it's a text message, not that Justchat app? Jesus, Abby, you need to cut back on the social media."

"I know, I know. Yes, it's a text message."

Caroline squinted at the display. "Oh! Poor guy. He should have bought her flowers."

Abby grinned. "Yeah, flowers from us. Wait! He still could."

Caroline flipped a light switch near the door. "Do you even know who that is?"

"No, but judging by the area code, he's local." She held the phone up and tapped in a message.

Sorry. U should have bought flowers.

She hovered a finger over the send button, hesitant to deceive the poor guy.

Caroline pressed a finger over hers and the message was gone, sent over the airwaves to a poor schmuck that needed to make good with his girl.

Badeep deep.

Right. What was *I thinking*? Listened to u, so obviously I wasn't. Guess I'm still a little chapped about the work thing.

Caroline peered over Abby's shoulder then yanked the phone away and tapped in a response before handing it back.

Har Har. Still could. New flower shop on main by PD

Abby punched Caroline on the arm and grabbed her purse. "You're shameless." She dropped the phone into it and pushed Caroline toward the door. "Let's get out of here. We've got a big day ahead tomorrow, and I really need a shower."

Caroline pinched her nose. "You *are* a little ripe. Have you told your family about the store opening? Are they coming?"

"I sent them one of the flyers we mailed out. They know, but they don't usually have time for these shindigs."

Abby had managed to hide the disappointment all day, but if they stayed much longer, she was sure to break down. The pain in her leg from her encounter with Ruckus served to muffle the more intense pain in her ego. None of her family had called with well wishes. Not one out of the six. Her new business—her new world—meant nothing to them. They were probably all still mad at her for quitting.

Her purse beeped several times on the drive home, but she ignored it. She should stop pretending with this guy. It was cruel. Whoever he thought she was, she needed to set him straight when she got out of the car.

But there were three more messages. Reading through them, her stomach clenched.

First message:

> What's a PD?

Second message:

> U have to go to games with me. She probably hated Astros. Should have seen it coming.

Third message:

> The real pisser. I made reservs at 8 for Sotby's. U know how hard to get? Screw her, I'm going. Wanna go?

Uh-oh. Now what? Abby wiped her thumb across the screen, as if to clear the message, or perhaps clarify it. Should she answer? He was going to expect someone to show up. It would be unconscionable not to set the poor guy straight. He'd sit there alone at that nice, expensive restaurant, the restaurant she'd never been to and probably never would because she couldn't afford it. *She* had no boyfriend to buy her tickets and take her there.

She'd regret her next step ... but she took it anyway.

> PD = Police Department. Sure. Meet you there.

She had lost her mind.

Chapter Three

"Now what?" Carter growled as his phone started ringing. He glanced at the display on his new phone and cursed himself for not backing up his contacts the past several months. Not only was he now *sans girlfriend* but he had lost every phone number he'd accumulated. Business *and* personal. He'd managed to copy the numbers for Jackson and a few others from his buddy Roger while at the office, but the number displayed matched none of those. "Thanks, Amanda."

He might not have a clue who was calling, but at least the phone was cool.

He let it go to voice mail; he'd deal with recovering everything tomorrow. He was going to dinner at Sotby's and, by God, he'd have a good time. It had taken three weeks to get the reservation and he wasn't about to let it go to waste. Besides, he needed to eat.

An hour later, he lounged at the bar of Sotby's, awaiting his table. He was a few minutes early and his reservation wouldn't be ready for at least thirty. A good thing because Jackson hadn't shown yet. Garlic, cilantro, and, oddly, lavender overpowered him. The deep mahogany finishes in the restaurant and the bright cheerful colors of the upholstery were elegant. It had been finished off with neon lighting tucked into various portions of the woodwork. The lighting cast a warm yet subtle glow in the room that enhanced the romantic atmosphere. Add the jazz music to the background that promised a night to remember and it would have been the perfect place for a celebration. *Would have been* being the key phrase. Now it was just an expensive place to eat and bullshit with Jackson.

"Got any Band-Aids? I lost a battle with a small horse today and have a hellacious scrape and bruise on my leg." From nowhere a leg was pushed into his line of view, shoved against his thigh. It wasn't the tiny bruise that caught his attention.

Her. Running Chick. Was she one of those lucky rich people who managed to eat here frequently? He couldn't contain the grin that swelled. If there was a God up there watching, Jackson would be delayed—indefinitely.

"Would a napkin work?" He held up the black cloth. "I'm really sorry about that. I had no idea he'd bolt after you. He's not mine—"

She waved off the napkin. "I know. I know. He's your neighbor's. Maddie told me she was going to have someone walk him while she recovered from the surgery. I expected some old miserly woman. Not you."

"She described me like that?"

Man, he really liked her laugh. Listening to it was like eating candy. You didn't want to stop. She must be meeting someone; she glanced around the room and then leveled on him. "No, not at all. I just, I don't know, jumped to conclusions, I guess. You're eating here tonight?"

"Yeah, meeting a friend. He hasn't shown yet."

"Me too. Although, I don't really know what he looks like." The door blasted open and she glanced nervously at the person entering until he was followed by a lady who seemed permanently attached to his hand. "How is Maddie, by the way? That foot thing sure turned into a big deal. Who would have thought? It's nice of you to help out."

Carter hadn't quite understood what the surgery on Maddie's foot had been, or why it handicapped her so extensively. A broken bone would be easily mended and less painful. Perhaps Maddie had low pain tolerance? "She's irritated as hell about being cooped up, but who can blame her. You're on a blind date?" He threw that last part in to make it sound casual. Would she notice?

She pulled off her jacket and threw it over her arm. "Um, sort of. You eat here a lot?"

He shook his head. *I wish.* "My first time. You?"

"Same here."

He had never seen her with her hair down. Nice. Black-ish, straight, and hugging her cheekbones like it loved being there. Normally, it was in a ponytail. The bartender moved nearer and rather than miss the chance, Carter held up a couple of fingers.

"What can I get you?" he asked Running Chick. "Wine? Daiquiri? Beer?" He wanted to text Jackson and tell him to take his time, but that would be rude. Rude to her—he didn't really care about Jackson. Only a loser texted someone when they were with a woman.

The fact he thought so brought a small amount of clarity to his breakup. He'd thought he was giving his all with Amanda and learning to trust. But he hadn't exactly followed his no-texting-while-with-a-woman rule … Had he simply been a loser, after all?

"Wine, any red is fine. Or maybe white. Wait, what's that?" She pointed to a glass in front of a lady at the other end of the bar. Frothy clear bubbles with green leaves and limes floating within.

"Mojito, I think."

"I'll take that." She pointed at the drink and held out a card to the bartender.

Carter pushed her hand down, surprised by the warmth of it. "Oh, no, you don't. It's the least I can do since I nearly put you in the hospital."

The noise in the bar was a gentle rumble; it would be bad form to be rowdy in a place like this. Or at least he assumed as much. He didn't know. He fit the place about as well as a glove on a foot. Overhead, jazz music, soft and sexy in a sleepy sort of way, wafted by. Perfect for elegant dining, good discussion—or great sex. Not that he was anywhere close to that, at the moment. In fact, he was probably in for a dry spell.

"Tell me about this blind date. Where'd you find him?" Was she doing the internet dating thing?

"Um, I didn't really. He's sort of a friend of a friend and just went through a breakup, I think."

He grunted. "Welcome to the club."

"You too?"

"Yeah, but it actually worked out pretty well. I got a new phone out of it. I've wanted one for a few months but couldn't trade up until my contract was due." He waved the phone back and forth. One of the new models with a larger screen, more memory, voice activation, and a high-resolution camera.

Her eyes lit up. "Oh, I've wanted one of those too! How does breaking up equate to a new phone? You weren't on her plan, were you?"

Uh-oh. No, that would mean it was long term and he was some sort of boy-toy jerk—the kind that had women pay his bills.

"Of course not. We only dated a few months. She threw my phone on the floor when she told me she'd met someone else. Not sure why *that* was my fault but, oh well." Okay, maybe the fact that he'd spent as much time texting as talking in Amanda's presence should have been a clue to his level of commitment. Was his social media usage why she'd looked elsewhere for attention?

"Good riddance." She held up the mojito the bartender had slipped in front of them and clinked his glass.

"Good riddance."

She wore pink polish on her nails.

"So, what does this guy look like? I'll help you find him." Carter surveyed the room, searching for singles, of which there were none.

"I don't know."

"Seriously? You have a blind date with someone and don't know what he looks like? Do you have his name?"

"Not exactly. I guess this wasn't very well thought out. To be honest, it was a last minute thing. I just kind of—caved. I thought he'd need cheering up. I know. Stupid, right?"

He wasn't going to say that, but he wondered if she really intended to meet the guy. Not that he cared.

"Not really. His loss, my gain." Okay, that was a cheesy thing to say.

"What about you? Where's your date?"

"Not a date. A buddy. He's supposed to meet me here. I'm a little early." He checked his watch. Fifteen minutes late. Odd for Jackson. Not that he'd complain. He'd rather talk to Running Chick. He held out a hand. "I'm Carter, Carter Coben."

She clasped his fingers in hers and he held tight. "Abigail Jeffries."

He ordered more drinks and took a sip, then searched the room for Jackson. If he didn't show pretty soon …

The maître d' tapped him lightly on the arm. "Your table is ready, Mr. Coben."

Carter whirled around, glass in hand. *Okay, make a move. Here's my chance. The one I waited four months to get it … and it took a dog to make it this far. If I wimp out now, I really am a dumbass.* He smiled at the serious face before him.

"Abigail, I really don't feel like sitting alone at a table for two." He took a sip of courage. "Why don't you join me? At least until one of the people we came here to meet shows up."

Seconds ticked. She could sit at the bar in this fancy place, talking to no one, and waiting—or she could be at a table with him. He doubted either option was what she'd planned, but option two was better than nothing, right?

"Okay, who wants to sit alone when everyone else is with someone?"

"Agreed."

"What a couple of losers we are." She stood and grabbed her bag and drink.

He shook his head. "Depends on how you look at it. *I* just traded up from an old friend that probably has forgotten all about this to one *really* gorgeous woman. Not exactly loser in my book." He touched a hand to her back to guide her after their host. The slinky fabric against his fingers tingled. The citrusy scent on her skin did other things to him.

Chapter Four

What is it about me that makes him feel comfortable telling me his girlfriend woes? Does that put me in the nice-to- talk-to-but-not-interested category? And why do all the good ones just see a buddy in me? Look at him, sitting there sipping his drink in his fancy clothes. He could model for *GQ*. Except for the fact most models were seriously lacking in personality and he had it in spades.

The waiter approached the table and asked for their order. She wasn't sure what to do.

Carter grinned and pointed at the parchment in front of her. "Go ahead."

She leaned forward and whispered, "But your friend will be here soon. Then what?"

He mirrored the move and lowered his voice. "Who cares? You snooze, you lose, right? Besides if—no, *when*—your date shows, you'll at least have your food on the way in case he turns out to be a real dork. Blind dates are awkward. This will just make it easier. And faster."

"Good point, but what if he's not a dork? What if he's awesome?"

"What if he has black teeth and hasn't taken a bath in days?"

Abby swallowed a giggle. "What if he has a six-pack to die for?"

"What if he looks like death, as in *The Night Stalker* or some other serial killer?"

"What if he has seriously killer bedroom eyes?"

"What if he has an STD?"

She rolled her eyes. "Maybe he's a male model … and he just says that to get rid of his annoying fans so we can be alone."

"Bedroom eyes. Male model. You like that kind of guy?"

"Hey, a successful model can make seriously big money and eat at places like this all the time."

"You're right—and give you fashion advice and shoe discounts. Maybe he'll date me instead."

She laughed, handed over the menu, and ordered. She knew she shouldn't say it, but—

"I get the impression this breakup hasn't really torn you up much, has it?"

The drink he'd gulped spewed from his mouth. "Why do you say that?"

"I don't know, you just don't seem all that sad, I guess."

His hair had a tendency to fall into his eyes and she squelched the urge to reach out and move the bangs so she could see them better. Only she was fairly sure direct contact with those eyes would be—yep, devastating. Damn. Whoever this girl was that ditched him, she was an idiot.

He shrugged. "Sadness is a waste of time. Who knows? Maybe I'll be seriously pissed tomorrow. I mean, I've been busy running over people with a dog—and meeting the same at a fancy restaurant. I'll have time to think about it later." Something about his eyes told her there *was* sadness, maybe it just hadn't hit yet.

There wasn't a single person in this joint without a date, except *them*. She wondered if his friend had ditched and if the guy she was looking for had chosen not to come … or was Carter *her* guy? No way. Not possible. No woman in her right mind would ditch this gorgeous piece of man. Dark, wispy hair that he obviously spent little time on, eyes that held a depth of intelligence, and the hint of dimples in his cheeks which alluded to a great laugh. No, Carter was a keeper. He couldn't possibly be the man she'd intended to meet. As if to confirm her speculation, her cell signaled a text message. She stuck her hand in her purse to check, then hesitated. *Nope. Rude. Just go with it.*

"Abs—"

"Abby." Not that she cared if he gave her a nickname. He could call her anything he wanted while he sat there looking all gorgeous and sexy.

"Sorry, Abby. I doubt you run for a living, so what do you do? You work around here?"

Yeah, she still basked in the glow of new ownership, and she couldn't contain the grin. "I just opened a flower shop down by the police station. We open tomorrow. We've spent the past couple of weeks stocking up and taking orders."

"Really? I actually hate flowers—they bring back a lot of shitty memories. Why a flower shop?"

He hates flowers? Who hates flowers? They smell wonderful, they're festive, they're great at attracting and keeping the right girl—

"I don't know. I spent the past four years working in Corporate America. I just wanted to get away from all the B.S. and have more control over my future. I have a horticulture degree. I had three choices: golf course, landscaping, or this. The first two would have been okay, but this seemed way more creative. While I was in college I had a couple of part time jobs. I worked for another shop for a while and did an internship at a landscape business. Loved that, but flowers are celebrative. The best moments of people's lives happen over flowers. Or plants."

"Yeah, hospital visits and … funerals."

"Okay, sadness too, but that's all part of life. What about weddings, dates, and anniversaries? I've been thinking about doing date packages too."

"Date packages? What does that mean? Here are your flowers and, oh, here's a date to go with it? Does that have anything to do with your interest in blind dates?" He had a mean little twinkle in his eye, which sent a jolt of nerves skittering down her spine.

She leaned over the table and slapped his arm. "Shut up. That would be an escort service and no, I'm not in *that* business. How many times does a guy want to take a girl somewhere really cool but doesn't have any idea where? Or maybe he just doesn't have the time to plan it all because he's busy. I think I could get some of the local businesses to give me discounted rates and I could include tickets and dinner with the flowers."

Their dinner arrived. There was still no sign of the people they were waiting on. She frowned at the door. "Your friend hasn't shown. You sure he had the right place and time?"

He picked up his knife and fork. "Your date appears to have blown you off too."

"Ouch."

He cut a piece of his steak, slipped it in his mouth, and closed his eyes. "Abby, if Jackson showed up right at this moment, I'd tell him to get lost. Why the hell would I want to eat with him? Look at you—much better date. Much better. Whoever this blind date of yours was, he's an idiot. Don't give him a second chance."

"How long have you known this friend you're meeting? Is he, like, a bestie?"

"Yep. I've known him since we were kids. And tonight he is officially a no-show. Eat." Carter pointed a knife at her plate while he continued to chew.

To be honest, since she'd ordered the mojito, she hadn't bothered to search for the poor schmuck she'd texted earlier. It was probably mean to call him that. Abby speared a shrimp and lifted it to her lips. Still, his loss had prompted her to show up. She wasn't sure why—probably empathy. Regardless, she was eating this dinner and glad for it. To be honest, Carter was the kind of guy she could see herself doing this with on a frequent basis. *If* she could actually afford to eat at this place, which she couldn't. Her diminishing bank account tapped her shoulder but she ignored it. Abby popped the shrimp in and ... yum. Wow. She'd wait a bit longer to worry about how to pay for this amazing food, which had no prices on the menu.

"I like your date idea. I'd buy that."

She bet he would. If he came to places like this, he probably had a whole slew of women to buy date packages for. What girl wouldn't go for this kind of wining and dining? Nice.

The low lighting and sexy jazz music was certainly conducive to a great date and romance. Which wasn't going to happen tonight—not for her, at least. This was simply a friendly dinner and she'd never been a one night stand in her life. Though she'd probably give it consideration if someone like him ever offered. Yikes, why did that thought surface? Ridiculous. Besides, he was practically inhaling that steak and she wondered if he was in a hurry to leave.

"Yeah, maybe you could use it to make up with your girlfriend."

He shook his head and grabbed his drink. With their eyes locked, he lifted it to his mouth and took a slow drink. "Why would I want to do that? She found someone else, remember? It's not like he just popped up before she told me either, she had to be lying about it for a while. Going behind my back, seeing this … guy, and not saying a word. Jesus, there's nothing I hate worse than dishonesty. I can take a lot of other shit but that's over the top. A deal-killer. Besides, I'm not that … whipped. The only thing I'd buy her would be a *breakup* package. Have any of those at your shop?"

"No." She laughed and nervously twisted the straw in her drink. Had his eyes darkened while he spoke of the lies? Whoa, intense. What did that mean?

He plopped the glass to the tablecloth. "Now that's a good idea. A breakup package. You could put really nice flowers in it, making it look all gorgeous, then send it to her at work. Everyone would think someone was being really romantic and sweet. They'd all stand around while she checked it out. She'd think it came from the other guy, until she opens the note and reads it."

She raised a brow. Hmmm. This guy had a vengeful streak. That might scare her if it wasn't sort of funny. "What would the note say?"

"I don't know—maybe 'the best thing about dating you was saying good-bye with these'?"

She shook her head. "No. No." She held out a finger. "How about 'the best thing about dating you was getting a new phone'?"

He busted out laughing and clutched his stomach. "That's good! Yeah. I'd buy that. Maybe even throw in a few chocolates and add a note that says 'hope these go straight to your ass.'"

Now *that* was funny. She couldn't help but laugh too. Maybe it was mean, but the woman cheated on him. He deserved to have a little tantrum. Only a little though.

"Okay, I'll do it." Abby's plate was empty. She had no idea how she'd plowed through the food so fast, but it was cleaned clear off.

He sobered. "What? I was just kidding."

"I wasn't." She pushed a paper drink napkin toward him. "I'll do it for free. Put her name and business address on that and we'll send it out tomorrow. I'll even deliver it myself and let you know how it goes." Obviously she'd drunk too much—enough to make her braver than normal at least. Or maybe she'd bonded with this jilted but gorgeous man in a strange, help-me-hate-her way. Was that a good thing?

He waved at the waiter to bring them more drinks; she wanted to decline more of the liquid courage but didn't. She'd made him nervous because he hesitated to answer. "Nah, that's okay. Just leave it alone. I don't want to make a scene."

Hmmm. He had a vengeful streak but he didn't act on it. That was … good. Only she really wanted to see this girl now. What kind of woman would be stupid enough to ditch this guy?

"Come on. You'll feel better. Besides, it's not like *you* cheated on *her*. Right?" Or was that what started it? How long had he dated this woman? She didn't remember.

He frowned for a couple of seconds then relaxed. "Right. But sending flowers is kind of—"

"Mean?"

"Yeah."

"And cheating isn't?"

He scrubbed his chin for a second and glanced around the room as if seeking confirmation. "Okay. Let's do it."

Chapter Five

Holy crap, she was a good florist. Abby smiled at the gigantic bouquet of roses, daffodils, and daisies. A touch of lavender made it smell heavenly. Too bad her family couldn't appreciate her talent as much.

She'd come in early to put it together. If she hadn't, she might have lost her nerve. Besides, Carter was nice and fun, and he even *paid*. She owed him her best effort. Especially since he'd shared a cab with her and stood there at the door of her apartment talking and joking and, for a second, he leaned in as if intending to kiss her. She'd wanted it, too. She'd moved closer and waited, but then the cab honked and he bailed.

She headed up the elevator of the building his ex-girlfriend worked in. Ex-two-timing-with-another-guy-behind-his-back girlfriend. It was a beautiful arrangement with a well-crafted message. Surely she wouldn't get upset? In fact, she might even laugh. Or say something ugly. Or get mad. Abby could handle that—despite the revolting roll in her stomach. If the woman dared say anything, she'd give her a piece of her mind. Who did she think she was, anyway?

She was ready for it when the blonde bimbo walked up. Okay, she wasn't a bimbo—rather, an attorney, according to the names on the wall. She was smart, big deal. She was still slime. Legal *and* cheating slime. Abby's stomach somersaulted in preparation for the confrontation. The woman took the flowers eagerly anticipating—something. A love note from her new guy maybe.

Only, the girl looked at the note and proceeded to ... *cry?*

Really? Oh, no. That wasn't what was supposed to happen. The girl was pretty. And shocked. And, dammit, Abby's forehead started to sweat. Then her palms joined in the perspiration and she rubbed them dry. She pretended ignorance.

This had sounded so much better right after she drank a gallon of mojitos. With *him*. Obviously she hadn't thought it through to this point.

The girl's hair was up in a fancy knot and her eyes were raining cats and dogs all over the lapels of her expensive suit. The note played through Abby's mind—they'd crafted each word together over lots of booze.

> Dear Amanda,
> Thanks for letting me off the hook before the hook sunk in further. The good news? I have a new smartphone! Even better news? I won't waste another minute of its service talking to you AND I have season baseball tickets to share with someone who actually DOES want to go. Have a good life.

"What's wrong? You don't like them?" Her gut tied up in knots. It had been funny at the time. Now? *I am such a bitch.*

"No, it's not that. It's just—he's really a nice guy. I shouldn't have gotten involved." Her nose had started running and she was babbling, a bunch of undistinguished phrases salted heavily with tears and hiccups.

Abby panicked and grabbed some Kleenex from the reception desk. She shoved them at the woman, who sniffled and blew her nose. The tears continued. "I mean, how was I supposed to know they were friends? They were both soooo … nice. I never thought. How can you help it?"

"Help what?" Abby had no idea where this was going, but at this point, whatever it was, she'd totally misjudged the ex. Or this woman had a stellar act going. The blubbering woman pushed the note toward Abby, who read it.

Should she mention that the woman reading the note had also been the woman *writing* the note? Devising every word in order to make a full impact. Shit. It worked. Her head ached.

"Falling in love with his best friend."

...

"What did you say?" Caroline was so engrossed in the story, she accidentally snipped the head of a rose rather than the stem. "Damn. Sorry."

Abby turned at the jingle of customers entering. "I wasn't sure what to say. I just stood there and patted her arm. I think I said something like, well, you can't really control who you fall in love with, can you. Maybe, I said he'll find someone else. I don't know. I panicked and ran."

"You ran away? Wow. You dropped that crap on her then bolted. Nice."

"Hey, you're supposed to be on my side. How was I supposed to know? Besides, you're forgetting she was going out on him. With his best friend, no less. She's not exactly an angel."

When a couple walked to the desk and waited, she stopped speaking and smiled. Had they heard the story? God, she hoped not. It was way too much drama for a business. "Can I help you?"

Thirty minutes passed before they'd selected their purchase and left. She was thankful to think about something other than Carter and his ex for a while. Still, she couldn't shake the shitty feeling in the pit of her stomach.

Caroline waltzed up to her as soon as the door closed behind the couple. "You can't tell him."

"I said I would. I told him I'd tell him what happened when I delivered it."

"So, you guys are meeting again about the hate flowers? Geeze, what a screwed up way to date a guy. How's this going to happen? Another fancy dinner and more mojitos?"

"Um, well, I'm not sure because we didn't exchange numbers. He knows where I live and work, but I know nothing about him."

Caroline got in her face and dropped her hands to her hips. "You like this guy, right?"

"Yeah, he was nice. Fun."

"Then you can't tell him his girlfriend ditched him for his best friend. Make something up. Anything. Don't let *that* come from you. He'll figure it out eventually."

"If he hasn't already."

Badeep deep.

Her cell signaled a message and Abby realized she hadn't bothered to look at it since the night before. "Shit, I forgot to get back to the random text guy."

"Wow, Abby. Your life is turning into one big story after another." She glanced at the text message on Abby's screen.

> Hey man, what happened to you? I waited all night.

Okay, at least in this one thing she had to be honest and decent. Maybe she hadn't started out that way, but she could fix it. Let him know she wasn't who he thought. She clicked in a response.

> Sorry, but I think you have the wrong person.

There. Whoever it was would realize the mistake and stop texting.

Badeep deep.

> Yeah, right. How much beer u had? Guess what, I met the running chick yesterday.

The running chick? Her stomach fell. Oh God, it *was* him? Wait. Not possible. Because he—

Caroline sucked in a gasp from her place looking over Abby's shoulder. "Holy shit, Abby! You're the running chick, right? You know what that means?"

Her hand shook and she dropped the phone on the counter and paced the floor. The answer was clear. "What?"

"Carter is—"

"The guy whose girlfriend dumped him for the ticket idea. Only, it obviously wasn't anything to do with the tickets. It was his *best friend*. And he's texting me. He thinks I'm his friend, the creep. Holy shit. He thinks I'm Jackson. Could this get any screwier?"

"Not likely—unless it was on television. How in the world did he get the two of you mixed up?"

"He said he had to replace his phone. That's all I know … maybe he transposed a number or something. Tell me, what do I do?" The door clanked open then shut. *He'll never forgive me for lying to him.*

A few seconds later it opened again. And again. In fact, they had a steady flow of customers for a couple of hours. Most of them were curiosity-seekers checking out the new business. Caroline and Abby worked solidly until lunch. When Abby's stomach growled, she checked the clock. "Caroline, why don't you get some lunch first. I'll cover until you get back." The stream of people walking by outside had picked up due to the noon rush.

"Maybe I should stay for another hour."

Abby waved her away. "No, go ahead. I'll be fine."

"Okay. I'll be right back, though." Caroline pulled her purse from under the counter then pointed at Abby's phone. "You should answer him, you know. He's probably wondering why you haven't."

"And say what exactly? That I'm just as deceitful as the lying, cheating woman that dumped him?"

"I wouldn't exactly say *that* but you'll think of something."

Chapter Six

Abby didn't have to think of a response to text because less than ten minutes after Caroline left for lunch, there was Carter. Coming in the door of her shop.

"Hey. Thought I'd stop by and see how the first day went."

Damn, he had a great smile. Great eyes too. In fact, pretty much great everything. Which made her nervous.

Badeep deep.

Her phone danced on the counter and she glanced at the message.

Caroline: Want me to bring you something?

She whisked the phone away before he could see the other messages and dropped it in her purse.

"Good. Uh, it's going good. We've had a fairly steady flow of traffic. Lots of people just coming in to window shop, though. It'll pick up once people know about us."

"You should advertise."

"We do. Are. What do you think?" She twisted the vase of a big creation she was working on, hopeful he'd forget to ask about the one she'd delivered first thing this morning.

He frowned. "I'm not the best person to ask. Flowers aren't my thing, remember? Well, tell me."

So much for forgetting.

"What?" She busied herself, adding more carnations, then reached for the ribbon. It needed a bigger bow. More color. She turned to look at the stash behind. Only he grabbed her wrist from her hip and pulled her around.

"Your delivery. What happened with your delivery?"

"Which one?" She gulped. Maybe he'd think there were more than one and—

"Mine, of course. Come on, spill."

"Oh, well…" She *really* didn't want to do it. She couldn't. No, someone else had to drop that bomb on him. Not her. It had been bad enough making Amanda cry. "She wasn't there."

He dropped her wrist and stepped back. "Oh. That sucks. So much for a reaction."

"I know. Sorry. That wasn't really how I thought it would go." Of course, neither was the real thing.

He walked around the store, touching and smelling. He picked up a couple of things and evaluated her work. "I like your store. You have a way with color and I like that you have a lot of plants and not just flowers. Plants last. It's nice. You'll do great."

"You think?" Her words came out in a squeak. Heat warmed her face and she cleared her throat.

"I know so." There were about three minutes of awkward silence before a customer walked in and Carter waved and headed toward the exit. "Gotta get back to work."

He stopped when the people entering detoured toward a row of shelves on the side of the store. He strode back and leaned over the counter. He whispered, his voice low and full of warmth, "I had fun last night. Your blind date was an idiot."

That was sweet. She grinned. *And* he was essentially calling himself an idiot without knowing. "Your friend was too, apparently. And whoever your ex-girlfriend is, she's a complete moron." He had no idea just how much.

"Are you running tonight?"

She shrugged. "It depends on whether I get out of here on time or not. If we close as scheduled, I will. Why?"

"Maybe I'll see you at the park."

"Maybe."

"Thanks for helping me out. I'm sure that delivery will make Amanda have more than a few regrets. Wish I could have seen it."

He waved and left.

• • •

Caroline was ticked off when she found out she'd missed Carter. "I want to meet this guy next time he comes in. Why didn't you tie him to the counter or something? Guys dig that kind of thing." She flung some red grosgrain at Abby and sulked. "This ribbon will work fine. If he comes back, use it. At least then I'll know who we're dealing with."

"We? *We're* not dealing with anyone—I am. And I'm flat out lying. He thinks I'm someone else."

"I doubt that."

"Need I remind you about his text messages?"

"That doesn't count. Text messages aren't personal. Showing up here today. That was personal. He made an effort. He came by to see you."

"He came by to find out what the ex-girlfriend said when I delivered the dump-me flowers." Abby wasn't foolish enough to think he wanted anything more than a little info on the delivery. Sure, he'd tried to kiss her before but that was just the result of mojito madness. What kind of regrets was he hoping Amanda would have? Regrets about letting him go? Or about cheating on him? Was he hoping she'd want to make up? Abby hoped not. He hadn't seemed too upset about the breakup at the restaurant. The opposite, in fact. He'd seemed totally—interested. *In me.*

"Did you tell him?"

"Of course not! I'm not that cruel."

"Be honest. Do you think he'd want her back if she was second guessing herself? If she felt guilty about it and she was just trying to get attention or something?"

"I don't know. Would you want to date someone who played head games? I wouldn't. Caroline, it's none of my business. If he wants her back, he'll go get her. Now, come on. We have work to do. Stop gossiping. Get busy."

Still, she was not getting involved with someone rolling off a breakup. Very bad idea. She glanced at the pile of inventory waiting to be unboxed and stacked in the back room for use. Abby snapped her fingers twice. "Time's a-wastin'." Her mother would have laughed to hear her use the favorite catch phrase. God, she really *was* more like her mom than she wanted.

Caroline snickered. "That's right, it is, old woman."

Her mom had referred the comment to her choice of entrepreneurship rather than keeping the nice corporate job in the family business. That job was conveniently populated with lots of young, sophisticated single guys. Guys that "are already making their way in the world and ready to settle down. After all, her clock has a lifeline—and time's a-wastin'."

Abby shot a glance skyward and cursed. "At least I have my priorities straight."

"You sure do. You ditched the fancy corporate job with huge benefits to tie on a hefty debt starting your own business. Now you hang out with crazy people like me. Meet random guys through text messages and chat sites then avoid all the ones your friends and mom try to set you up with."

"Maybe you both should just butt out. I don't want a man right now. I need to focus."

"Yeah, well, sometimes focus is improved by expanding your interests. I wasn't talking about a permanent man—just a man. Any man would probably do you good at the moment and who knows, it might even fine-tune that focus a bit."

Abby hitched a brow and turned her lips to a frown. "Seriously? This coming from the girl who's sick of the revolving door of men she's been hanging around?"

"Okay. Okay. Do as I say, not as I do." Caroline grabbed a box opener and slit the first box open. "Speaking of wasted time, you should call your mom. She probably misses talking to you."

"Yeah, I'll get right on that." Her voice dripped sarcasm because they both knew she wouldn't. Abby had taken enough advice and criticism from her parents for the business start-up. She had no desire to call and get another dose anytime soon.

She'd finally and effectively squelched the questions. Caroline didn't mention Carter or her family the rest of the day. Of course, that didn't stop Abby from thinking about them or, actually, Carter, for hours.

She skipped her evening run so she wouldn't have to face him. She'd catch up later. Or maybe she'd start running in the morning. By nine she'd bathed, had slipped into an old T-shirt and sweatpants, and was camped in front of the television awaiting the news report.

With her laptop balanced on her crossed legs, Abby decided to log into the Justchat site and take a glance. How pathetic was she to text and chat more than she actually *talked* with men? She shrugged. Hey, it removed all the complicated parts. The man from a few days ago, "Traveling to Survive," had left her a short message and asked her "What's up? My life is crazy today, how about you?" They'd exchanged a few short notes over the past day and she was starting to look forward to the responses. He seemed nice but she was thankful the chat site kept all her personal information secured. Sometimes initial niceness hid a whole slew of weirdness. Who knew what kind of people lurked on the site?

Why had she chosen the name "She Loves Dogs"? The guy probably thought she owned a house full. She shrugged. For someone with no dogs at all, it was wishful thinking.

She clicked at the keyboard.

Just when I thought I'd heard and seen everything, I get surprised. Today, I met a woman who completely fell apart over a breakup with her boyfriend. Not because she missed him, but because she was involved with his best friend. Crazy, right? She was completely destroyed about hurting the guy. Seems like she should have thought of that earlier?

Ironically, I happen to know the guy and can't understand what she was thinking because he was perfect. Should I say is instead of was?

Speaking of escaped moments, forgot to ask you where you live? Hopefully, somewhere really exotic like an island out in the Mediterranean or a cabin in the mountains. Me? I'm from Austin, Texas, the state capital that definitely puts the weird in Keep Austin Weird, but I live in Houston now.

The news flashed on the television and she watched the highlights for a few minutes, then returned to the laptop. The screen flashed a message pending in the app bar at the bottom so she clicked it.

Traveling To Survive: LOL. And I thought my life was complicated! Wow. That must have been awkward. Not from the Mediterranean though I hope to go there some day and hang out on that island. Lots of sand, wind, and crystal blue water. Sounds fantastic. Cabin in the mountains? No, but I go to Aspen to ski every year with some friends. You ski?

Small world. I live in Texas too … not one of the weird ones. I think Curious, what does a woman from Houston who hearts dogs do for a living?

As much as she'd like to "just chat," she had work to do. That question could wait. Abby grinned, pulled up her last project plan,

Text Me

and delved into work while listening to news highlights from a car accident that had piled up the freeway, and a burglary downtown.

Badeep deep.

Uh-oh.

She bobbled her head from the laptop to the television, then to her phone sitting on the table—rather, *dancing* on the table. She needed a distraction, anything to keep her from delving deeper into the text-o-drama. What should it be? She glanced toward the kitchen. Ice Cream. Gotta have some.

She flung herself off the couch and went to the refrigerator. Unfortunately, she hadn't thought to buy any the last time she was at the store. In fact, she hadn't even gone to the store in about three weeks. She picked up a Ziploc bag of something green and black and sniffed. Gross. She pitched the unidentified object in the trash. Nothing to snack on. She slammed the door shut and returned to the couch.

Badeep deep.

She ignored it again. For about ten seconds. Then it beeped once more and she realized that if Caroline was texting, it might be important. Maybe she'd had an accident on the way home? Or perhaps she was sick? Or, God forbid, there was a fire at the shop? She snatched up the phone.

Or just a message from Carter.

> Hey, you still there?

Well, that one she could answer honestly. She tapped a finger to her chin twice. Should she?

> Yeah, I'm here. What's up?

> I sent u 3 msgs and got zilch

Sorry. Busy.

No prob. Did u read them?

Yeah. U met running chick. Who's that?

U don't remember?

Should I?

The girl at the park. One I see running all the time.

Abby stared at the screen, realizing she was about to cross that line again. It was wrong to snoop, but the guy *was* talking about her. He had been nice—and funny. In fact, he hadn't seemed the least bit torn up about the ex-girlfriend. *Amanda*. Gorgeous Amanda.

Oh yeah. What about her?

Amazing.

She stared at the display as warmth flowed into her body. She grinned. *He thinks I am amazing? Really?*

He wasn't so bad himself. She typed in a few letters then backed them out. What would a man say to compliment another? Would it be considered gay to tell him he was pretty amazing too? Yeah, probably.

How would a best friend respond? Okay, well, technically the person he thought he was texting was a seriously shitty best friend, so she wasn't sure it mattered what that man would say. She keyed in the next thing that came to mind.

No warts or missing teeth?

Seconds ticked by.

No and not any moles either. So far. I haven't checked everywhere yet.

Yet. Abby tapped her feet in a quick happy dance. That sounded promising. Hmmm. So, he wanted to check her for moles? She grinned. Now there was a new game. She shoved the reminder of his recent break-up aside.

LOL. Good luck with that.

Abby snickered. This was fun. Dishonest, but fun.

U don't think I have a chance?

Of course he had a chance. In fact, if he'd made the move the other night and actually gone in for the kiss, she might have … what, let him check her for moles? Of course not. Well, she wasn't sure. She clicked at the keys.

Go for it, man. Screw Amanda

She didn't feel the least bit regretful about that statement. Nothing dishonest there. She meant it. He deserved better.

Amanda who?

Chapter Seven

Carter watched ESPN highlights and drank the last beer he'd pulled from the fridge, which happened to be the *only* beer in the fridge. Actually, it was the only thing in the fridge at all, other than takeout from Hunan Joe's. He wasn't sure how long the box had been there but the contents couldn't be edible. Surely sushi had a finite expiration date and, judging by memory, it was overdue. Best not to look.

Preseason highlights were on for baseball and the Astros looked … pitiful. He didn't care. He'd watched them for years and they always turned it around eventually. Who knew when it would happen?

The tickets sat on his coffee table, a reminder of how badly he'd tanked with Amanda. The message from Jackson glared at him as if to say *sayonara, sweetie*. He should be remorseful, or at least miss her. He didn't and that seemed a little strange. In fact, he was … relieved. Which was even stranger. Was that callous? Or had she merely met expectations?

Jackson was right about Abby. He should go for it. And he would. Tomorrow. Twice in one day would be creepy. He'd taken the dog to the park but didn't bother to search her out.

When the highlights were over, he picked up the new phone and pecked another message to Jackson before heading to bed.

> Don't 4get about game Sat.

He didn't wait for an answer; he was too tired. He wished he could say work had been a drain and he'd put in a rough day. It wasn't true, though. All of his days were rough, and this was no exception. The only difference was his mood. It had lightened just a bit after his dinner with Abby. He tore off his clothes, dropped them in the closet, and crawled into bed. Sleep came easily.

• • •

It never occurred to Carter that Jackson hadn't answered the earlier text until he was on his way to the ballpark. Work had been stressful the remainder of the week; piles of contracts and meetings that promised significant growth in his fledgling customer list had snowed him under. Not to mention the weather had turned ugly and, other than racing outside with Ruckus, he'd barely stepped foot past the door of his apartment. He'd searched for Abby a couple of times while out. Had she stopped running? Or was she avoiding another meeting with him? Probably just busy.

Maddie had growled at him every time he showed up, and it was evident her solitary confinement had worn her nerves thin. Fortunately, the boot on her foot would be off in a week and she'd be able to move around again. That would improve her mood. He shrugged as he drove. Maybe she lived alone because she was perpetually grumpy. Ruckus seemed happy and loved though, and was getting easier to corral on their walks. That would be over soon. He'd have no excuse to scour the park for Abby as she did her run and that was disappointing.

He braked at a light four blocks from Minute Maid Park and sent a text to Jackson.

> Meet me by the gate at the east entrance.

The light turned and he continued to the closest lot and parked. His phone beeped as he walked toward the field. He looked around for his friend's familiar face. Nothing.

It wasn't like the guy was hard to find either. He was three inches taller and as big around as a string, not an ounce of fat on him. Not much muscle either. What he lacked in physique, he gained in personality though. Carter hated to admit it, but his best friend had a flair for flirting and could charm just about anyone he met.

> Sorry, man. Can't make it. Work thing. Maybe next time?

Crap. If he'd known earlier, he would have given the tickets away. The extra one in his hand would go unused this time. He cursed again.

Oh well, no reason to waste both. He strode in and watched the game—alone. Thankfully, the Astros won. He thumbed a quick message before leaving.

> U missed a great game. Ur off the guest list now.

No reason not to put a guilt trip on him.

> Yeah, listened to it while I worked. Can't believe they waited until the sixth inning to make a run. How was it?

Carter stubbed his toe on the curb as he crossed to the parking lot where his car waited. He swore, the adrenaline of victory waning under the pain. The prior day's weather had wet the concrete such that it smelled damp. Still, the faint aroma of barbecue at the bar down the street masked it enough to tempt.

He considered going for ribs and a beer then shrugged. He, too, had work to get done.

> Awesome. They're out of town for two weeks to Seattle now.

He dropped the phone into his console and drove home with the intention of firing up his laptop for a few hours. Maybe he'd stop and ask Maddie if she wanted to go to the next game. She probably needed to get out. Hell, he could just give the tickets to her and let her take someone else. Or he could take someone other than Jackson. There was a thought. He grinned and flipped on the turn signal. He suddenly had a need to spice up his apartment.

With plants.

• • •

Other than the shrill of sirens from the cars tearing out of the police department, Abby hadn't seen a lot of excitement for a weekend afternoon. Of course, she over-thought the implication. Was this the sign of a business slack that could be trouble? She had no idea, but she hoped it was only the prior day's rain that had potential customers sidetracked.

Still, she'd been able to listen to the game and now was whistling to the blare of Miranda Lambert's latest tune. Actually, she alternated between singing the parts she knew and whistling the ones she didn't. With no customers, she wasn't worried about offending.

The display shelf by the counter had to be rearranged to make room for twelve bridal bouquets and boutonnieres for the Taylor-Babbinet wedding. She grappled with baby's breath and roses, gasping then cursing when she caught her finger on a thorn.

"Dammit! Missed that one." Abby thrust the blood drip on her fingertip away from the lace ribbon and leaned over the counter for a clipper to cut the little bugger. Her fingers wouldn't—quite—reach.

"Whatever it is, I'll get it for you."

She jerked upright and dropped back to the floor. As she whirled to see who had entered while she danced and whistled, her elbow snagged a crystal vase and water sloshed onto her pants. The vase teetered, threatening to fall.

"Uh-oh." Carter apprehended the vase just before it tumbled from the edge. Unfortunately, the entire contents had already dumped onto his shoes—and pants.

"Holy crap, you startled me." Abby scrambled to collect the flowers and tossed them on the counter before heading to her stock room to get a towel.

"Sorry about that."

"Did you—" She stopped herself from finishing with *have fun at the game?*

She hadn't wanted to see him and have to set the record straight, but here he was. In the flesh. "Um, you want to buy more flowers for your girlfriend?"

He snickered. "Nope. Over. Done. Stick a fork in her. I was just out and about and thought I'd get some plants for my place."

"No flowers? We have some great arrangements over there and they smell wonderful."

He briefly glanced where she pointed but shook his head.

"Flowers die too fast. I want something that will last—that I can't kill."

"Okaaay. Well, almost anything can be killed with the wrong care. Plants are kind of a personal thing. If you get ones that fit your habits they flourish. So, are you high maintenance or low and easy?" She meant to say low maintenance and easy-going, but it came out different.

"Hmmm." Carter rubbed a finger and thumb across the leaf of a braided money tree. "Easy? I guess but not *that* easy. High maintenance, definitely not. Not sure what you mean by low but I'm willing to give it a try."

Then he had the nerve to *grin*. Seriously?

"Low *maintenance* and easy-*going*, goofball. As in, don't give me something I have to water every day because I'll probably forget. High maintenance would be someone that has a set routine and never varies from it. I once knew a guy whose entire life revolved around his watch. His alarm went off at 6 a.m., he showered until six fifteen. He dressed in fifteen minutes and promptly brushed his teeth at six thirty, following with a comb through the hair at six thirty-five. He left work on time and ate dinner at seven every night regardless of where or with whom. He couldn't handle variations. He could do high maintenance."

Carter grinned. "Sounds boring."

"You have no idea." Yikes, did she really say that? She thrust a hand over her mouth and tasted blood from her finger. Should she add she once considered marrying the bore?

He lifted the money tree and inspected the pot. "I guess he penciled in sex around nine p.m. on Wednesdays and Saturdays so he could be promptly asleep by nine thirty? Did he also kiss good-bye at six forty in order to be out the door by six forty-one?"

He did not just say that. Blood dripped to the floor, reminding her she still needed to dress the wound.

"I wouldn't know." Technically, she did know and he was spot on, but for some reason that was TMI at the moment. There was no reason to discuss something that had been over for two years. She pulled a paper towel from the roll on the counter and wrapped it twice over the thorn prick then cupped it in her fist. "A guy that can handle the high maintenance type—"

"Of plant."

"Yes, of course, the high maintenance type of plant—can probably go with something that needs to be watered more often and on a set schedule. Those kinds of plants wither quickly if their schedule isn't kept up and they have to wait for attention. They're more finicky and needy."

"Needy for attention," he repeated with his back to her as he bent over a fern that perched on the floor.

"Yes, as far as care goes." He baited her with an innuendo. In a way, it was entertaining. Also dangerous. With his back turned, she had ample time to soak in the way the jeans slung low on his hips and cupped gently against areas that—her eyes jolted upward as he whirled to her with a wide grin.

"What about you?"

Her mouth went instantly dry. "Me?" she squeaked.

"Yeah, what would you suggest? High maintenance or low? If you were choosing a plant, which one would you go for?"

"Well, I'm not a good judge. I work here every day and can pamper them as much as they need."

"Do you?"

She had the distinct impression he meant something else, and she wasn't sure what. "Do I what?"

Her knees wobbled when Carter strode closer, pulled the towel from her hand, and wiped the blood gently from her skin. "Do you pamper your plants? Do you give them the attention they crave right on schedule whenever it's needed? Or do they suffer and wither, awaiting that precious care they yearn for, only to have it denied until they're so shriveled they can't function?"

Abby swallowed the gigantic lump in her throat. His fingers were darker and rougher but they stroked intimately against the injury.

"I always pamper the things I care about but, for the most part, I'm a low maintenance kind of person. Sooo," she dislodged herself from his grasp and picked up a philodendron, "this is the only kind of plant I'd bother with at home. It's easy, undemanding, and still perks up when I douse it with water. No matter how poorly I manage it. Here, at work, is a different story."

Carter tsked. "Sounds like you're one of those lucky few that can keep professional and personal lives separate."

Okay, that's it. He made no sense and all of this tiptoeing around *something* was fun, but weird. "Okay, Carter, what exactly are you getting at? You want a plant, take this one. Or not. That money tree you had earlier was good too. And easy."

"Easy works."

"Stop it."

"Stop what?"

"Aargh, you know what. Stop all this innuendo. Buy a plant. Or don't buy one, but stop the word games, *capisce*? I'm busy." She grabbed a water spout and headed toward one of the shelves. The plants didn't need watering, but it kept her mind elsewhere.

"You didn't look busy when I got here, you looked—happy. Like you were in your zone."

She was glad he hadn't mentioned the particular zone she joined included dancing and singing wildly to country music. "I was, thank you."

He lifted the money plant to the counter along with the philodendron. "Just curious, what happened with your blind date the other night? Did you ever figure out why he didn't show?"

Yikes. Am I really going to lie to him again? No, it's time he knows the truth. After all, it's not my fault he texted. I just ... answered. Tell him. NOW.

Carter dug into his wallet for cash. "So, have you heard anything more from Amanda, our friendly lying, cheating ex-girlfriend? Does she want me back yet? Did she ask about me?"

Okay, maybe not. He'd hate me and he's obviously still into her. Abby cleared her throat and shot a quick glance at the sky for forgiveness.

"No. The blind date did show, though. I was with you."

Chapter Eight

Carter wanted to smile but didn't. Would it be wrong to high-five a woman for getting ditched by a blind date? Probably.

"He saw us and left?"

"Not exactly."

It would have helped if he could read her expression but her back was turned. She was pressing keys and scanning the barcode on his plants.

"Well, did you tell him you were there? Did you set up another time to meet?" He grimaced and pretended to sympathize. "What kind of man just leaves without at least *trying*?"

Her shoulders hefted up and down as she slammed the drawer shut with his money inside. She held out a hand and dropped change into his palm. "Water these guys once a week. Keep them out of direct sunlight, maybe near a window but not right in front of it. There's some plant food in the soil already, but you'll need to add more in three months. Other than that, they should do great."

He lifted the plants and anchored one on each hip, realizing he'd made a slight tactical error. It was two blocks to his car and they were beyond bulky. Should have picked smaller pots. If he could get them there without dropping them, they'd have to hang out the window for the short drive to his apartment.

Abby glanced at the clock on the wall above the door. "Uh-oh, I'm late! Not exactly the best way to make an impression." She walked him toward the door in a rush. "Sorry, I have to close up."

"Another blind date?"

"No. Something much more important. A wedding."

Huh, what? He jerked to attention and she rushed to gather flowers into a box. Oh, of course—a wedding delivery. He stood outside the window, watching for a second, until one of the pots slipped from his hip. He grabbed hold, trying not to let it spill as it clunked to the pavement.

"Carter, you busy this afternoon?" Abby stood in the doorway, her black hair hanging in wisps over her eyes.

"Just getting my plants settled into their new home. Why?"

"Want to help me load this stuff into the van?" She tossed her head toward the box she'd filled.

He scooped up the dirt he'd spilled on the sidewalk, dropped it back into the pot, and wiped his hands. Going to a wedding was about the last thing he wanted to do—outside of visiting a dentist. But he guessed he could help load the truck. "Sure. No problem."

Abby grabbed one of the plants. "I'll drop you off on the way to my delivery so you won't have to carry these."

An hour later, Carter frowned at the white tablecloths and twinkling crystal above them. How he'd allowed her to talk him into helping her load *and* unload the flowers was a mystery. She'd been describing the place to him, talking nonstop about how exciting it was, and telling him it was her first wedding since the opening.

Then his mouth got ahead of his brain, and perhaps the stupidest thing ever leapt off his lips. "Why don't I go with you and help you get set up just to make sure it goes smoothly?"

Once the words were out, he couldn't take them back. He wanted to, but it was too late. She'd busied herself securing the plants, boxes, and ribbon before closing up the truck. When the door clanged shut and she turned, he considered a quick escape. He assumed she'd say no. She hadn't, and somehow it wasn't the least bit awkward.

That, in itself, was confusing.

"It's just a wedding, not a funeral. Don't start hyperventilating." The scrape of cardboard on the truck bed brought his attention back to the present, as she hefted the box of flowers and handed it to him.

He blinked. "I wasn't."

"Your face is as white as those lilies. You can leave if this weirds you out. I can manage on my own—it's not like I haven't done it before."

The comment slapped him back to reality. What was it about these things that made most guys run for the hills? He shrugged. The permanency, of course. In his experience, permanent never worked. No more than trusting—he'd tried that with Amanda—another one of Roger's stupid ideas. *You need to get past what happened to your sister and trust people. Accidents happen. It's not like Carley intended to deceive everyone.* Yeah, right. That's exactly what she intended. And apparently Amanda too. The woman in front of him now wasn't asking for his trust or permanency. She was simply asking for a little help. That was easy enough.

"Unless you want to drive me back, I might as well help. I'm already here and if it bothered me, I wouldn't have volunteered. You do a lot of weddings at this place?"

He glanced around the room. They were in the alcove of a historical landmark, a building that had once housed the elite socialites of Galveston. Presently, it was a museum by day, open for tourists, and available for parties after hours. An unusual but attractive site with flowers and ribbon trailed throughout.

When he turned back to Abby, she shook her head. "This is just the reception hall. The wedding is at the Catholic church, a very formal affair. We'll go there next and deliver the bouquets, corsages, and flowers for the vestibule. Can you grab the other box too? I'll get the door."

"It must get old after a while." He moved away and let her latch the door behind.

"What? Weddings?"

"The smell. You spend all day around all these and probably get tired of it. I always thought that was why girls liked flowers—because of the scent. It covered up all the ugly smells."

She grinned. "Well, that's definitely a plus but no, ah, you obviously haven't bought many of them, have you?"

Carter plunked the box on a table and began distributing the candleholders to tables. Should he tell her he'd seen enough flowers for a lifetime at family funerals? "Only when I had to."

"Flowers, candles, scented oil, room fragrances—they're all an aphrodisiac. They set the mood."

He liked the sound of *that*. "Mood for what exactly?"

She avoided eye contact. "Whatever. Dinner, asking for a date, going beyond the date—"

"To?"

"To whatever. A guy can't go wrong with flowers."

A deliveryman from the food caterer strode up and asked where to put his cargo. Abby pointed toward a door, stating to check there for the family. The creak of his dolly wheels across the tile broke the silence.

"Don't you notice the smell of a room or a person?" She quirked a brow as she placed the last flowers, with an ornate candelabra, at the main table. Actually, he *did* notice. He'd noticed her scent the minute she ran past him ages ago but never thought about it until now. Flowers, however, weren't the same.

He shook his head, not ready to make that admission. "Unless there's food involved, nope. Now, if you filled this room with *eau de barbecue* or maybe *la scent de steak*, you'd have me in a second. My heart would be full."

Abby threw a stem she'd cut from the arrangement at him and gathered the boxes. "No wonder you're single."

"What? That's not romantic?"

"Not even close. Next thing you're going to tell me is your favorite smell is sweaty gym clothes after a workout."

"Nope. After a weekend baseball game. That's the best." He took the boxes and stacked them in her truck while she fumbled for the keys. With them in hand, she tapped against his chest.

"Maybe you should try flowers with the next girl and see if it lasts longer."

He rubbed the spot she'd thumped. "Ouch." On a whim, he grabbed the hand with the keys inside and pulled her to him. He ran his cheek along her neck and sniffed. "You're assuming I want it to last long. Maybe I should test your theory and see what you smell like. See if … "

It wasn't the smell that caught him off guard. Nor was it the closeness. With his cheek against hers, the first thing he noticed was how soft she was. Amanda had been all woman, but she'd been so concerned with makeup and hair she often felt … starched. Abby's hair was soft and wispy against his cheek, suggesting silk against his roughness. It rendered him unable to speak or move.

She stepped back and he lost his balance for a second then righted himself. The look in her eyes was mostly alarm. But there was something else. Maybe a little—*fire?*

He straightened his shoulders and grinned. "Nope, *nada*. You smell like dirt."

"And you smell like deodorant with a little sweaty gym socks thrown in." She strode to the driver's seat and hopped in the truck, waiting on him to get in the other side.

When he did, he threw his arm across the back of the well-worn seat and let his fingers rest against her shoulder. "See, you like it. It's sexy, right?"

"Seriously?"

"Come on. Girls love tough men and tough men don't smell like flowers."

"Are you telling me you're a tough guy? Here? Delivering flowers with me? Shouldn't you be at a boxing match or at the gym? Besides, maybe guys aren't that into flowers—but has the deodorant thing worked for you so far? I doubt it. It never hurts to add some cologne and send flowers or gifts. Maybe you should try a different approach. "

He bristled. She had a point. "That makes two of us."

"What's that supposed to mean?"

Her tone of voice elevated. Should he stop before he said something incredibly stupid? Besides, who was he to give love advice? He'd just been ditched for someone else.

"Now you're trying to say my blind date ditched me because I smell bad?"

"Whoa, that was a leap. Honestly, my guess would be the guy showed up, took one look at this," Carter pointed a finger at himself, "and realized he was way out of his league. He probably thought there was no way you'd go out with him after talking to me. Smell had nothing to do with it."

With both hands on the wheel, she stared at him as if he'd lost his mind. Seconds ticked by. "You really believe that? That someone would look at us and think we actually belonged together?"

He winced. Of course not.

"What difference does it make? We're not."

"Not?"

"Together." He said it, but for the life of him he couldn't tear his eyes away until she started the truck and put it into gear. An awkward silence sat between them as they went to the church. He helped her carry in the boxes and waited while she distributed them. He had no desire to seek out the wedding party and intertwine himself in their day. He'd never met them, so it would have been even more uncomfortable than sitting in the truck in silence.

It didn't stop him from staring at her as she worked and *that* was ridiculous.

When she turned down the block toward her shop, she took her foot off the gas. "Where to?"

"Huh?"

"Your car or your apartment?"

His mouth dropped open. Was that an invitation or his perverted mind playing tricks? She pointed to the back. "For your plants. I told you I'd drop you."

Whew.

"Two blocks down on the left."

"What did you think I meant?"

It wasn't what she meant; it was what he thought that had him confused. He'd spent all of a few hours around her and, for a second, he'd actually thought she wanted sex—what the hell was wrong with him? That was like going from zero to fifty in a millisecond. Not going to happen. Not to mention he had a slight problem with commitment. An ideal problem in this situation. Quick and over might work. Could he do that?

Carter noted the meticulous way Abby managed her shop and how she'd helped him with Amanda. Her laughter and the way she'd almost cried when she looked at the wedding fiasco they just left.

Nope.

Chapter Nine

At ten the following Monday, Abby's phone announced a series of text messages but she was tied up. Literally. She had ribbon everywhere as she readied another group of deliveries for her next wedding rehearsal. A call came in for a funeral and she switched gears to prepare a suitable wreath.

"Are you going to answer any of those messages, or do I have to listen to your phone bleep all morning?" Caroline's snarky response wasn't really impatience over the noise.

If Abby knew anything, Caroline wanted to hear the latest on Carter.

"If it bothers you that much, answer it yourself." She hadn't been serious but when Caroline dove over the counter for her purse, she squealed and intercepted.

Caroline's spiked hair ruffled as she tried to grab the device away. "Don't tell me to answer then change your mind. You know I'll do it."

"Yeah, and if I remember correctly—that's how this all started. You answered a random message from a mistaken guy and somehow I ended up in a big mess of confusion."

"You know, a lot of people would say it wasn't a mistake—in fact, if you believe in karma or fate—it was bound to happen. No mistake involved."

"Oh my God, the next thing I know you'll call yourself some type of messenger or medium. He got me all mixed up, that's all. I should never have answered. Correction. *You* should never have answered. He would have eventually figured it out."

Caroline grinned. "Hey, you're the one that decided to actually go to the restaurant, not me." She held up both hands and widened her eyes in a challenge. "Don't blame me if you can't hang with it."

"Hang with it? What the heck is that supposed to mean? Hang with lying my ass off to the guy?" Abby whipped the phone up and scrolled through the first messages. From his friends. For some reason, she was now in a *group* text. Would one of them see the errant number and expose her?

"No. It means—you should tell him. Tell him about the messages, only do it in person so you can spend a little more time with him before he realizes you've been spying on him all this time."

"I wasn't spying."

Caroline raised an eyebrow. No words needed in that expression.

"I wasn't! *He* texted *me*, remember? I didn't start it. Nor did I run over him with a dog. If you ask me, he's the one that started it all. Besides—"

Caroline snipped ribbon loose and tied up a yellow bow for the funeral arrangement. "Let's don't forget you still haven't told him about his girlfriend either."

Abby huffed. "Ex-girlfriend. And seems to me, the person that should tell him is her. Or maybe his best friend."

"Who happens to be you at the moment."

"No, not me."

"You're answering his texts as if you're him."

"OKAY. I won't answer them anymore. Besides, his real friend is a jerk."

"And you'll tell him?"

"Tell him what? About me *not* being Jackson—or at least not the Jackson he thinks he's texting? Or about his ex-girlfriend's reaction to the flowers? Or maybe the reason why she broke up with him is because of *Jackson*. The friend, not me. Or maybe that the blind date I thought I was meeting actually was him, which is why he never showed. Only he did. Which one? And remember, I *tried* to tell him about the texting." Abby's voice had risen to almost a yell by the time she stopped for a breath. She gulped a couple mouthfuls of air.

Caroline patted the flower arrangement, nodded her head, and shrugged. "Hey, ease up before you pop a blood vessel. I don't know. Pick one. I wouldn't throw it all at him at once. He might pass out. Or deck you."

Badeep deep.

The store phone jumped into action, ringing simultaneous to her text message. Abby groaned and surveyed her phone's screen again, which gave Caroline just the break needed to grab it and run to the back of the shop.

She pointed at the desk. "Answer that."

Abby checked the store phone, recognized her parents' number, and silently thanked her decision to put the added expense of caller ID on the bill. She wasn't ready to face the music yet—she still wanted to bask in the fairy tale idea of business ownership.

"Holy shit!" Caroline's head was glued to the texts. "Did you see these group messages?"

"Some of them. Hey, I thought you said I needed to stop spying and set him straight."

Caroline's voice was mockingly low and masculine. "There really is a running chick? Yeah, nearly killed her with the neighbor's dog. You weren't with the neighbor? No, just helping with the dog. Good. No warts? No, she's nice. Seeing her again? Already did. Twice. Damn, that was fast." Caroline giggled. "You know one of these guys is a real jerk. He said, 'So the tits *are* real?'"

"What! He did not!" Abby ran to her side and peered over her shoulder. She rolled her eyes at the words. "I thought you were joking."

"Nope. It gets worse. Look." Caroline handed over the phone and Abby read the others.

Well, are they?

Carter: Not answering

Is that I'm sleeping w her so can't tell or don't know 'cause she ditched me 2?

Carter: Screw you

Oh, well good luck w her. You'll get there

Carter: Should I repeat?

Lunch at Fadi's. Who's in?

Me

Me but can't go til 12:30

Me too

Carter: U just want the details

Damn straight

12:30 then

Carter: I'm busy

Rog, drag him w u

No problem

"That's it," Abby huffed. "I'm calling him right now and getting out of this."

Caroline yanked the phone away. "You're just mad because he thought your boobs were fake. Think about it this way—they're so perfect, he didn't think they could possibly be real. From a guy, that's a compliment. Besides, you're so upset if you call him now, you'll bite his head off. No, I have a better idea. I think we should crash this lunch party. Grab your purse."

Abby dropped her hands to her hips and shook her head. "No."

"Why not? We could pretend we were just in the neighborhood."

"Who'd watch the shop while we're gone? I'm not closing just so we can continue this horrible charade."

"I know! I'll go talk to him and tell him about the phone mess-up, and you can stay here."

"You'd do that for me?" Abby didn't believe a word.

"No, but I'd eavesdrop and see what he's saying about you. How's that for a friend?"

Abby rolled her eyes. "And you tell me *I'm* bad."

The door jangled as Caroline yanked it open. "Oh, honey—you haven't *seen* bad yet. This is better than any damned reality show! Be back in an hour." She waved fingers and rushed out before Abby could stop her.

Abby wanted to laugh. Abby hadn't described Carter, and Caroline had yet to meet him. So Caroline had no idea who she was looking for.

• • •

A shadow appeared in Carter's doorway and he checked the time. It had taken all of three minutes for Roger Freeman to walk down the hall to his office.

"You ready?" Roger leaned against the door, catching his shirtsleeve on the latch.

Roger had worked with him since college and been a friend throughout. Carter used that term loosely because Roger had a lot of frustrating quirks. Still, there was very little about him that Carter didn't know, and vice versa. Neither could run away from their pasts. Fortunately, there'd only been a few times when he wished it possible. Roger had fallen off the radar for a while during their senior year and just after. Carter knew little other than there was a girl and he gave up asking after the first attempt. Roger nearly bit his head off when he pried.

Whatever his friend's problems or past, not too many men in his world were reliable enough to recommend for a job. Roger had been one then—and still was. He was a real ass around women, but when it came to work, there weren't many Carter trusted as much as Rog. It didn't make sense, the women thing, to a lot of people.

Carter knew it was an act, a front. Roger hadn't a clue how to behave because he'd never had a girlfriend—except maybe that one time—and very likely never had many second dates. The guy had the most horrific manners around women. It had to be nerves because he was great around clients. Or maybe it was intentional. Who knew?

"I said I was busy. I meant it." Carter buried his head behind his laptop screen.

"You're always busy. Whatever it is, it can wait until after lunch. You haven't gone with us in over a month." Roger untangled himself from the door latch and dropped into the chair across from Carter's desk.

"We're meeting with the bank at three and I haven't looked at—"

"The lease for the property on Bellaire? I have it memorized." Roger leaned over and closed the folder Carter had splayed open. "Let's go."

Carter sighed. Roger was right. Amanda had been demanding, to say the least, which was ironic, considering the situation. How had she found the time to monopolize his time as well as someone else's? He'd all but given up his friends after dating her a month, not something he was proud of. He owed it to the guys to mend the fences and make sure he wasn't that stupid again. No girl was worth it.

He grabbed his keys and followed Roger out.

Fifteen minutes later they were seated at a table near the window of Fadi's, gulping down iced tea and Mediterranean food. The place was famous throughout the city. Not just for the taste of the food but for the quantity. No one left hungry.

• • •

It came as no surprise when Abby's phone beckoned only minutes after Caroline left. She debated answering, but her curiosity interfered.

"Okay, tall, dark, and handsome? Or blond, blue-eyed, and short?" Her voice was matter-of-fact and hushed.

"Not playing this game, Caroline. It's bad enough to answer the messages, but a recon mission? That's over the top. Get back here."

"No can do. I think I can figure it out, anyway. There're three or four of them, right? So that rules out a few tables. All the ones full of women can be crossed off also." Caroline mumbled something and Abby assumed she was paying for her lunch based on the sound. "You're really not going to help me?"

"Nope."

"Okay, you leave me no choice. I'll just have to go around and ask them."

"No! Don't you dare!" Her last word was silenced when Caroline cut her off. She dialed back but no answer. When the phone lit up with texts, she breathed a sigh of relief. And laughed herself into the flowerpots.

The first message from Caroline had a picture of an older man with silver white hair that curled over his shirt collar. He wore a tie and had a napkin tucked into his neck to protect his clothing—a smart move since a deluge of drips soaked into it. Her message read:

> This one?

A second later, there was a picture of the man sitting with him, a bald crown over his dark side locks. Bushy eyebrows and moustache suggested the only spot he didn't grow hair was on top. The man was talking with food in his cheek in the picture.

> Or this one?

Abby giggled. As *if*. She tapped a brief **no** to each. Caroline was obviously enjoying this way too much—three more pictures of similar men came through. The man with the shaved head and eyebrow tattoos was interesting, and answering *yes* was tempting. The response would have been wasted, since she had no way to see Caroline's reaction.

Abby's stomach rumbled, reminding her *she* wasn't eating and she added a few keys to the last response.

> Bring me something back when ur done sightseeing.

Another picture came of four men at a table, mid-twenties and up, with the caption

> Eureka.

Abby panicked. The fun screeched to a halt. Caroline had taken the picture of herself in a booth—and the men were behind her in the adjacent one. Carter was one of them. Her mouth fell open. Dammit!

Caroline texted again.

I'm right, aren't I?

Fortunately the door jangled and Abby was saved from answering. She dropped the phone into her purse and went back to work. She decided it was time to set a company policy regarding phone usage during work hours. One that included no texting or calling that harassed the owner. Since they were both owners, it would be critical they set the standard for future staffers.

Chapter Ten

"Where the hell is Jackson?" Roger asked their other two friends when he slid into the booth. David Fender and Garth Satrose exchanged looks and shrugged. Carter thought the lengthy silence odd.

"I asked him," Carter said, albeit it was in the same message everyone else had.

"No idea." David tore off a hunk of pita bread and scooped hummus. He shoveled the entire thing into his mouth and tore another. "I haven't talked to him in a while. Was he joining us?"

Carter glanced around the restaurant. The place always smelled of garlic. The hum of voices during the lunch hour made it difficult to talk. "He never answered."

David concentrated on the hummus and spoke through a mouthful. "He's been pretty busy lately. Some big thing at work."

Carter shrugged. "He's texted several times but hasn't said much about work. He was supposed to meet me at the game last weekend and skipped. Glad to hear business is picking up for him."

Roger stared over his tea glass as he sipped. "He's texted? What'd he say?"

David and Garth exchanged another look. David nodded at a girl sitting behind Carter in the booth. "Check that."

The girl was taking pictures of herself. Carter glanced over his shoulder just as she snapped. *Click.* He wondered if she'd be surprised at having a guest in the photo.

Roger leaned in over Carter and made his famous pig face—the camera clicked again. A quick gasp told him the girl responded as Roger hoped ... the thud of the camera hitting the table meant she'd grown tired of her self-portraits. Or didn't like the background.

Carter shoved Roger's arm. "Back off, Rog. You've already photo-bombed enough."

"Hey, just trying to make it interesting. Come on, tell us."

"Tell you what?"

"You know—tell us about runner girl."

"Nothing to tell."

Roger sniffed at something he'd pulled from the food line. "Not sure what this is but thought I'd try it. So, no warts, no moles, real boobs, and she has all her teeth. Does she speak English?"

The two men across from them coughed and Carter sighed. "That's your idea of the perfect girl? A foreign born person who doesn't understand you but has a great rack?"

Roger shrugged and popped an olive in his mouth. He bit down then frowned and pulled out the pit. "I didn't say that. It's just—I mean, we all saw her at the park, remember? She's out of your league, man. There has to be something wrong. If she has trouble understanding you, maybe you won't blow it as fast."

"What's that supposed to mean? You think I blew it with Amanda?"

"No, actually—it sounds like she was the one blowing—"

Carter coughed. "Don't even say it, gutter slave."

David finally swallowed his mouthful and spoke. "You didn't waste any time changing gears."

"Damn. You're like a revolving door. Maybe you should take it a little slower next time."

"Slow wasn't the problem. Maybe I shouldn't listen to Jackson's advice. The guy was full of shit."

Garth glanced at David then cleared his throat. "What do you expect from a guy who talked us all into buying season tickets so he could use them?"

"Huh?" Carter stopped chewing. "You bought Astros tickets too?"

"No, mine are for basketball. And David bought football tickets. What about you, Rog? What did you get?"

Roger sighed. "Soccer. Well, the guy's no idiot. Why spend the money if someone else will?"

Carter shook his head. "That's rich since he's the loaded one in our group. Why'd he stand me up last weekend?"

David laughed. "Because he's—"

Garth slugged him in the arm and furrowed his brows. "Shut up."

"What? Someone should say it." David rubbed his shoulder. "Shit, you didn't have to punch me, asshole."

"Say what?" Carter asked.

Garth lifted his phone. "Yikes, David, we need to get back. All hell is breaking loose at work." He pushed hard against David, almost sending him to the floor.

"Hey! Let me finish."

"No time. Move it."

Carter blinked and stared after his two friends as they all but ran from the restaurant. "What the hell was that about?"

Roger slid from the booth and moved to the other side, opposite Carter. "No idea." He shook his head and stood as soon as the chick with the camera rose from her spot behind Carter and went for a refill. He pointed at Carter's cup. "Want more?"

"I'm fine."

It took Rog a full five minutes to fill his cup, add a bunch of sugar, and get a straw—which he normally never bothered to use. All the while, he hovered next to the spiked hair woman. When she placed a lid on hers and headed for the door, he finally returned. For some reason, the entire dance the two had just played reminded Carter of hanging out at the park hoping to run into Abby. Why hadn't he just talked to her? It would have saved him the past three months with Amanda. Maybe.

"Take a picture next time," he told Roger. "Then you can stare at it all you want. She probably thought you were stalking her."

He shrugged. "Hey, she's cute. I think I know her, not sure."

"Then why didn't you say something?"

"I said I wasn't sure. Hair's different. Say what exactly? You look just like someone I used to know—that's a great line. Or maybe, I'm a tea guy, how about you? Or sooo, you hang out here often? What about—hey, that's a cute cup you're holding?"

"Anything's better than nothing. Just curious, Roger, were hers real?"

"Huh? What? Oh, I-I don't know, I wasn't looking." Roger's face turned the color of a stop sign. "Hey, aren't you going to Bangkok next week to work on that contract for the sports equipment guys?"

Carter nodded. Good change of subject.

...

Abby was with customers when Caroline rushed in from lunch and dropped a bag of food beside her purse. She had little opportunity to eat for another hour and even then, more customers were out front with Caroline. Between the two of them, they barely spoke until the end of day. Caroline said the luncheon outing wasn't a big deal and she'd left because one of the guys was leering at her. It gave her the heebie-jeebies.

Abby wanted to pry Caroline with questions, but that would be desperate, which she certainly was not. In fact, she hadn't cared one way or the other if Carter and his friends thought any part of her anatomy wasn't real. It was ridiculous. Nor was she concerned whether Carter actually said anything about her. He was still on the rebound, and rebounders were a bad bet.

Chapter Eleven

Carter braced for takeoff and closed his eyes. Flying was a ritual, or so he told himself. He'd been on a number of airplanes as the business grew. No matter where he sat or how big the plane, he was borderline claustrophobic the moment he clicked the belt around his hips.

He mentally voiced the numerous things he always did—thankfulness for his fortune, blessings for his friends and family, and promises to be his best self. Just in case he crashed and met his maker. If any of the guys he hung around knew what went through his head on a plane, they'd label him a sap for sure. Still, it had worked for him thus far; he had no intention of switching gears and breaking the good fortune and smooth flights. A small part of him believed karma was a good thing. Or at least nothing to mess with.

When the plane leveled off at full altitude, he pulled his laptop from below the seat and read through his presentation. The company had put him in charge of this venture and, with their new confidence, it was critical he prepare adequately. This was a contact Jackson knew and he was counting on that to be a good referral. They needed this contract if they were going to stay on target and minimize their production costs.

He'd called Jackson twice to discuss the project and gave up. As a last resort, he sent Jackson a quick text to let him know about the meeting, half-hoping he'd join him on the trip. No answer. Not like the guy.

A week and a half later, he reversed his flight routine and headed home. His laptop was filled with notes, copies of building plans and designs, and the longest to-do list he'd managed since starting his job six months earlier. He was exhausted and Jackson had been a no-show. It would have been irritating as hell if he hadn't been too busy to think about it.

The ten-hour flight managed to satisfy his need for sleep but had done nothing to rest his mind. Swirling thoughts of work made him anxious. As the plane taxied to the gate, it dawned on him he'd thought of little else the entire trip. Not a single time had his mind wandered to Amanda or their breakup.

Then he passed the airport florist on the way to his car and he realized his thoughts *had* been on a woman. Or maybe not his thoughts, but his dreams. Only the woman was surrounded by flowers and ribbon, and she'd done some pretty crazy things with them.

Abby.

Once he reached home, he checked his watch then dialed Information. With the number in his phone, he dialed Jeffries Florist. The minute she spoke, he felt the smile behind the words.

He grabbed an apple from his backpack, took a bite, and spoke as he chewed. "I'd like to voice a complaint."

"Oh, no! Whatever it is, we'll make it up to you. I promise."

"You promise?" He swallowed the apple and grinned.

"Of course. How can we make it better?"

"Well, I was in there a couple of weeks ago and bought some plants from this girl. Nice looking, good salesperson—but real bossy."

Did she just suck in air? "Carter?"

He laughed. "Yeah, how's things, Abby?"

"So, you're not really complaining?"

"Well, I do kind of have a problem." He glanced at the brown leaves drooping on the philodendron. "I've been on a business trip for a while and one of the plants is losing all its leaves. I watered it before I left but I think I killed it."

"Which one?"

He told her and she proceeded to tell him it would perk back up with water.

"Perk—okay, sounds good. Hey, did you ever get a chance to meet that blind date?" He rolled the apple, seeking for a good spot to bite again.

"Um, sort of." She quickly changed the subject. "I heard Maddie got her boot off and is walking now. I don't need to worry about you losing control again, do I?"

Hmmm. Losing control. He wasn't sure how to answer. He grabbed a cup from the cabinet, filled it, and doused his molting plant. "You mean with Ruckus?"

"Of course, what did you think I meant?"

"No idea. Listen, I was actually calling about business." The thought popped into his head mere seconds before he spoke, but it was still good.

"Yours or mine?"

"Um, both. We moved into our building less than a year ago and it's pretty empty. I wondered if you guys did corporate plant maintenance?"

"You mean watering, pruning, and all that?"

"Yeah. We need to spruce it up. So, do you?"

Seconds ticked as she considered his question. "Of course, but I'd need to come by and look at the space and give you an estimate. We'd have to charge for delivery, but other than that and the monthly care fee, it would be hands-free. No way you could kill them."

"Great. Come by tomorrow at eleven." He rattled off the street address and told her where to go once inside. "Oh, Abby—you can tell me about the loser blind date then too. Over lunch."

He clicked the phone off before she could refuse and headed to the fridge for a beer. He'd completely forgotten to mention the baseball tickets and ask if she'd go. Again.

Chapter Twelve

Listen, asshole. There r games in 2 wks. If u plan to go, say so or I'm asking someone else.

Carter figured that would get Jackson's attention. He didn't understand it. The guy had seemed more than willing to take the tickets off his hands when Amanda dumped him, but then he just disappeared. Carter had called him also, but it went straight to an automated voice mail. If not for the texting responses, Carter would have thought he was hurt—or something else was wrong. He frowned and pecked in a few more words.

Answer me or I'm coming by ur office and making a fool of you

He waited a full five minutes.

Ding.

That would just make a fool of u, not me

Should I tell ur boss you took a picture of her changing clothes in the car for yoga?

Carter expected a smartass response, but nothing came. At all. He still had no idea about the tickets.

The blinking icon on his screen reminded him that it'd been a while since he'd looked at the Justchat application, not that he had time for any chatting with his crazy schedule. Still, he should at least respond if there was a message. He tapped the open key.

> She Hearts Dogs: Sorry it's been a while, crazy week. I don't know why I chose that nickname … wishful thinking, I guess. I live in an apartment where no pets are allowed. Always wanted a dog. What about you? You live with any other creatures?
>
> For a living? Own my own business. Just getting started and it's a little scary.

Impressive. He keyed in a response.

> Everything in life is scary if you think about it too much. Just keep moving. You'll do great. Take my word on this: No one ever fails that doesn't give up.

Yeah, it sounded a little too preachy but she obviously needed a little encouragement. The pop-up surprised him with an instant response.

> She Hearts Dogs: Thanks! Think I'll print that and put it in my pocket. May need to refer back to it whenever I start to question my sanity.

Carter chuckled, mainly because he should probably do the same. He clicked in a short answer.

> Sanity? What's that? No such thing in today's world. Though if you're starting out on your own, I'd say you're pretty sane. Brave as hell too. Why haven't I met you yet?

He watched the screen till a response popped up.

> She Hearts Dogs: Awww. Wish that brave thing were true. The reality is I come from a large family where everyone jumps right into

the family business straight out of college. I guess I'm the only rebel. I tried it for a while but wanted more. The thought of doing it for the rest of my life was worse than eating worms.

Not sure why I couldn't force myself to take the safe road—life would have been a lot less complicated.

Yeah, well, complications happen regardless. He shrugged. When the office phone blared, he jolted. The receptionist announced Abby's arrival. He thrust his phone into his pocket, grabbed his keys, and headed to the lobby.

She had her hair pulled into a ponytail and some silver hoops dangled from her ears. Was she wearing lipstick? Her lips were a little full anyway, but that was certainly … attention grabbing.

She met him halfway across the floor and reached a hand out to shake his. Fingernail polish, a skirt, and—heels. He flicked a glance at the tight lines of muscles just above her knees. It was a paradox. A damn teaser how her legs could be so toned from running yet he knew the skin to be soft, not hard. Or at least the skin on her face and arms, what little he'd touched.

Damn if there wasn't a perverted desire to skip the office tour and get her out of the office. Alone. Would it terrify her?

"You look good." It was the only thing he could think of because, for some stupid reason, he'd lost his voice and just stared like an idiot.

"Thanks." She grinned. "It took twenty minutes to scrub the dirt from my fingernails. I finally gave up and just painted them." She held up five digits and wiggled them in his face. Was that why she always wore nail polish?

The receptionist watched with a dark scowl. Carter put a hand to Abby's back and pressed her toward the elevator, speaking loud enough to calm curious ears. "Okay, let's take the tour. We have about twenty areas I thought could use something. We're not touching the individual offices. Just the community spaces and meeting rooms. The lobby you saw. The rest is this way."

When the elevator doors closed, she turned toward him. "You know the person who greets visitors sets the tone for your business. It's the first impression one gets."

He lifted a brow and leaned against the wall. "What are you trying to say?" He stared at the red polish as she pushed a loose hair back from her face.

She shrugged. "Nothing. Maybe she was just having a bad day."

Badeep deep.

The noise came from her phone and she reached in her purse, shuffled around, then turned as the elevator opened. "Sorry about that. I turned it off."

"You can answer it if you need to. It might be business."

"No, Caroline's taking care of things. No one would call me. Show me." She held those shiny nails out and gestured him to lead the way. Which, for some reason, sent heat straight to parts of him that wanted those nails anywhere and everywhere *but* the public meeting rooms of his office.

He led her down the hall to the first room, the employee kitchen and lounge. Thankfully it was empty. The minute the door clicked behind them, he snagged her fingers and held the nails up for inspection. He turned the thin fingers in his and watched as her eyes flared.

She bit into her lip and the lipstick seemed to—beckon.

"I like it. The red. It suits you. Cheerful." It was a stupid thing to say but hell, if he didn't say something, he was going to *do* something really stupid. Their eyes locked. Oh, hell, why not. He reached out and slid his fingers behind her head, wrapping the ponytail between his thumb and fingers. He yanked her close and dropped his mouth on the lips that had him tied in knots the minute she walked in. *Holy shit.* She tasted like apples. And sin.

Or maybe heaven. He wasn't sure because as soon as their lips touched, she opened up and stroked her tongue against his.

It shocked him and turned him on instantly.

...

Abby hadn't really planned to attack him. He kept staring at her mouth, then her legs, and finally her fingernails. It was seductive the way he kept looking around as if trying not to stare, then returning—to her.

She told herself it was business and she'd dressed appropriately. Sure, she could have just worn the pants and tops she had on at the shop, but that wasn't professional enough and she wanted to make an impression. It was just about the job, she tried to convince herself.

With their tongues wrapped together in a swami dance, there wasn't anything the least bit professional in her head. Nope. Carnal, perhaps.

When he let go of her fingers and palmed both sides of her face while he walked her backward against the door they'd entered, her thoughts evaporated. There wasn't anything businesslike in that kiss. Not that kissing was *ever* businesslike in her world.

She curled her toes in the heels and was certain she'd topple right off them if he let go. Which he didn't. He stepped away and searched her face for a second then came right back. Into another one of those hellaciously wet and delicious kisses. The door handle dug into her back and her weight twisted it. Her ears were ringing and his lips continued to rattle her nerves. And the handle at her back.

Bang bang bang.

The door handled twisted again.

"Hey, unlock the door," a female voice complained.

Carter released her so fast Abby fell forward on her heels. She quickly gained control and smoothed the skirt then felt her head.

Her ponytail surely was a mess. She didn't dare turn, just cleared her throat. "Um, I think we could probably put a couple of ficus trees in this room. They'd do quite well. What do you think?" She rubbed a hand over her burning mouth, worried lipstick was all over her face.

Carter nodded. "Let's look at the other spaces." He motioned her out the door and down the hall.

The next room had four people in a meeting. Heads swiveled when they rushed through the door, taking in her hair and dress. He waved a hand. "Sorry, just evaluating the room for plants. This one doesn't need much."

They stepped out and hurried toward the next. Her face was heated as she fully expected the next room to be filled too. All of whom would take one look at them and know she'd just given him a tonsil lashing. When the door opened, she was relieved.

It was empty.

"Thank God." Carter let out a breath.

She whirled on him and glared. "What exactly do you think you're doing?"

He grinned. "I was about to ask you the same question. Only maybe I should just—"

Damned if he didn't drop his mouth to hers *again*. Only this time he twisted the door lock shut behind her. She had no idea how much time passed while they played tonsil hockey. Nor did she care. In fact, it hadn't really been a surprise when she drew back and his hand was on her waist—inside her shirt.

When his other hand slid up the outside of the fabric and a thumb stroked across her breast, her mind cleared instantly. In fact, her entire body jumped to attention. *His* attention. Her ears thundered like a freight train. Ironic, because if this didn't stop soon, she was going to be run over with the "stupid" disease. The stupid disease that might possibly see them both naked on that humongous mahogany conference table behind him.

"Um, Carter?" She shoved against his chest halfheartedly.

For a second, he didn't budge. When he finally stepped back, his eyes were lidded and soft. Was he having the same stupid thoughts? He glanced at the table and ran a hand through his hair. "Sorry about that, Abby. I wasn't really planning to … "

She looked at the latched door and raised a brow.

"Okay, maybe this time I was, but before. In there," he gestured down toward the employee kitchen, "that wasn't planned. You should—"

She glanced at the time on her phone. "I should go. I have to get back. You can just send me a floor plan and tell me what you want in each room. I can work off that." She scrambled in her bag and pulled out a card. "Here's my e-mail address. Just send it there."

She flipped the latch and whipped open the door. She needed to get away. Fast. Far enough away so she could catch her breath and put everything in perspective. Only he grabbed her arm and held her tight.

"I promised you lunch."

"I never said yes."

"So, say it now." He leaned his forehead against hers and damned if she didn't want to turn that latch back into place. She didn't.

"Just lunch?"

"Sure. You hungry?"

Did he really just ask that? She bit back the groan. She wasn't hungry *before* he kissed her. But now? She was ravenous. Only there wasn't a restaurant within miles that would satisfy her craving. Did it matter she wasn't who he thought? Instead, she was lying and cheating and hiding important details at every turn. Or word.

Correction, *she* hadn't really cheated. His best friend had. Only he thought she was the best friend. Her head started to throb. *No.*

He hadn't thought she was anything other than herself. *She* was the one that had things all messed up. She had to tell the truth—but it was so incredibly *complicated*. He was texting her as the friend, she knew about the ex's relationship, and she'd never said a word. Plus she was deceiving him by continuing to send messages and respond when he did.

This was all Caroline's fault and Abby intended to tell her so. Had she not sent that first message, this would never have happened. She would never have gone to that restaurant looking for him. *But the incident in the park with Ruckus had nothing to do with that.*

Carter grinned. Some of the lipstick had actually wiped off on him. What would his office think? She reached up and stroked it away with her fingers.

This was all wrong. She wished she could ditch the entire project, and him. Only, she needed the work. She needed any work, really. She couldn't afford to turn down a job simply because one of her clients gave hot-as-hell kisses that made her want to—a crazy image of him flew through her mind. Naked.

"Yeah, I'm hungry."

Chapter Thirteen

If the scent of flowers was an aphrodisiac, then Abby's red fingernail polish and lips combined to be the ultimate visual topping. Better than walking by the lingerie store on Fifth Street. She wrapped the nails around her tea glass and brought her lips to the edge for a sip. *Bam.* Gut-wrenching heat that made him want to taste them again. He didn't dare look away.

He'd followed her to a diner she recommended and was surprised they had the same taste in food. Simple, easy, and a nice quiet atmosphere where you could talk. He noted the way the booth walls rose and wrapped them in a perceived solitude. They could probably take up where they left off at the office and not a soul would notice. Maybe just another taste of those lips. He scooted toward her.

She adjusted the same amount. In the other direction. Okay, message received.

"Carter, have you been here before?" She looked around the room.

Was she seeking an escape? He wouldn't blame her if she did. The kisses were just a spur of the moment impulse. He glanced at the lipstick on her tea glass. They were an impulse driven by the need to taste that. Was he sorry? Hell, no. He'd do it again in a second.

"Sometimes. Listen, about my office—"

"Like I said, just send the blueprints and tell me what you want. I'll get it done. I can probably deliver everything by next week, depending on what's on the list. Will that work?"

He shook his head. "No. I mean, sure, but that wasn't what I meant. I was talking about—"

She swept those fingernails out and laid them over his hand and squeezed. "Don't. Let's not talk about that. Please."

He registered the desperation in her voice. "Okay."

"Good." She gave a weak smile.

Carter watched her movements with interest. "So, just curious, how did a Midwestern girl end up down here?"

Abby shrugged. "Dumb luck, I guess. After graduation, my parents gave me a week-long trip to Europe. It had always been a dream of mine. Of course, they hadn't trusted me to go alone, so my brother, Jason, chaperoned. I met Caroline in Edinburgh. You know, Scotland. She was making a trip down the famous pub crawl from the castle … and we were shopping for kilts. I had made a bet with Jason and he lost. The pay-up was to wear a kilt as long as we were in Scotland."

"Did he?" There was no way in hell he'd put a skirt on, but one had to admire a guy that wasn't afraid to.

She giggled. "Technically, yes. He had swim trunks under it. Said it was too windy over there and he wasn't interested in baring his ass to the world. It was ironic, coming from a guy who later strode down a nude beach sans the very same swim gear."

He swallowed hard. Had she been on that beach too? That thought was pretty damned—interesting. "They have nude beaches in Scotland?"

She choked out a bit of her drink and covered her mouth with a napkin. "Of course not. It's cold and windy there year round. Who'd want to think about swimming in that climate? No, that was later. You know what they say, when in France … "

"Do as the locals do." He *really* wanted to ask if she'd done so but decided against it. "That must have been one hell of a trip. Scotland, France. You met Caroline there?"

"She had just graduated too…from journalism school. Said she was going to explore the world and write first-hand experiences. She had a grant from some newspaper that was supposed to turn into a news journalist job in New York eventually. She stayed with us until Italy then took off for some exotic island I'd never heard of. I can't remember the name."

"Pretty brave for a girl that age."

"She's never been shy. Her dad had been a journalist and she thought it sounded glamorous. Although he disappeared when she was a kid so it doesn't seem too great to me. She called me a month later and we talked for hours. Apparently, she was coming home—to Texas. She wanted me to visit for a while. I couldn't wait to get away from home. My parents were driving me crazy. Every time I turned around they'd invited some random young "successful" guy for dinner and conveniently left me alone with them."

He hitched a brow. "They were setting you up? Why? You'd just graduated. They should have been helping you find a job, not a date."

Abby cleared her throat. "Actually they wanted to do all of that. I was supposed to join the family business like everyone else…and I did for a while. Then one day I sat in this meeting with these arrogant jerks and realized that I'd very likely be in meetings like that for the rest of my career. And my parents wanted more than a date—they wanted a husband. There was something freakishly boring about it. Apparently, in their book, any girl that isn't married when she leaves college is likely to be a spinster forever. Not to mention, they hated my idea of studying landscape architecture … thought it was useless."

"Wow. Supportive."

"Yep. Not much has changed either. Anyway, I came here and Caroline introduced me to an old boyfriend that got me a job, so I stayed. She and I roomed together for a while then went our separate ways. Caroline was more a night owl and I was too much a morning person. She's still my best friend ever, though."

An odd partnership if you asked him. By the way she'd talked at their dinner together, Caroline was wild to the point of crazy.

Abby was the grind-master work-a-holic. Okay—crazy was the common denominator. "What do your parents think about the new business? They must be happy for you, being an entrepreneur and all?"

She dropped her eyes to the table then looked away. "I don't really know. They haven't said a word so far. Before I opened, they had a lot to say—none good. They thought I was making a mistake putting all my savings into a business. Now, no call, nothing. I think they ... forgot."

"Parents never forget that kind of thing. Maybe they've tried calling and missed you?"

She shook her head. Her teeth scraped over her lip and trembled—was she on the verge of tears?

"Nah, I am one of the middle in a brood of five. They forgot. Or maybe don't care? It doesn't matter. I gave up waiting on their approval years ago."

Based on her expression, that was a lie. She still wanted approval—in fact, he'd bet she was craving a little at the moment. "Then it's their loss. You'll be the talk of the town soon."

The waiter arrived and took their orders then disappeared. No, this idle conversation wasn't going to work. He had to say something. He thrummed his hands on the table. "I'm sorry. I have to say something. I'm not one to—I just—Shit." He ran a hand through his hair then lifted his lips in a grin. "It was fun, okay? That's all I wanted to say. It was hellacious fun."

She took another sip before answering. "It was, wasn't it?"

Their food arrived within seconds and they ate and talked baseball and about her shop, and he told her a few things about his work. She had the most animated way of talking. Her hands, eyes, face, and even her feet kicked into the conversation sometimes. He noticed because she'd added the red polish on her toes too. They peeked out of the heels that showed off her slim ankles when she slid sideways in the booth.

Lunch ended so quickly, he wanted to order again. Unfortunately, the time on the wall made it obvious they both needed to get back to work. Her car was near and she left him at the restaurant door in such a rush, he was barely able to say goodbye. Maybe she feared he might try to kiss her again.

Back at work, things got crazy in a heartbeat. Roger followed him as soon as he stepped from the elevator, advising that their project deadlines had changed. The customer he'd seen last week liked the presentation and needed product faster. Therefore, they needed him to rework his proposal. Yikes. Roger rattled off the details and handed him a paper with notes then told him to call them.

"Oh, and that was the running chick earlier, wasn't it?"

He nodded, not willing to say more.

"You brought her here? What were you doing in the lunchroom? Lindsey said you looked like you were making out. Don't tell me you did it on the table, I'll never eat in there again."

Carter's mouth fell open. "Seriously? You guys are gossiping simply because I gave her a tour of the office? Grow up. She has a plant service that does corporate maintenance. I asked her to give me a quote." He strode around his desk, dropped his keys on the top, and fished through the stack of paper and phone messages.

"Yeah, and what other kind of maintenance is she doing for you?" Roger's raised brow was more than annoying.

Carter wadded the paper he'd just read and tossed it at him.

The guy darted out the door but not before throwing another question at him. "Hey, did you find out if they're real?"

Carter growled and shook his head. When his cell beeped with a group message from Roger, he glanced at the screen and ignored it. Childish idiot. None of his business.

• • •

> Carter took runner in lunchroom. I mean to lunch

Abby didn't care much for Carter's friend, or his comments. What a slimeball. Carter did NOT tell them that, did he? Abby stared at the screen, her face heating. The message was a reply to the lunch message from before. Was that what the whole thing was about? A guy's curiosity on the status of her breasts? We'd just see about that, wouldn't we?

A dozen other comments flashed after the first, which made her blood boil more. Nothing from Carter though. He was irritatingly silent. She wasn't sure whether to be glad or furious. What a bunch of losers. Well, according to the rule "judge a man by the friends he keeps," Carter was given a verdict. Over. Not that they'd even started anything yet. Or would, because she wasn't interested—not anymore.

Still he'd kissed the brain cells right out of her head. *And gossiped to his friends immediately after.* She'd fix that. Why not? His friend had already screwed *one* ex, why not make it two? Technically, she wasn't an ex but still—she picked up the phone and punched in a message.

> Oh, they're real alright. Perky too. U should see the rest of her.

There. What do you think of that, Mr. Kiss-and-Tell? Her stomach clenched. She should feel better about standing up for herself with a bunch of sex-starved gossiping never-left-high-school boys. She didn't. A flurry of text responses chorused and she couldn't bear to see what other gross remarks they'd made.

In fact, the rest of the day her body ached with the realization she'd been a conquest in his circle of friends. Something they'd goaded him to prove, and he'd done it. He'd done a hell of a job too. All she could think about was that damned lunchroom door and his mouth trailing kisses across hers while his hands did other things. *Dammit. I'm such an idiot.*

"Well, you sure showed him." Caroline gave her the eyebrow-hovering look that plainly said *and made a fool of yourself to boot.*

"Who cares? Those guys are a bunch of teenagers—talking about things like that. He set me up to go out with him so he could test out their theory. You think they made a bet on it? I mean, look at these babies. Can I help it if I have kind genetics?" Abby thrust her chest out and lowered her eyes to observe. Genetics were only part of it, and Caroline knew as much. She ran several miles a week and spent at least another hour at the gym every other day. Releasing the breath she'd held, Abby grimaced. She'd had little time to exercise since the store opened and she needed to get back to the routine.

"Well, if they made a bet, I wonder which way he picked. Real or bedazzled?"

"Does it matter? I mean what kind of guy does that? The wrong kind, obviously. No wonder the chick dumped him for his best friend." Abby threw a hand to her mouth, embarrassed at the insult. "Do you think that was a set-up too? Maybe one of the guys goaded him into it just to see what would happen?"

"Wow, did you really turn that jaded over night? Talking about the silicone hills on a woman isn't the same as stealing her."

Abby rolled her eyes. Caroline didn't get it. "Need I remind you he wasn't just talking about them? He was actually tasting and feeling and—"

Caroline held up a hand to stop the conversation. "Please, spare me the details. I don't want to know. Okay, wait, yes, I do. Exactly how far *did* he get? I mean, were you horizontal when he felt you up? Or just getting started?"

Abby threw the tape dispenser at her. Fortunately, it was plastic and Caroline was fast. It missed, glancing off the corner of a pot before hitting the floor and splintering.

"Way to go, boss. Should we chalk that up to employee theft—or abuse? Now we have to buy a new one."

Whoosh. The door burst open. The steady rain had prevented the normal pedestrian traffic from venturing through; the only customer that would step in had to be serious. Abby scraped the broken plastic into her palm, dropped it on the counter, and turned to make a sale.

"You slept with Jackson?" Carter's face was ashen as he stomped forward, splattering drips across her floor.

"Excuse me? Is that really a question you're entitled to ask? Who I've been with? I mean you hardly know me. Just because you—we—oh, forget it. Look, you had your fun. Now get lost." Abby whirled around and disappeared into the stockroom. Where did he get off asking? He was the one that locked her in a conference room, kissed her brain cells dead, then embellished the details. What did he care who she slept with? Or didn't in this case. It wasn't like he'd made it that far. Thank God for that. At least she hadn't been a total moron and had held onto at least one or two cells of gray matter. She'd never been the type before and wasn't likely to start now.

The door to the stockroom bumped her behind when it closed at her back. Her hands shook. She'd squeezed the plastic so hard it carved a small cut in her palm. The patter of Caroline's shoes was the only sound in the other room. Her muffled voice followed. "Soooo, I'm Caroline."

Abby peered through the one-way glass window in their office, thankful she'd had it installed. Of course, it had been for an entirely different reason. She wanted to make sure they'd see customers who entered if they were in the stockroom.

At the moment, it was also convenient for watching Carter fume. His eyes widened as recognition hit. He didn't take the hand Caroline extended. His were shoved in his pockets and didn't budge.

"Caroline, huh?" His eyes narrowed. "Tell me, Caroline, who likes to take pictures and spy on people—how well does Abby know my friend Jackson, really?"

Caroline's head started to turn toward the window, then she corrected herself. She squared her shoulders and straightened. "Um. Well, I'd say she has his number memorized. Just like you know which parts of Abby's anatomy include implants, you sorry turd."

His mouth dropped. He blinked his eyes twice. And left.

Badeep deep.

Yikes. Should she look at the message? Was there any point in doing so? They were done. Toast. And she had work to do.

Badeep deep.

Oh, hell. She grabbed the phone from her purse.

Chapter Fourteen

We're done man. Couldn't just leave this one alone, could u? Let me know when u grow up. Till then, go to hell.

He crammed the phone in his pocket and stomped through the drizzle to his office. This wasn't the first time Jackson had tried to horn in on his date. It had been a game since high school. He hadn't really cared then. Much.

Jackson was charming and everyone drew to him like flies to sugar. It wasn't too far-fetched that when Carter had grown tired of someone, they clung to Jackson's supportive nice-guy routine. Not to mention, the guy was filthy rich and hadn't needed to work full-time his entire life. How they'd become such good friends was a puzzle.

Well, not really. He remembered it vividly. Jackson moved into the house at the corner of his street when they were ten. Since everyone else on the street had daughters, not sons, their friendship was a no-brainer. And a necessity for both of them unless they wanted Barbie dolls and bows on their heads. The competitiveness seemed healthy then. Even in college, it had pushed them to succeed—be their best. Not with girls, but elsewhere.

This was too much, though. Over the line. Carter frowned. He had no idea there'd been a line 'til now. Abby was it.

Abby was it.

The phrase caught in his head. He swallowed the boulder in his throat. Was she?

...

For a few weeks, Carter managed to throw himself so deep into work he barely looked up. The only thing he took time for was—more work. And he watered the damn plants. He hadn't a clue why, but he did.

He also decided to keep chatting with the girl who loved dogs … but didn't have one. She was a lot less complicated. Pretty witty too. He almost rolled in laugher when she told him about her siblings. He liked her attitude. In fact if he could match *her* personality to the physical attraction he had for Abby—well that would be interesting. Physical attraction only lasted so long, though.

At some point, Abby delivered the new order to the office accompanied by spy girl. Together they arranged the foliage quite well. He was gone then and every time since. The receptionist kept him aware of the scheduled visits and any questions or concerns she mentioned. There were few. One tree died and was replaced shortly after delivery. The ones in the kitchen had *issues*. Per the note, someone was dousing them with coffee, or some other beverage. If it continued, mold would grow and they'd have to replace them as well.

He didn't care. In fact, he had half a mind to tell her to take them all back. He started to write the note several times but couldn't finish. One such note glared at him from the desktop when she arrived for the weekly watering. Crap. He looked at his watch and realized he missed his escape. The rap on the door was shortly followed by the door easing open, and she popped in.

Her eyes widened. "Oops. Sorry, I thought you were out. I was just watering—"

He motioned her in. "Help yourself." He returned to the computer screen, noting her movement in the reflection. *Shit*. Was this as awkward for her as him? It shouldn't have been—they hadn't done anything more than share a few kisses. A few searing-hot-nearly-took-her-clothes-off kisses. Yeah, no biggie.

With her back turned, he barely caught the words. "You're wrong, you know, I haven't … been … with anyone in over a year. A year and four months. Not that it's any of your business. So, whatever you thought—it wasn't right."

The chair let out a squeal as he turned and leaned to stare at her back, which still made him want to touch her. Dammit.

"Seriously?" That was a hell of long time. So … if that were true, then anything between her and Jackson was ancient history. How could he hold that against her? Or him either.

"Seriously. And don't think I'm proud of it either. I just don't get involved that easily. Or deeply."

Two more raps on the door announced they had a visitor. Holy shit. Speak of the devil. "Jackson. What are you doing here?"

Abby sucked in a quick gasp and turned her back, which caught Carter off balance. Her shoulders were stiff and she hunkered down. She was hiding from him? It had been that awkward?

"I thought we should talk. I know I probably should have done this earlier but I wanted to give you a little breathing time to digest the situation." Jackson stood at the door as if ready to escape. His face was sullen. "It wasn't like I meant it to happen."

Carter glanced from Jackson's face to Abby's back. She was a post. He held up a hand in protest. "Let's don't talk about it, okay? I don't want to know."

"I met her a long time ago. Before you did, actually. It was just—random. We were having fun and then somewhere along the way everything changed."

Carter hitched a brow. "Changed?"

Jackson shifted feet and glanced at Abby's back. "Yeah. I would have told you but it all moved so fast and all of a sudden you were asking about a—"

Abby shoved an elbow in his back and spilled water down Jackson's pants. Not just a little either—she doused him good. *Did she really do that? Wow.*

"Oh, uh. Sorry about that, Jackson. You should probably go change or something, right?" She stared at the wet spot. Jackson's mouth opened then shut. He darted back to Carter's face with disbelief.

Seconds ticked as the two men glared at each other. Acceptance finally kicked in and Jackson shrugged. "Yeah, I guess I should. Later, man." He stood but hesitated. "Where's Roger? I need to kick his ass."

"I have no idea. Probably his office. Why?"

Jackson left without answering. When the door was closed and the room quiet, Carter cleared his throat. "I gather things didn't work out very well between you two?"

She held up the empty pot and grinned sheepishly. "Not one bit. So, um, I'm out of water. I'd better go refill. Sorry about the mess. I'll come back and clean it up later." She rubbed a foot over the wet spot on the carpet then slipped from the room.

She didn't return as promised. When Carter went searching, the only person available was spy girl. Caroline. She eyed his approach warily.

"She left, didn't she?"

"Yep. I don't know what you said *this* time, but I'd recommend you seek out some dating advice. You suck at it."

"Apparently I do," he admitted. As he walked back to his office he heard voices in Roger's.

Jackson's voice, loud and clear, thundered. "That was the stupidest idea ever."

Roger stayed calm. "No. Give it a little more time. I think it'll work out. Besides you could have done a better job with your part, you know. Mouthing off like that wasn't cool."

"Maybe not, but how was I supposed to know she'd do that? You'd better know what you're doing. Personally, I think it'd be better just to lock them both in a room and let 'em duke it out. Or whatever else comes naturally."

A chair leg screeched on the floor and steps approached. Carter strode to his office, grabbed his jacket, and left.

Chapter Fifteen

Caroline wasn't letting Abby off easily, no matter how long a day they'd had at work. She snatched Abby's purse from the counter and held it captive. "Drinks are on me tonight, girl. You need one. Or ten maybe. Let's go."

Abby trailed down the street after her. "What I need is a kick in the ass. How could I do that to him? I mean the guy has already been through hell with his shitty best friend. Here I am lying to him every time I turn around. It's awful. I'm a horrid person! And he's incredibly … nice."

"Is he? I thought you were still pissed he felt you up and blabbed about it. Now you think he's nice? Make up your mind. Do you like him or not?"

"Yes. I mean, no." She sighed. "I don't know. Except for that fake boob trick, he seems pretty decent. Fun too. I mean, we like a lot of the same things."

"Yeah. Dogs. Running. Flowers. Baseball. Jackson. I mean you, of course—not the other dweeb."

They scooted into a booth at the back of the bar and ordered a round of beers.

"I know, right? Although, he's not much on flowers. I even like his smartass friend Roger. I've talked to him a couple of times at the office. He kind of grows on you once you get used to him. All I've done is lie, lie, lie. Carter will never get past that. I can't believe I dumped that entire pitcher of water on Jackson, but hell, at the time it seemed safer than telling the entire story."

"You have to be kidding about Roger."

Abby laughed. Of everything she said, Caroline picked up on *that*? "It's hilarious actually. He's like this totally obnoxious misfit of a guy who can't help blurting out the most inappropriate things in front of a woman. What's odd is if you just observe what he does otherwise, he's got a big heart."

Caroline rolled her eyes. "Sure. I believe *that*."

"He does. Every time he says something totally wretched, the secretary apologizes and says he's really a closet teddy bear. He loaned her money to fix her car when someone sideswiped hers in the parking lot. She's fifty and has three kids in high school. Her husband left and she's barely able to pay her bills."

"He wants to make sure she shows up for work. Big deal, that's a win-win for both."

"It was twelve hundred dollars, Caroline. Not exactly a homerun for him, in my book. Oh, and he thought you were cute." That caught her friend's attention.

"Me? Cute? Ha, that's a laugh. I haven't been cute a day in my life." She shuddered as if the words insulted. Abby noted she swallowed a grin and avoided eye contact.

"Well, he thought so. He even asked if you were seeing anyone."

"Was that before or after he asked if *my* boobs were real? Or maybe he was still ogling yours?" Caroline gulped a couple of swallows of beer and raised her glass for a refill as the bartender darted by.

"To be honest, he turned ten shades of red the first time I met him and didn't have the balls to look me in the face which was kind of odd, considering he had no way of knowing I'd read the messages. It kind of made me wonder what else the dirtbags were saying outside of the text messaging. Then I ran into him in the hallway and he was forced to acknowledge me. Very polite, as a matter of fact. You should talk to him."

Caroline shook her head so hard the spikes on top rattled. "Not on your life."

Abby shrugged. "Your call."

An hour later, they were still in the booth. A plate of nachos sat in front of them, half eaten. Abby licked the sour cream from her thumb. The beer glasses had been recycled more times than Abby could remember and she'd switched to water.

Not Caroline. "Hey, I'm off tomorrow, remember? I don't have to get up early. Here's to you, boss."

"Technically, we're partners."

She held up the empty beer glass, peered at the drips in it and shrugged, then clanked Abby's water. Caroline leaned forward over the table and winked. "You should stay out late tonight. Real late. Like maybe go water his plants or give him, I mean them, a little tender care."

"You're wasted. And talking crazy." Crazy but still an enticing thought.

"Hey, you said he had a good set of tonsils. That's not something one should waste. You know what I mean? Besides, you told him it had been a while."

Time for a subject change.

"Forget him. Listen, I've meant to talk to you about this—we need to do something to drum up business. Even with the loan, we'll have a hard time making it through the end of the year unless we do something more. I was thinking we should advertise. Maybe take on some more office maintenance projects like Carter's. What do you think?"

Caroline shrugged. "Sure. I still like the breakup package idea. That was stellar."

"Yeah, and mean. I can't go through that again—it was excruciating."

"For you or her?"

"Both. Besides, that might make things worse rather than better. How would you like to be the place that sends out hate flowers? Talk about a bad rep."

"Okay, the date thing then. Tell you what, while I'm off tomorrow, I'll draw up some ads for you. I do Photoshop pretty well. I was real good at making prank pictures in college. I should show you some of them. It's not an easy thing to—"

Abby thrust a finger in her face. "I don't *even* want to know. If you feel like taking a stab at an advertising campaign, I won't stop you. Just don't bring me anything that will get us into trouble, okay?"

Caroline had a mouthful of nachos when she nodded. The sour cream on her bottom lip was in direct contrast to her complexion. She wiped it with the back of her hand and slipped out of the booth. "We should do a blog too, and maybe do promotional things on it. I'll give it a shot and show you next week. See ya. I'm done. Be careful walking home, okay? Or go get your tonsils checked again—that would be fun."

She winked and was gone.

• • •

A few weeks later Abby smiled at her phone display then dropped her chin onto fisted hands. She'd opened the Justchat app. It was time to officially give up on Carter. With all the lies she told, he'd never forgive her. She wasn't even sure she wanted him to, knowing the crap his friends had texted about her. Totally childish and so … so … caveman. The Jackson-dousing incident had sealed the lid on the entire fiasco. Besides, *this* guy had no baggage. Yet. Why couldn't everyone be like the chat guy? She left the messages on her screen as a reminder that not *all* guys are dumbasses.

> Traveling To Survive: You said a while back that life would be less complicated if you'd taken the safe road … less complicated equals BORING. Doesn't sound like you (from the little I know). I'm traveling out of the country for a while with work. Will try to talk but may not have a chance. Be good … and brave.

She Hearts Dogs: Perhaps YOU should be brave if traveling … and safe. My curiosity is killing me—you're not some kind of military spy or diplomat, are you?

Traveling To Survive: LOL. I wish. Nothing that exciting, just an average-joe-business-guy with customers in strange lands. Talk to you later.

She-Hearts-Dog: Later

She kept smiling when the next customer entered then acknowledged a small crowd window shopping through their store before she rushed off to Carter's building for the scheduled maintenance. She left Caroline in charge. Her friend had done a great job, not only with advertisements but also inventory. While Abby hadn't looked, apparently the blogging thing was getting a lot of followers too. After the nacho and beer night, Caroline had recommended they add in a few gift items. Things that would catch someone's eye in the window and offer an alternative to flower gifts—or complement them. They now offered amazing jeweled gift boxes that could be included or center-pieced in a bouquet or plant for any occasion. Perfect for, say, an engagement ring or anniversary item.

The beer and nacho night had been a great idea, one they chose to repeat twice. In the kitchen/break room at Carter's office, she felt the dirt in the ficus tree she prepared to water and fertilize.

"Great," she muttered. "Is it that hard to dump coffee in the sink? Plants don't need caffeine. Neither do people." She reached in her pocket for the fertilizer stick and hoped it would counteract the mold.

"That depends on whether the person has spent two days on an airplane with a bunch of people who don't speak English."

She squared her shoulders. She hadn't seen Carter since the come-to-Jesus meeting with Jackson. Purposely avoiding him had been difficult at first, but then the office buzz said he was overseas on a project. Guess he made it back.

Good, it was time to put this thing between them to bed. Ahem, scratch that. Time to put it in the past. "How was the trip?"

He shrugged and the shift of his shoulders was laden with stress and fatigue. "Long." Judging by the shadow on his face, he'd come straight to work from the airport. Without a shave.

She swallowed hard. Hadn't bargained for the sexy, scruffy look.

Nor the way his eyes seemed to dig right into her head and pull all sense away. She cleared her throat. "Have you talked to your friend Jackson lately?"

He shook his shaggy hair. "Nope. I've been away for work. Haven't had time. Normally we keep up through text messages but—I've been busy."

Even with the lapse in time, he was hard to ignore. He scratched his head with vigor and smiled. "Abby, do you like baseball?"

"Huh?" She was brain dead. What did baseball have to do with anything?

"Baseball. I have tickets to the Astros for tomorrow night. Do you want to go?"

"With you?" Still brain dead.

He snickered, "Yeah. Unless that's a problem. I could give you both tickets, I guess, but I was kinda hoping to go."

"But you bought them to go with—" Oops, she snapped her mouth shut before she said *her*.

"I bought them because I like baseball. If you can get away from the shop, go with me. If not, no problem, I know you're busy." He stepped away from the wall in the lounge, stuck his hands in his pockets and turned to leave. "You look great, by the way."

"I love baseball."

He'd already stepped through the doorway. He turned back. "Yeah?"

"What time?"

"I'll come get you around six-thirty. Will that work?"

She nodded. Would he last nine innings? The man was a walking zombie. She hoped he got some sleep before the game.

...

By the third inning, the Astros were down by five and had gone through two pitchers. This wasn't going to be their year to make the playoffs unless something big happened. Carter frowned at the display over the stadium. Hey, if they couldn't win, at least he had good company and plenty of beer while he watched. Abby seemed filled with nervous energy. Every time a ball appeared to head for the stands, she leaned into him and clenched his arm. The Astros couldn't seem to seal the deal though. On the last one she groaned and slapped the counter. "Oh, my God. Get it out already!"

He laughed. "You're really getting into this, aren't you?"

"I love baseball. My brother played and I went to all his games. Dad took me. It was probably the only thing we did together, mainly because my sisters were too girly to stand the summer heat. When I was in college, that was all Dad and I could talk about without arguing."

Carter sighed.

"What? Something wrong?"

"No. I just think I died and went to heaven. I've never been around a woman that enjoyed it as much as I do."

In the fifth inning. A loud tune played and the overhead screen flashed the words *KISSCAM!* The ballpark cameras then searched the crowd and zoomed in on couples, enticing them to kiss—or not. Young. Old. In-between. It didn't matter. While the new pitcher warmed up, they watched and laughed.

"I love the kisscam! It's so fun."

"Everyone does. It's hilarious when they zoom in on two people obviously not comfortable with each other—say a brother and sister."

"Or a first date."

Carter nodded. Abby's eyes lit up as she grinned at the next photo. She'd worn lipstick again. Not the red she'd had on at his office that day, but a pale pink. Still, it had the same effect and he wished the camera would settle on them.

Instead, it found an elderly gray-haired twosome. The man leaned over the woman, bent her back in her chair, and kissed the hell out of her. Both laughed the entire time and when they sat back up, the woman gave a big thumbs-up to the crowd, who applauded vigorously. "That was definitely *not* a first date."

She laughed. "I'd love to be on the kisscam. With someone I actually *wanted* to kiss, of course."

Touché. She stared in admiration at the pitcher, who was now ready to sail the first pitch past a ready batter.

Her concentration amused Carter. He reached a hand under her chin and pulled her face around. "You don't need a camera for an excuse to kiss someone, Abs." To prove his point, he leaned down and brushed his mouth lightly against the pink of hers. He'd thought the passion from before a fluke. At least he wanted to believe it, because the last thing he needed was to get involved with another woman. Only, this wasn't really *involved*—she was just—fun, he guessed. He wasn't sure how to describe Abby, nor what the proper term was for his thoughts. Thoughts concerning her polished fingernails against his skin. He groaned and pulled away from the kiss.

"What? What's wrong?" Her half-lidded eyes were no longer focused on the ball field or the score.

He grinned. "Nothing's wrong. See—who needs a camera? Want a beer?"

She nodded and he trotted up to the beverage stand. He wasn't looking for an escape, but a little breathing room—or thinking room—was necessary.

It had been ages since the kisses at his office and, as much as he'd wanted another right away, her involvement with Jackson had cooled those jets. Or he thought so, before he went away for a month to manage the project overseas. He was snowed under the entire time with work, yet he still managed to think about her. He chalked it up to an overstimulated and over-worked imagination. It hadn't made sense that kissing Abby actually set off anything more than just a desire for temporary female companionship.

He could see her in the seat while he ordered and paid for the beer. Her ponytail, pulled through her cap, was sweet and cupped against her neck. Tonight's kiss wasn't what he'd expected. It had been an experiment, driven by a need to prove the unimportance of the ones in his office. The experiment failed miserably.

Beers in hand, he returned to the seat and handed hers over. "Abby, just to be sure there are no more surprises ... Are you seeing anyone right now? Like Jackson or Roger, or any of my other friends?"

Her eyes popped open and she spit the gulp of beer back into the cup as she choked. "Roger? Are you kidding me? You really think I'd date—him?"

He held up a hand and shrugged. "I never would have thought you'd go for Jackson, but obviously you did. Roger? He's really a nice guy once you get to know him. Most girls don't ever get to that point because he sucks at first impressions."

"You're right about that." She set the beer down and entwined her fingers on her knees. "I'm not seeing Roger—or Jackson—or anyone at the moment. Are you?"

"I'm not sure. There's this one girl." He winked and took a sip from his glass. "She's cute and likes everything I do. Kisses great, but … "

Abby's hurt registered and he knew he'd better not take it too far. She looked away.

"She always has dirt under her fingernails. It's not a big deal really because she works with plants. She covers the dirt by painting the nails with this awesome red polish. Pretty sexy actually."

"Is that right? Another plant girl."

"Not *another* plant girl, just one, and then she has this amazing way of humming when she kisses—it's almost like a purr."

He grinned as she frowned and shook her head. The ponytail bounced across her shoulders. "I do not."

"Oh, yes you do. It makes me wonder what you do when you—"

She landed a quick jab to his rib.

"Ouch." He rubbed where her elbow landed.

"Keep wondering, buddy, 'cause that's not on the radar at the moment."

He hitched a brow. "It's not? Not even a remote possibility?"

Abby scraped her teeth across the pink lipstick, which he knew tasted of candy, and his body went rigid. The announcer overhead boomed out, "Okay, folks, it's time for the seventh inning stretch. Everyone stand up—and streeettttcccchhh."

They stood together. She lifted her hands above her head and thrust her chest out, and damned if his eyes didn't try to roll back in his head. He grabbed her hand and groaned. "Let's get out of here." Carter pulled her toward the steps.

"Huh? Now? Where to? You have an emergency?"

"Yeah, an emergency need to find out exactly where that purring and stretching leads. Are you with me or not?" It was her fault, really. She'd leaned into him all night, brushing the warmth of her arm against his. She spoke in that soft way she always did and he loved it. He glanced at the scoreboard. Yeah, he loved the Astros, but they could manage without him this time. "I can take you home—or *home*. Your choice."

She stepped against him, her hand in his, her chest against his back. He looked over his shoulder and registered the glint in her smile.

"Well, I always did think the seventh inning stretch was a critical part of the game. A game changer, sort of."

"It could be."

The drive to his place usually took about thirty minutes, depending on traffic. When she slipped her fingers inside the buttons of his shirt on the way, he jammed his foot on the gas and they managed it in twenty. Thank God there weren't any cops along the way. He would have landed a ticket for sure. He rushed to the door as soon as the car was in park, not willing to give her time to back out.

It was pathetic and pushy. He couldn't help it—she'd been on his mind for weeks. Invading his work, his sleep, everything. It had to stop, and tonight it was going to. He'd get her out of his thoughts for good.

As he opened the door, Abby slid her fingers around his waist from behind and dug those fingernails into his stomach. He clenched his eyes. Okay, maybe she wouldn't be completely out of his thoughts, but he'd work on that later. After he investigated that awesome purring thing. He whirled her around, slammed the door behind them, and plunged his mouth to hers.

· · ·

Abby was about as close to losing her mind as she'd been in ... forever. When she'd wrapped around him from behind, he groaned. There was a mountain of heat between them just as it had been in his office, but *this* time she needed confirmation. She strung her fingers in his hair and pulled back softly. When his mouth moved down her neck and he pushed the neck of her T-shirt aside, she pulled harder. "Wait."

"Huh, what's wrong?" The grogginess in his voice wasn't sleep but restraint. Thick and waning restraint.

"I need to know something."

His gaze mirrored the same passion burning in her.

"Sure. Tell me." He stepped back, his arms wrapped loosely around her waist. "If you're worried about protection, I have it." He nodded toward a hallway that most certainly led to a room she wanted and feared at the same time.

"No, not that. I mean, um, that's good. I just need to know that whatever happens between us stays that way. Okay?"

"What does that mean?"

"I mean, I don't want our—whatever this is—fodder for man talk." Short of telling him she'd read all those texts about her, she couldn't exactly detail it out. Still, she wasn't interested in any other gossip about ... body parts or performance.

"You think I'd do that? Christ, Abs, has that happened to you? Someone talked about you that way?"

"No." *Just you, that's all.* She panted as his hands took a soft turn north toward the skin under her breasts. "But—"

"Trust me, I'm not like that." He delved his mouth against hers, his tongue wet and searching for a response, and she forgot everything.

What exactly had she wanted him to say?

He released her lips and trailed kisses across her cheek and down her neck, over her collarbone, clamping down on the soft pebble of her breast. She yelped and clung to him so tight his heart beat rapidly and his breath rasped as he licked her flesh. She kissed his cheek. His ear. Anything she could get her mouth against while she held him.

Abby blinked away the fog when Carter lifted his head. Her shirt had somehow ended up on the floor. His too. While his hands fumbled with the clasp on her bra, she stroked his chest and moved to the zipper on his pants. The cold rasp of metal sent her blood skyrocketing, but before she could reach in and grasp the spot she wanted to touch, he grabbed her wrist.

"I'm sorry." She tried to control her breathing. "Too forward, right? We should stop."

"No. No, it's not that—we just need to—relocate. Come on." He entwined his fingers in hers and pulled her behind him to a dark room with even darker furniture. Everything about it was incredibly male: the sheets, the furniture, even the smell. It was all *him*. Which heated up things even more. He grabbed something from the floor and tossed it aside before she stepped forward. "It's a little messy, sorry."

She giggled, more from nerves than anything else. "Well, at least I know you weren't planning this."

Chapter Sixteen

Carter's over-stimulated nerves finally got a message through to his brain and jogged him awake. Silver shards of moonlight filtered through the blinds and cast a striping of color across his bed. And the body sprawled over him like a blanket.

He brought a hand up and stroked the tickling hair away from his nose and smiled as he soaked her in. Now that was a picture he wouldn't easily forget. Nor the time they spent together before he did the unthinkable—fell asleep, sated and exhausted.

Her fault, but he wasn't placing blame. More like awarding it, he supposed. The flight home, late night at the ballpark, beer, and the warmest skin *ever* wrapped around him. Not exactly a bad way to wear a man out.

Badeep deep.

The glow of Abby's cell shot through the room. Who sent her text messages at six a.m.? His cell buzzed and danced on the counter as well. Okay, who was he to judge? He ignored the message and trailed his hand down her back, letting it rest in the small spot at the base of her spine.

"You awake?"

In response to his question, she slid her leg up his thigh and rested it across parts of him that drew to attention. *Wow.* The rest was over. Would she be interested in another seventh inning stretch? The first one had been a blast.

"Yeah, now." She pushed up on an arm and shoved the hair from her eyes.

Her skin was pearlescent in the light, goading him to touch. Which he did. He reached up and cupped a hand over the swell of her breast and trailed a thumb across it. He liked that she watched.

"I should go."

"Now?" It was hard to pass up a chance to make her do that humming thing again. Besides, they had another hour or so before work.

Badeep deep.

"Yeah, someone's trying to find me." The glow from her phone lit the room again.

"Here, I'll get it. You can answer and then we'll—" He slipped her leg away and pulled up, dropping his legs to the floor.

"No!" Abby bolted toward the glow, snatched it up, and hit a button, plunging them back to moonlit darkness.

"Wow, you move fast for this early. Too fast for me. I'm not awake. Come here." He motioned her to join him, but she reached for the pile of undergarments at her feet.

"Can't. I need to go take a shower and get ready for work. I, um, take a while." She yanked on her bra and panties then went in search of her other clothing. When she returned, she twisted her hair back into the ponytail he'd slipped it out of the night before. Another message lit up her phone and he wondered if that meant something.

Or perhaps *someone*. A pit opened in his stomach. *No fucking way. Not again.*

She had someone looking for her. And she didn't want him to see who.

...

The following week, Carter walked into the office proud of the fact he hadn't picked up the phone and called her any of the fifteen times he'd considered it. Should he have at least checked to make sure she got home okay? Yeah, right. Home to whoever was trying to find her? Most guys would probably love to be a girl's wild side. The fling. The one-night stand. Why did he have a problem? He shrugged as rain pelted his office window. He didn't. But he *did* have a problem with lying.

He was relieved he had a flight out on Thursday afternoon and the rain would clear by then. He'd be in Thailand by nine a.m. the following day—which was actually the same day due to the time change. A little distance and reflection would do him well. And a hell of a lot of work.

As if he didn't have enough problems, Carter's thoughts wandered to his mom. His latest attempt to convince her to sell the house and move in with him hit a brick wall. "An old woman like me doesn't need to cramp the style of her young and single offspring." It had been a relief, though he argued just enough to seem sincere. She'd hate the city anyway. Their meager home in the hill country wasn't much, but it didn't require a long drive anywhere and there was ample grass and freedom. Plus, she had a plethora of neighbors to meddle with and check on her.

If her health was good, that would have been enough. It wasn't and he chastised himself for not visiting her before he boarded the plane. He was all she had left and guilt plagued him for not visiting more than a couple times a month. It had been a week and half with the past trip and now that would stretch to three weeks by the time he returned.

Not good.

He made a mental note to ask one of the guys to go by and check on her while he was gone. Roger or Jackson would probably be okay with doing so. They'd known her for a few years and she loved them like family.

When the airplane taxied to a stop, the thought disappeared. His customers waited on the tarmac and whisked him to their office, thrusting him into business meetings and planning discussions until well after dark.

He nodded off on his way to the hotel when the jet lag finally caught up. The driver woke him long enough for Carter to get to his room, and he was in a deep slumber within minutes of entering.

• • •

"You didn't explain anything, you just ran like hell?" Caroline's raised brow exuded her disapproval. The garden-gloved hand on her hip punctuated it. "And now you're wondering why he hasn't called? Seriously, Abby, what did you expect? Even if he wanted to see you again, taking off like that certainly makes it look as if you didn't."

"What was I supposed to do? I had to get a shower before I came to work." Maybe it wasn't exactly the full story, but there was truth in the words.

Caroline didn't buy it. She shook her head and ratcheted her brow higher. "Yeah, sure. Whatever you say."

"Besides, it's been almost a week. He could have called any time he wanted. I'm always here." Abby grabbed a bag of top soil and started filling peat pots for seedlings. "He could have stopped by too."

"Yeah, if he wasn't on the other side of the world."

"What are you talking about?"

Caroline ran a box knife through the seal of the delivery that arrived the day before. She pulled the flaps open so she could reach in and unload the contents. "He's in Thailand again, according to Rog. Left Thursday."

Abby spun around with a clump of soil in her palm. "Rog? You mean Carter's friend Roger? You're calling him by a nickname now? I thought you despised the guy."

Caroline shrugged. "It's kind of hard to avoid talking to him while I'm doing the plant maintenance. I mean, he's right there. So am I. I try to ignore him as much as possible, but he won't take a clue. Besides, after you took off like a whirlwind and left his buddy tied up in the sheets—"

"I didn't tie him—"

Caroline held up a hand. "Oh, please—metaphorically speaking, of course. I know you're too straight-laced to tie someone to the bedposts. Assuming he had bedposts. Did he?"

"Wouldn't you like to know."

"Rog said he was going to be gone for at least a week, very likely two. They have some big project going on over there and apparently Carter's commuting on a quarterly basis. He was hoping he'd get to go too, at some point."

"He told you that? Wow, you two are getting pretty cozy."

"Hardly. He's a toad."

"A toad. What the heck does that mean? You know what they say about frogs and toads."

Caroline leveled a bored gaze on her. "No, I don't."

"You have to kiss a lot of them to find your prince."

Caroline rolled her eyes, yanked off her dirty gloves, and grabbed her purse from the counter shelf. "You sound like my grandmother. Besides, been there—done that. Not doing it again. I'm going for a sandwich before I throw up. You want something?"

"Nope. I'm good."

Been there, done that? What the heck did that mean? The door flung closed behind her and Abby enjoyed a few minutes of silence before a set of customers waltzed in and needed assistance. Her phone announced a text message while she worked, but she ignored it until they were gone. When she finally lifted the screen to read it, she gasped. Could things get any more complicated?

> Carter: Jax, can you go by and see Mom? I'm worried she's not taking her meds. She probably needs a couple of refills on the blood pressure stuff too.

She stared at the screen, expecting it to bark another order. Wow, now what should she do?

By Caroline's information, Carter would be gone a couple of weeks minimum. If his mother was out of medicine, well, *that* could be dangerous. Especially blood pressure medicine. If Abby ignored the message, she'd never forgive herself if something happened to her. She frowned and shook her head, trying to admonish the growing plan. *No, I am not getting involved.*

She told herself that at least three more times that afternoon but it didn't stop her from visiting his office. With the intention of checking on the struggling plant in the lunchroom, of course. When Roger just happened to walk in for a soft drink, it had been easy to ask questions. Too many questions, if the look on his face meant anything.

Still, she'd gleaned enough to get a town name. From that, the Internet told the rest. Sunday was her planned day off, so she'd make the trip then.

Normally, Abby kept Caroline in the loop on everything. Fortunately, she hadn't asked how the day off would be spent. It was a relief not to tell it; there'd be a mountain of comments and teasing.

Chapter Seventeen

It had taken forty-five minutes to go from city sidewalks to country slumber and Abby had to blink to make sure she wasn't watching it on the widescreen in her living room. Taking a short road trip had been enticing since it had been months since she'd done anything other than work. Okay, except for Carter. She'd done Carter. She took a hand from the steering wheel and slapped her face for the picture she'd planted in her head. Technically, she wasn't sure who took the initiative on that little fiasco, which she aptly wrote off as TBF—*The Ballpark Fling*. She grinned through her stinging face.

It wasn't as if she had so many that names were required. In truth, it could have also been named the *new business fling*, or the *texting guy fling*, or even the *great fling of 2014* … or perhaps her entire life? No, that was depressing. Still, *TBF* sounded good. She shrugged. Or maybe just *The Carter Thing*. Actually, she'd never had a fling before so simply calling it *The Fling* would have sufficed but where's the fun in that?

She assumed the reason why it was so great was the result of such a long lapse. Or maybe her ex hadn't really been all that great and she wasn't worldly enough to know. Had she been more like Caroline and moved through guys like a lawnmower, maybe her mind wouldn't keep conjuring up crazy images and she'd stop sighing all the time, wishing for those images to be real again. *Crap!*

She swerved the wheel sharply to avoid the missed turn. The tires squealed a bit on the wet concrete but managed to veer into the fenced drive. The only marker had been the mailbox. Thankfully it had huge numbers. Large enough for a blind person to make out in the rain.

So this was where his parents lived. Or at least his mother. She knew little about his father—siblings either. Would it anger him that she came? They barely knew each other. Not to mention if she told him, she'd have to explain how she knew to go.

She'd just take care of the immediate medical concern and get out, without telling anything to either of them.

It was a nice house. Abby had imagined some clapboard white farmhouse with chickens when she reached the last turn. There had been one or two of those on the way, and it would have fit. Wrong. The house was brick and stone. Austin stone—one of her favorites. The light tan and white gave a warm welcome. Abby's stomach twisted as she noted the entrance wasn't visible. Instead, the drive wrapped around the house; she'd have to pull to the back. No hiding or turning around.

When her tires crunched behind the home, she gasped. The car rolled to a stop. The house was on a hill overlooking a steep drop to a creek bed. Water trickled along, a natural fence between the house and the pasture on the far side. A horse jerked his head to measure her interruption then dropped it back to eat his fill of the tall grass surrounding his hooves.

"Holy cow, what a view." She let out a soft whistle and climbed out of the driver's seat, stretching her arms above her head.

"Isn't it though? I don't think I could ever give it up." The voice startled Abby.

She peered across the car's roof to seek the owner. She narrowed her gaze.

There. In the shadow of a side building across from the house sat an older woman. A bowl rested in her lap as she worked her hands on the contents—contents which were hidden in its depths. "Are you lost?"

Abby pushed the door shut and stepped toward the woman. "That depends. Are you Carter's mother? Carter Coben?"

The woman lifted her wrist to push hair from her face. A wasted effort because the wind plopped it right back. "Yes, that's me. Is something wrong? He's not hurt, is he?"

"Oh, no. He's fine. I'm just here because—he asked. He had to go to Thailand for a few weeks and said you might need a prescription or two filled. I just wanted to come by and—check."

The woman stood gingerly and placed the bowl on the chair she'd vacated. She grabbed a walker that had been out of sight behind the chair and moved to meet Abby. "I'm afraid I haven't met you before. Are you a friend of Carter's?"

"Uh, sort of." Abby had no intention of explaining. Something told her this woman probably wouldn't approve of the new TBF designation assigned to her son. She quickened her steps and moved to hold the woman's arm. "I'm a friend of Jackson's. Carter asked him to stop by and uh, I offered to come instead. I hope that's okay. Jackson's been a little—busy lately." *If only she knew.*

"That's so nice of you. I do need a couple of things. Thanks for stopping by. Let's go inside and I'll give you the list. Is that okay?"

"Sure, Mrs. Coben."

"Call me Becky, honey."

That was all it took for Abby to gain the woman's confidence. Thank God she wasn't a burglar or a murderer. This old lady wouldn't stand a chance against someone with ill motives. The faint smell of dust caught Abby's attention. She looked up and noted a pickup approaching with a white cloud of dust trailing behind.

Abby changed her mind about Becky's safety when the driver leaned out the door and waved. "You okay, Ms. Becky?" The rifle in his back window was enough to ease any concerns. Or scare off a dumb kid with bad intentions.

"Yeah, yeah. All's well. This is a friend of my son's. Apparently he's over in the rice country now."

Abby mused at the way the woman offhandedly bragged about her son. Pride mixed fairly well with feigned exasperation. She imagined the entire countryside knew as much about Carter's travels as Becky.

"Rice Country. Where, Louisiana?"

She laughed, a worn but lively sound. "Thailand." The woman took her hand from the walker and waved him away. "Get back to work, Bruce, before you run out of sunshine."

The truck dashed away in a cloud of dust. Four hours later, Abby finally headed to fill the prescriptions after touring the house with Becky. She'd heard a zillion family history stories and gotten a brief lowdown that Carter had lost a sister AND father when he was younger. It made her cringe to hear such personal stories about him. No child should get hit with that so early in life.

Abby was only slightly disappointed when the pharmacist informed her the doctor mentioned he was dropping Becky's meds by the house on his way home the next day. Great. So the trip hadn't been necessary. It had definitely been entertaining. Except for seeing two dozen photos of a young Carter. Now she had a face to put with the asshole friend, Jackson. She'd been too much of a coward to look at him in Carter's office, but she took ample time surveying the photos.

She just didn't have the heart to tell anyone he actually *wasn't* a nice guy. Nor was he a good friend. In fact, all those pictures of him just made the truth larger and somehow sadder. How could a man who grew up with Carter steal his girlfriend? Wasn't there some kind of code about that? Or maybe it hadn't been the friend's issue—maybe Carter hadn't really been vested to begin with.

By the time she arrived back at her place, the sun had disappeared and stars twinkled as a reminder they saw her. And Carter. And his mom. It was comforting in some way. She showered and lounged in front of the television for a dose of late night news before sleep. Carter probably should know Becky was okay.

She grabbed her phone and typed in a quick note to ease his concern. He responded immediately with thanks. Amazing thing—technology. A message like that could travel around the world in seconds. She turned the phone to silent and clicked the light off before snuggling into the sheets.

Abby seriously needed advice and not the kind that Caroline gave. Sitting up in the dark, she retrieved the phone and opened Justchat.com. After sending a series of messages, she waited for eons for an answer. The clock made a clicking noise as the time changed. Still, no answer. She watched the screen and waited, the bright glow of the display casting an iridescent light across her face.

> She Hearts Dogs: Hey, there. Sorry I haven't talked in a while … very busy.

> Traveling To Survive: No worries. Me 2.

> She Hearts Dogs: Need some advice. U up for it?

> Traveling To Survive: Ok but don't sue me if it doesn't work out.

> She Hearts Dogs: LOL. U ever been dishonest with someone because u think it's best for them?

She set the phone down and padded to the kitchen for a drink of water. Upon returning the flash of blue showed an answer. Should she read it? Her stomach rolled but she lifted the phone.

> Traveling To Survive: Honestly, yes … but now, not sure I'd do it again. U probably aren't going to like this answer … but here's the thing … it is not up to u to decide what's best for someone else. Only you. So whatever ur keeping from the person, just realize it's not yours

to keep. Tho if I don't know what it's about, I can only guess at how to handle.

Should she tell him? He'd probably hate her too. She shrugged. Better him than Carter, right? She sucked in a deep breath and started typing.

She Hearts Dogs: OK but don't hate me ... need ur help on this. Remember the girl that got involved with her boyfriend's bestie? Well, I got to know the boyfriend (now ex) and now feel like I should tell him about the ex and his friend. Feel like I'm lying.

Traveling To Survive: Hmmmm. OK. See what u mean. That's a toughie. Truth is u R lying. BUT this isn't your story to tell. How long has he been friends with the asshole?

Abby giggled because that was exactly the name she used on Carter's lame friend.

She Hearts Dogs: They grew up together.

Traveling To Survive: Damn. Seems like that happens a lot nowdays. Well, I'll let u off the hook on this one. That's the OLD friend's bad, not yours. Maybe u could get him to tell it?

Yeah, right. *That's* not happening. Another message flashed on the screen.

Traveling To Survive: Now ur turn. Need some feminine advice. Ready?

She Hearts Dogs: Sure. This isn't relationship advice, is it? Because I'm not the best person to ask about that.

Traveling To Survive: Nope. Not exactly. How hard should a person work at a friendship? Hypothetically of course. If you find yourself constantly going the extra mile, do you keep trying? Or give up?

She Hearts Dogs: Is this a potential date thing or a buddy?

Traveling To Survive: Buddy

She Hearts Dogs: Ok. That's easy. Never give up on your buddies and they won't give up on you. Why would that be considered feminine advice though?

Traveling To Survive: Because I don't want to ask a guy—sounds soft. Hey, you think we should meet some time? Would love to buy you a drink or dinner. What d'ya think?

She Hearts Dogs: Hmmm. You don't think that would ruin our budding romance?

Traveling To Survive: Is that what this is? Really? I thought we were just chatting. JK.

She Hearts Dogs: That's the point. If we meet, we are no longer "just chatting." Don't you think the anonymity of it all is kinda nice? I mean we can say whatever we want to and not worry about impressions. It's liberating.

Traveling To Survive: Liberating from what? Okay. We'll keep chatting then. Let me know if you change your mind though. I can still chat even if I actually know who I'm chatting with.

Abby dropped the phone as if it were on fire and rolled over in the bed. She scrunched her eyes closed and pondered the thought of meeting someone now. Someone *else*.

The display on the phone blasted the room in light and she rose to see it. She pulled it closer and read.

> Carter: Sorry about losing it. Think Abby's involved w someone.

Huh? Where the heck did he get *that* idea? Especially after the other night. She wanted to let it go but hell, she was so far over the line with the texting, it didn't matter.

> Did she say that?

> Carter: Not exactly.

> Then call her and ask.

> Carter: I can't. None of my business. Wanna get a beer when I get back?

She frowned. Why would he think that after all that happened? Oh, yeah. She told him as much when he asked about Jackson. Idiot. How was it possible a random guy she never officially met could cause this much havoc in her life? Abby tossed the phone down. She really hated this Jackson guy. In fact, if she ever saw him again, she planned to tell him exactly what she thought. And the girlfriend too. Still, her chat buddy was right, it was their drama to tell—not hers. She grabbed the phone again and added a message before settling back into the bedding.

> CALL HER.

Chapter Eighteen

Her cell light blasted her again around 11:00 p.m. and she groaned. Without sound, it simply danced around on the nightstand. More annoying than if it rang. No one ever called this late unless—she pulled herself up. An emergency. That would be the only reason. She grabbed the phone and blinked to focus on the screen. It had been forwarded from the office phone. She started to ignore it, but the incessant buzzing wasn't to be denied.

"Hey, Abby, It's Carter." The low rumble of his voice made her heart jolt. Yay! He took her advice. Correction, Jackson's advice.

"Um, Carter?" Stupid to ask because one, he told her and two, she knew that voice—intimately. Still, she didn't care to give away the fact she'd *wanted* him to call and why the hell he thought she was involved with someone else. How to get to *that* discussion without giving away her spying efforts? She sat up in bed and leaned against the headboard.

"Wow, your voice sounds good. Listen, I'm sorry I haven't called. It's just that—work has been crazy. I'm in Thailand."

"I heard. What's it like over there?" She imagined tons of short, thin, dark-haired women fawning over him and playing karaoke while drinking shots at a bar—a bar where everyone sang American songs in strange accents. Having never been anywhere near there, she had nothing to go on but scores of movie clips. Yeah, it wasn't exactly politically correct to generalize but—it wasn't like she voiced the thought.

"Crowded. Too crowded. How's the flower world going? Business good?" His words were distant and awkward. Yet comforting.

"It's fine. Listen, we need to talk about that night after the game." She wasn't sure where to start or how to tell him about the mistaken messages. If she told too much, he'd realize she'd seen everything he said about her. That might be TMI for the current situation. Would he get mad? Of course he would. He'd hate her and that would be unbearable.

His breath whooshed out in a sigh. "It's okay. Look, I don't know what you have going on, but I just wanted to tell you I was thinking about you. When I get back, we'll talk more."

She frowned. He didn't want to hear it? "Why not now? Anything you need to say can be said now, can't it? Why wait? I mean, what's the point in dragging things out. If you want to know something—or tell me something, it's fine."

Silence.

"I can't right now. I mean, there's something I want to talk about, but it needs to be in person. Not when I'm on the other side of the world. Have you kept up with the Astros this week? I haven't had time."

Geez, did he really want to talk sports? He could do that with anyone—even the asshole Jackson. As much as she enjoyed the game, that wasn't on her mind at the moment. What *was* on her mind was the full night of unbelievable sheet gymnastics they'd partnered in. Right before she bolted out the door because she wasn't ready to *tell the truth*. Regardless of her chat buddy's advice, it was wrong to continue the lie.

"I need to tell you something." What was the right way to say it? *Oh, it's not me that's involved with your best friend, it's your ex.* Or perhaps, *listen there's one thing I can't deal with and that's cheating.* Nope, too strong. Besides, they weren't involved in a relationship per se—that would likely scare the hell out of him and he'd think she was talking about him. Even if it was intended to reassure.

"No, you don't."

"Yes, I do. There's—"

"No, you don't. I don't want to hear it."

"You don't?"

"No."

Abby frowned. *Dammit, I wanted to tell you.* She chickened out. Again.

"Okay, then I guess you aren't interested in the fact your friend Roger has the hots for my business partner?"

"Seriously?"

Abby could have sworn there was a touch of relief in his voice. "What, you don't think she's attractive? Or maybe not good enough for your horn-dog friend?"

He laughed. "Hey, now. Of course she's nice looking—a little too severe for me but certainly someone that would catch a guy's attention. Come on, though, she's three almonds short of an Almond Joy, Abs. Rog isn't a horn-dog. He's just a little—confrontational. At least until you get to know him."

"Oh, I get that. I saw it right away. Still, there are some things a guy just shouldn't say. Ever." Or put in a group text message. To ten of his friends.

"Yeah, well. He's an only child and his parents haven't been around much since he was about thirteen. No one really gave him a lot of direction, other than the guys. I wouldn't exactly call that the best school for manners."

Carter had told her none of those simple details about himself. In fact, had she not been to see his mother—she would never have known anything of his childhood. Was that a bad sign?

"Good point. Anyway, he's been following her around your office like a puppy dog whenever we do the maintenance. It's cute, but awkward. Especially because she hasn't even noticed."

"At all?"

"Nope. It's weird. I almost think she intentionally avoids him. You seriously don't think she's attractive?"

"What do you want me to say? I think she's super-hot? If she weren't your partner, I'd probably call her up? Are you trying to push me off on her?"

Uh-oh. *Hell no.* "No, of course not. Besides—"

"Or maybe you want to do a threesome? Is that it?"

Yeah, right. Every man's dream. She detected the mirth in his voice and wasn't giving him the satisfaction. "That's it. You caught me. Only that would be assuming we were actually going to see each other again, which is a big assumption on your part. Considering the fact you're on the opposite side of the planet and haven't called me since—"

"The first time?"

"Technically, you need to add an S to that last word mister. Unless it was so unimpressive you've already forgotten." And yes, it had rankled her he hadn't called, then run off for weeks. Which meant he had no intention of calling.

"I'm talking to you now, aren't I? Oh, and Abs, I remember it all. Every. Single. Time. You want me to give you the number? I can, you know, but would that be your number or mine? I also remember the way you feel, the way you hum right at a particular moment, and how you bolted out of my apartment like it was on fire when your phone rang. So, no, I didn't call. Mainly because I wasn't sure if you wanted me to. You're the one who said it was none of my business."

"What was none of your business?" Okay, now they were getting somewhere, and she definitely liked the part about him remembering everything. Was that in a good way? A *best-sex-ever* way, or just a yeah, it was nice but let's *don't*?

"Who you're involved with."

"Well, that was when you accused me of being involved with your friend—"

"Which you were."

Ugh. Gross. That would actually NEVER happen. Still, she hadn't cleared it up because that would mean she'd have to go back to the truth-telling part, which he seemed hell-bent on preventing.

"I told you about him and that's what we should talk about. There's a lot there you don't know and I need to tell you because—"

"Look, Abs, I can't hear it at the moment. Sorry. I just can't. It would—"

"Okay. I get it. You don't want to talk about us. You don't have to say it over and over." Technically, as much as she wished otherwise there was no *us* but still, he wasn't interested in hearing her explanation, so she'd not give it.

"What us? Shit, Abby. Are you really going to do this to me on the phone? I mean, at least Amanda had the cajones to say it face to face. That's—cold."

The light bulb went blaringly bright. Oh. He thought she was dumping him? How any two people could have such ridiculously bad communication issues was incredible.

"The *us* I was referring to included two people. Only two ... and you were one of them, okay? I wasn't sure what it was, that's all. I—"

Holy crap, she needed to get off the phone before she said something really stupid. Before she spilled her guts and started some sort of mouth-explosion of words like *missed you*. After all, she barely knew him.

He sighed softly. "Oh. I thought you intended to tell me something else."

"Like what?"

"You were still involved with someone, I guess. I suspected the reason you jetted out when the phone rang was because that someone was looking for you. You know, it was pretty deflating."

"You seriously think I'd do something like that? I mean, I helped you with the flowers for your ex. Who, by the way, seemed really upset about your delivery."

Dead silence. *Oh shit.*

"I thought you said she wasn't there."

Oops. Okay, she could do this. It was time to spill it all—she was a pathetic liar and trying to keep it straight was exhausting—didn't some famous person say "If you don't lie, you won't have to remember what you said"?

She sucked in air and lifted her shoulders for courage. "I lied. That's what I needed to talk about … "

More silence.

"So she *was* there?"

"Um, yeah, but it was incredibly awkward and she was crying and blubbering about what a nice guy you were and—" *Then she said she was in love with your best friend.* Abby bailed out before adding that final stake to the heart. She couldn't do it.

"You didn't tell me about it. Why?" There was an edge to his voice.

"It was awkward. Crazy. If I told you, I wasn't sure what you'd do. Especially after the thing with Jackson, which is actually worse than you thought. It wasn't a long time ago, it was recent but … "

There was another long pause.

"Recent?" His voice hit a new octave. "Shit. You're still … " The silence on the phone made Abby's stomach crawl as she waited for him to speak. "I shouldn't have called."

"You're upset." She assumed he was desperately trying to get her off the phone after she'd spilled the beans. Was that because he planned to call the old flame? Had her admission made him want to win her back? Her *o*mission about Jackson was critical—yet, she couldn't say it. She growled. *Why the hell should she? SHE wasn't the one that screwed Jackson.* The one that likely was tangled up with the sleazebag at the very minute they spoke.

"No, no. Um, okay, maybe a little. I don't know." Another thundering pause. "Christ. Hell, yes I'm upset. What did you expect?"

Click

He was gone.

"Crap."

Chapter Nineteen

Carter anchored headphones in his ears before starting the treadmill. When he reached the steady pace he liked, he turned up the volume and focused on the lights outside the glass. They blurred and bounced as he moved. Running outside was one of the primary things he missed while away. In a city this size with traffic, people, and the constant blur of activity, an outside jog would surely put him in the hospital.

Thailand had a zillion charms about it, and he hadn't minded the travel. Almost everywhere were people that had a smidgen of English under their belt, so while he tried to learn the basics of the language, it hadn't hampered him much. The charm could easily be misconstrued as chaos, frenzy, and overcrowding. Not to him.

He loved the way they did business also. People were as driven to succeed—as he was. They worked hard, meticulously applied themselves, and had little tolerance for lack of effort. Not to mention that most of them took their health as serious as their business. Therefore, he had no trouble accessing a gym and working out whenever needed.

The only thing that annoyed him was the music. Pop music in Thailand was nothing like home. More of a dance, electronic thing that made his head throb. He glanced at the time on the treadmill. He'd gone more miles than intended. It was ironic since he had debated not working out when he left the office. He needed something to take his mind off work. And Abby's revelation.

Carter shook his head and kept jogging. Four miles. He'd gone four miles while he mulled over her words. *I lied.* That's all she said—as if it wasn't a big deal. He could think of a small number of reasons she would withhold Amanda's response to the flowers. Two that made sense. Either she thought he'd be more upset by it and she hadn't wanted to make it worse—or she felt sorry for Amanda. Then there was the thing with Jackson: *it wasn't a long time ago.* He lifted the towel from the machine and rubbed his head. That didn't take into account Jackson's admission.

There had never been a reason for him to suspect Amanda was involved with someone, yet she was. Of course, his work had been crazy busy so he hadn't paid much attention. More like basking in his overall success. He still felt the kick to his gut when she told him. Now he recognized it as a kick to his ego rather than his heart. It was a kick he probably deserved for being inattentive.

It hadn't compared to when Jackson stunned him by revealing his relationship with Abby. What exactly was that relationship anyway? Jackson said he'd been with her before, but was it after Carter mentioned her? After Jackson knew he was interested? Knowing it was in the past helped a little—but only a little.

When Jackson told him to call Abby, he'd thought the motive sincere. Until she started telling him whatever she had to say. He wasn't up for it. Not again. Amanda was history, but Abby still touched a nerve. If she was involved elsewhere, he wasn't ready to accept it. Not after the way they'd connected during the last weeks. The whole thing blindsided him. Ironic since his friends all thought him notorious for short-term interest in women.

Four and a half miles. His breathing was labored and sweat ran down his neck then trickled along his spine. It reminded him of Abby's fingers as they had trailed there. *Dammit.*

He hit the Stop button and headed to the shower before going back to his hotel. A little cold water would do him good. There was a twelve-hour difference between home and Bangkok, which meant he had about forty minutes before his scheduled video conference with Roger. He needed to get his head back in the game and focus. This was the biggest project he'd ever managed, and it was going to be kick-ass. His career depended on it.

His phone signaled a chat message from his new friend and pseudo-counselor.

> She Hearts Dogs: Well, leave it to me to screw it all up.

He grinned.

> What happened?

He thumb-typed.

> She Hearts Dogs: I told him. Why did I do that? I mean you tried to warn me but NO, did I take your advice? Of course not. I blurted it out like an idiot.

Carter checked the time to make sure he could still respond and delved into the chat screen. He wasn't really in the mood but he'd give it his best shot.

> Repeat ... what happened?

> She Hearts Dogs: He hung up. Mad.

Man, she's really grinding over this and she didn't even *do* the cheating. Noble. He sighed. What to say? He thought for a second then answered.

> He'll get over it once he realizes where the fault belongs. Next time, listen to me. OK?

> She Hearts Dogs: OK. Gotta get to work. Bye.

• • •

"Good morning," Carter said as Roger joined the conference. Roger had their client, John Gazman, beside him. John waved.

"Good evening to you." Nine p.m. in Bangkok meant Carter was already half a day ahead of Roger and the rest of his team. Roger looked freshly showered and battery-charged, which was about as far from Carter's current state as possible. Still, he'd fake his way through.

"Okay, let's get started." The men jumped into the project plan and talked about the various orders and deadlines required to meet their needs. An hour and half later, John had excused himself. Carter and Roger went over their internal needs, with Carter giving a list of research items, some small assignments for other members of their team and a status report for the board. "So, what's this about Abby's partner?"

Roger stopped tossing a wadded paper and pulled closer to the camera. "Which partner?" He frowned and shook his head, a clear warning to hush.

Carter laughed. "I'm pretty sure there's only one. You know who I'm talking about. She said—"

Roger rolled his chair to look toward his credenza. "What exactly *did* you say, Abby?"

Carter snapped his mouth shut. *Oops.* He forgot. With the time change, they were on morning time and right in the middle of plant maintenance. Yikes. He waved sheepishly when she leaned over Roger's shoulder. "Hey, Abby. What d'ya know. There's the pretty little liar in the flesh."

Her gloved hands were filled with a water can and a fertilizer/plant food bag. "Watch it. I could douse your friend here if you provoke me."

Roger crossed his arms over his chest and leaned back. "Spill that and I'll make *him* pay."

Abby dropped her brows in a brief glare at the camera before shrugging. "I'm counting on it. I just told him you noticed her. A lot."

Roger rolled his eyes. The chair screeched as he lunged to a stand. "I'm going down the hall to get the team started on this list. You need anything else, just send an e-mail or text me." He held up a stack of papers with scribbled notes, waved it then disappeared.

They were alone. Or at least he thought they were—in two separate rooms, on two separate continents. Just the two of them. And a ticking time bomb.

"Not sure, but I don't think he liked the idea of us talking about him."

"Ya think?" She shifted from one foot to another and set the bag of plant food down in Roger's chair. Hopefully no dirt would spill because Carter was pretty sure Roger had light colored pants on. The man was really into khaki.

"You sure you're not reading it wrong?"

She plopped the water can on the desk, sending a few drops to the floor. "I'm sure." She paused to glance at the door. "You guys use Skype a lot?"

He nodded. "It's a good way to hold a meeting without flying around the globe. It keeps things personal. I use it to talk to a lot of people. If I could get my mom to use a computer, I'd Skype her too."

"She doesn't have one?"

"Oh, she has one. She just never turns it on. What about you, do you ever use video-chat or Skype to visit with family or friends?"

She nodded. "Sometimes. On my tablet. I have family spread out all over, so once in a while we use it. With my business, it's not really necessary."

While she looked fresh and energized, he was anything but. He ran a hand over his head and rubbed his neck. "So, what was it you wanted to tell me? Another one of your big stories? Just curious, is there an organization called Liars Anonymous? 'Cause if there is, you should sign up. You seriously have a problem."

Abby moved the bag of dirt to the floor, dropped into Roger's chair and leaned forward. Even angry, the pixilated image was nice, but he would have preferred the real thing. She sighed. "Look ... whatever you thought about my leaving the other day, it was wrong. I just had to get to work, okay? Don't read anything into my actions."

"Or your words either, right? Got it."

"Okay, got everything," Roger's voice jolted both of them away from the screen.

Abby jumped from the seat, apologized for taking over, and grabbed her things. She tossed an obligatory wave and headed toward the hall.

"Hey, Abs?" Her image had disappeared and Carter wasn't sure if she was gone or not.

"Yeah?"

"Take it a little easier on the next guy, okay? He might not be as easy to let go of you as I am. Oh, and send me your info and I'll be happy to plaster it on the bathroom stalls in the bars around town when I get back."

"Yeah, thanks."

"Wait, I think I still have it." He yanked his wallet open and looked through the pile of receipts and cards. Yeah, it was there. He yanked it out and held up the card, "Got it. Never mind."

"She's already gone," Roger said. "That was fun. You're a real jerk, you know. Good thing you're not here, I might have to kick your ass. You know, this isn't what you think, right? I can explain everything. It's actually a funny story."

"Ha. Ha. You don't know what you're talking about. Doubt you could explain *or* kick my ass. That woman's a habitual liar. Besides, from what I hear, you're all talk and no action. So, tell me what you have." Carter flipped open the folder in front of him and grabbed a pen to jot notes.

Roger frowned and pursed his lips before he started reading through the information Carter had requested.

They dove back into business mode.

...

A few mornings later and back on his own turf, Carter glanced at the time on his phone as he hurried toward work. Damn it. Late. He was never late. Or at least never *used* to be late. The wind slashed his face as he passed the newsstand. He glanced at the front page on each stack, a habit and sometimes his only chance to see what was going on in the world. National news showed nothing. Local news was a family of socialites talking about their family business. *Wait.* He slammed the brakes on. Was that Abby?

Holy shit, it was. Right in the middle of the group. He grabbed a paper and scanned the text underneath. His stomach dropped. Jennifer Jeffries. As in Jennifer *Abigail* Jeffries. As in the hateful woman that had gotten him fired months ago, thanks to Jackson's outburst. Seriously? They were the same person? Vile rose in the back of his throat. No way. No fricking way. Well, that explained Jackson's ranting in the meeting—and to think Carter'd been stupid enough to stand up for him.

He strode into the office and slammed the paper on Roger's desk. "Take a look."

Roger jolted. "Good morning to you too."

Carter punched a finger at the picture. "*That* is Jennifer Jeffries. *The* Jennifer Jeffries that killed my project and sent me packing. She is also *Abby* Jeffries, a.k.a. Abigail Jeffries … a.k.a. Satan."

Roger picked up the paper calmly and shook the page to straighten it. Carter stared at his face which had gone almost as white as the paper. "Um, yeah, that's definitely her. She looks good, don't you think?"

"Good?" Carter thought his head would split open. "Good!" He tried to think of words. None would come. He sputtered for a second, then turned on his heels and strode away.

Chapter Twenty

Abby tied her running shoes then slipped the ear buds in. The sun hung low over the trees outside. She couldn't remember the last time she'd gotten in a few miles and she needed it desperately.

Lifting the screen to choose her playlist, she noticed the flash of a chat message. Should she respond? Another glance out the window answered the question. She grabbed her keys and headed to the park.

She planned for three laps and was nearing the end of the second when she looked up. Shit. Carter. Good. He's talking to the dog. Maybe he won't notice. If she just took a long drink of water as she passed, maybe he'd think she hadn't seen him either? Too late to do a U-turn.

She lifted the bottle and drew on it. Four steps more and she'd be past and could drop the camouflage. She drew another sip and got—air. Rats. Empty. She forced her attention on the pavement and tossed the empty bottle at the trash receptacle as she passed.

Yay. Awkwardness over. She picked up the pace to make a fast retreat.

"Hey! Pick that up!"

Ignoring the sound, she slipped an earbud lose but kept running.

"Get back here and pick up your trash, woman."

Abby slowed to a stop and turned to see the empty water bottle roll into the grass. She'd missed the can. "What's your problem?" She dropped a hand to her hip. Sweat trickled down the side of her face and a light breeze cooled the dampness away.

Carter approached. Abby checked the path behind. Should she back up and run? His face deepened to a ruddy shade.

"I don't have a problem. You do. Do you always toss your trash all over the park and leave it for someone else to trip over? Or maybe for a dog to choke on?" He thrust a forefinger at the empty water bottle that glistened at the edge of the sidewalk. "Pick that up."

When he loomed over, she stumbled backward. "Good grief. It's just a water bottle. I missed. I wasn't *trying* to put it there."

"Just a water bottle. Right. And if everyone threw them on the ground, the entire park would be covered in trash." He wrapped his fingers around her forearm and yanked her toward the offending bottle. When he stopped, her toes were against it. "Pick it up." He repeated.

Seriously? He was going to force her as if she were ten years old? Not happening. Abby yanked her arm free, stuck her nose in the air, and turned. She took three steps and tossed a response back. "Pick it up yourself if you're gonna get all Godzilla about it."

Abby slipped the earbud in place and increased her speed to get the last lap in before dark. The sun was barely a sliver behind the trees when she rounded the corner and returned to the spot he'd accosted her. She glanced around, half expecting Carter to be there.

He wasn't. Neither was the bottle.

She let out a whoosh of air and relaxed.

Bang. Thunk. Her head stung, then her arms, then—*oh my God.* A rain of debris fell over her shoulders and head. Something wet and sticky trailed down her neck then dripped to her arm. Gross. She kicked a few things as she slowed and they bounced and rattled. The clatter startled a group of people standing nearby and their mouths fell open.

"What the hell?" Abby whirled to see—Carter's chest. His arms were above his head shaking the contest of the trash receptacle. *All over her.* She growled and yanked the plugs from her ears. "Are you CRAZY?"

Carter dropped the can to the ground with a thud. "No, just sick of people like you who don't see how every single piece of this adds up. One bottle here. One bottle there. A candy wrapper," he retrieved a McDonald's bag from the ground, "a half-eaten meal. If we all throw our crap on the grass like you, this is exactly what it'd look like. Is that what you want? You happy?"

Abby swiped the goo from her arm and threw it his way, then pulled her shirt free from her slimy, plastered skin. The sucking noise it made assured her there were plenty of *un*-empty beverages in that trash pile. "Seems to me this is more about *you* being happy, isn't it? This isn't—"

"Everything okay here?"

Abby whirled, ready to give the nosey onlooker a piece of her mind. Uh oh. Her face heated. A bicycle cop.

"Yes, sir." Carter's voice held the respect she'd missed earlier. "I mean ma'am. We're fine. Just was trying to help the lady clean up her mess."

Abby hitched a brow and threw him a glaring scowl. "My mess?"

...

Caroline rolled her eyes while she scraped the box cutter along the cardboard. "So, now you're picking up trash in the park for a month?"

Abby still smelled the garbage though she'd showered twice since. "It was that or pay the $500 littering charge. It's only on Sundays so shouldn't be a problem for work. What else was I supposed to do?"

"And he's going to be there too?"

Hope not. "I don't know. We can show up whenever we want to. I doubt he goes at the same time. He hates me."

"Of course he does. You slept with his best friend."

"Did not!"

"As far as he knows, you did. Plus you lied to him about that AND about the ex-girlfriend. Kind of makes you sound a tad on the manipulative side."

"Or just plain crazy."

Caroline held up her hands and widened her eyes. "Wasn't going to go that far."

• • •

Without her nightly run, Abby should have been gaining weight and losing energy. Of course, to do that she'd have to actually eat once in a while, and not just work. Energy was highly overrated in her book; she chose to substitute pigheaded perseverance. Not to mention a few lengthy chat conversations with her unknown chat pal at night, which kept her away from the potato chips. Besides, the conversations were more fun. He seemed incredibly interested in her family and she described each of her siblings in detail. She attempted to pry details as well but was stonewalled.

The only drawback to the excessive chats was waiting until almost midnight to take a shower and climb into bed. Not to complain, but the guy had said he was on a business trip to the other side of the world and it was morning for him. He was frustratingly chipper. She had to be nothing more than haggard, yet he didn't seem to mind.

The chats stopped after the fourth day and she assumed work took over. Of course, she stayed awake *hoping* for a message anyway and chided herself for caring. She had no time for a relationship. Especially one filled with unknowns.

Caroline's proficient advertising, blogging, and tweeting had sucked in quite a few more weddings, funerals, and even the occasional anniversary party or other event.

It had been over a week since Abby spoke to Carter. Good riddance. She wished she could stop sighing though.

She glanced at the time. She had a couple coming in just before closing to look at their bridal offerings. They'd also asked about catering options. Abby had never been into the food business and hesitated to get involved, but Caroline jumped in and took over the call when she started to decline. "Sure we can cater—we can do the whole thing. No problem." She winked at Abby as she led the phone caller astray. That had been a week earlier. She'd led a few more down that path since and Abby cringed at the risk involved.

"Why the heck did you tell them that? Neither one of us knows shit about catering and the only thing you cook is Hot Pockets." They'd lose the customer in five minutes when they showed up, but Caroline wasn't to be discouraged.

"Don't get your panties in a wad, honey. My cousin is a fabulous cook, and she's done a few weddings. Mostly for family, but she said she wanted to branch out. She just got a catering license. If we can get more business out of it, I say it's time to branch."

Abby rolled her eyes and grimaced. The woman was prone to jumping off cliffs without a parachute. "Well, you know we can't afford to lose a customer before we get them, right?"

"Pshaw. Calm down. We aren't losing anything. Have faith, girlie."

Easier said than done, but Abby caved when Caroline's cousin, Samantha, stopped in and showed them her catalogue. Which was a photo album filled with all the things she had cooked before. Hopefully they were as yummy as they appeared.

The door flew open and wind rattled the plants, ribbons, and wind chimes near the counter. Their couple had arrived. And so had Abby's chance to get a piece of Carter's friend Jackson.

Her eyes popped and her heart plummeted. *No way. Not them!* She searched for a place to hide, noting the tall fern by the back door. "Caroline, can you take over for a minute? I need to—" *Run for it.* She ducked behind the fern and sidestepped to the back room. *Holy shit. Now what?*

She looked at the calendar, registering the names, and realized she had no idea what Jackson's last name was. And, of course, Caroline hadn't bothered to get first names.

Abby watched through the same window she'd used to spy on Carter as Caroline and Samantha greeted them. Her ears burned and the flush on her face made it impossible to concentrate on what was said. When Caroline excused herself and approached, Abby took several short breaths to calm the nagging dread.

"What the heck's wrong with you? Are you sick or something?"

She shook her head.

"Then let's go talk to these people. It's a big sale. Let's get it done."

Abby threw a hand to her mouth as her throat clammed up. "I c-can't. It's *them.*"

"Them who?"

"That's Carter's ex. The one who dumped him! And that guy—is Jackson. The *real* Jackson. I dumped a can of water on his crotch! And I sent her hate flowers. I can't go out there. No way."

Caroline peered through the glass at the couple holding hands and making goo-goo eyes then burst out laughing. Not just a soft chuckle either. A full throttle, loud and obnoxious, belly laugh.

Abby grabbed some baby's breath and tossed it in her face. "It's not funny. If I go out there, there's no telling what they'll do—or say. I was horrible to them and I mean *horrible.*"

Caroline laughed until tears rolled down her cheeks then she gulped a few times before stopping the tirade.

Abby grabbed her arm and squeezed. "Knock it off. Get a grip. I *can't* go out there."

Her best friend and business partner wiped the moisture from her eyes and sniffed. "Why not? How many times have you said you wanted to give him a piece of your mind? Tell him exactly what you thought of how he treated Carter? How *she* treated Carter? Well, here's your chance. Go get 'em, honey." With a wave of her hand at the one-way glass, she disappeared back into the room and spoke loudly to their new customers. Who would likely be old customers in the next few minutes. "I'm sorry. Abby will be out soon. She's taking care of something. We'll just wait."

Which they did for at least fifteen minutes until Abby finally stopped hyperventilating and got her wits together enough to make an entrance, since Caroline refused to let her off the hook. She tried to approach quietly and unobtrusively but her soon-to-be ex-friend nipped that in the bud.

"Ahhh, there you are! It's about time. This is our owner and manager, Abigail." Caroline homed in on their faces as Amanda and Jackson turned. Well, if their expressions were any sign of their compatibility, they were made for each other. Both mouths bottomed out and their eyes rounded to the size of quarters.

"You!" they both said in unison. Yep, two peas in a pod.

Caroline attempted to maintain a straight face—unsuccessfully—while Samantha darted a glance around the group.

Abby's face went hot as a habanero, and she tried to smile. "Hi."

Chapter Twenty-One

"You know her?" Jackson's eyes changed from love-struck goo to dark frown.

Amanda ignored his question. "You're the hate-flowers girl. Don't tell me you sent Jackson some, too."

Abby rattled her head back and forth then found her voice. "No, he got a bucket of water on his crotch."

Amanda's brows followed suit and once again, the two were on the same wavelength, which happened to be a deadly stare-down of a soon-to-be-out-of-business shop owner. "Seriously?"

Abby wasn't sure where to start, or even if she should. "You two are engaged?"

"We're here to discuss a wedding, aren't we?" The two broke their confrontational stance and Jackson shifted to look at the floor. "So, do you make a habit of sending hate flowers to ex-girlfriends, or pouring water on their boyfriends? Or did Carter just sweet talk you into it? Hmmm?"

"Of course not. He didn't talk me into anything. It was my idea. I met him at the restaurant and we had too much to drink, then we started talking about all sorts of things and he told me about you and how you ditched him for another guy then we started—I don't know. It seemed like a good idea at the time. Then I delivered the flowers and you started crying and saying what a great guy he was and you seemed like you *missed him* and I thought, wow, maybe she wants him back or regrets it. I didn't know. So, I didn't tell him what you said because—well—that's *your story* and I don't want anything to do with it. But he keeps texting and Jackson i.e. me keeps answering."

Jackson popped his head up. "I'm not answering anything. I haven't heard a word from him since they broke up. I was afraid to talk to him. I went by there and tried, but you—doused me."

Caroline and Samantha had now imitated the same expression as the young couple and all four looked like they were about to belt out the high note in the church choir. Abby could have tossed a half dollar through each of those gaps. "I had to shut you up. You were telling him about our relationship and I was afraid he'd find out—"

Amanda's face went white and she spun around. Slamming a hand on her hip, she swung her head side to side. "Did she just say *our relationship*? As in you and her?" Her hair swayed as she pointed her perfectly manicured finger between Abby and Jackson.

Jackson raised both hands and stepped back. "I don't know what the hell she's talking about. She's crazy, if you ask me. I'd never seen her before I stopped by Carter's office."

Abby stepped forward and punched a finger at him. "He thinks I'm you, dumbass." She swung to Amanda and moved the finger her way. "He thinks I'm you, too."

Caroline popped up onto the nearby counter and swung her legs as she grinned. "This is getting gooood."

Abby growled, "You're no help. You're the one who started all this lunacy. Why don't *you* tell them?"

Caroline grinned. "Oh I think you're doing great, partner. You're on a roll. Don't stop now. Just take a breath and keep going. Samantha, what do you think?"

Samantha sidled up to Jackson and hitched a thumb his way. "I'm with him on this. I think she's crazy."

"I'm *not* crazy. Gullible, maybe, but not crazy."

Amanda sighed. "So Carter thinks you're Jackson, or me, or— what was it you said?"

Abby rolled her eyes. "Check. Check. Check. You win the prize. He thought I was Jackson and he kept texting me. Only it wasn't you," Abby pointed to Jackson, "it was me. Then Caroline grabbed the phone and answered for me. Thanks for that, by the way. Remind me not to ever call you when I *really* have a problem.

Then he thought I was you, Jackson, and kept texting. I answered again because *she* had just dumped him and I felt bad for him."

Abby stopped for air. "Can you believe that? He sees me running at the park for what, five minutes, and now they all want to talk about the status of my breasts?"

The two lovebirds gave each other a crazy-woman-talking glance.

Caroline snickered. "Well, they are good ones—as far as breasts go. I mean, from what I can tell and all."

"How juvenile. So, I just texted them back that they weren't fake. Only technically, it wasn't me texting."

Jackson put two fingers in his mouth and whistled twice, then made the time out sign. "Whoa. You mean you're the running chick from the park that he talked about?"

"Oh, great! So, I say fake boobs and running in the park and you automatically know who I am? What the hell else has he said? Yes! I'm running chick. So, I answered his text. Only it wasn't me answering because he thought I was you, and when I told him they weren't fake—well, he put two and two together and figured I'd slept with you."

Amanda's face shriveled up and she squealed. "*You slept with her?*" She threw her purse over her shoulder and marched toward the door.

Two steps away, Jackson grabbed her arm and yanked her back. "Hell, no! I didn't sleep with her. I don't even *know* her."

Abby followed. "He's right. He didn't. Carter just thinks he did because your intended went down to his office and marched in and confessed."

Both of them turned. "Confessed to what?"

"To being with me before Carter was, only—"

Amanda thundered, "So you were with her?"

"NO!"

Abby continued, "Holy crap, you're dense. Listen up, girl. He confessed—only it wasn't me he was confessing about—it was *you*. Get it? When he said he'd met *her* before Carter, he was talking about you. Carter and I had been sort of seeing each other so Carter thought it was me—because of the texts. He hasn't got a clue it was you, because I never had the heart to tell him. Apparently, neither has lover-boy here. When you cried over the flowers, I just—chickened out."

The sound of Abby's cell broke the seconds of silence that followed as she tried to settle her pounding heartbeat. Without thinking or looking, she grabbed it and answered.

"Abby?" As if it couldn't get any worse, guess who. Carter.

Oh shit.

Chapter Twenty-Two

Carter stared at the montage of traffic and waited. Was Jackson going to answer or what? They hadn't spoken in a long time, and it was about time to actually *talk* rather than text. Not to mention he needed to discuss the project for a few minutes and get background on his client—something Jackson could likely provide.

"Hi, Carter," said a definitely feminine not-Jackson voice he was familiar with. Too familiar with. Had he dialed wrong? He checked the display. Abby answered *Jackson's phone?* "Hang on a second." Her voice became muffled as she spoke to someone else. "You need to tell him. Straighten it out. It's not my place to air your shit." Obviously that was to Jackson.

Carter growled and raised his voice. "What are you doing answering Jackson's phone?"

"Technically, it's not Jackson's."

He heard a muffled noise on the other end then Jackson spoke, "Hey, Carter. What's up?"

"You son of a bitch." He punched the End button and hung up. *So it was true.*

He was an idiot to think maybe there was a woman somewhere who Jackson hadn't screwed or at least charmed into wanting him. Why would Abby be different? Was the entire time spent with Abby just a fluke? His imagination? No, there was a connection—he was sure of it. *Am I forgetting the night her phone went crazy and she ran out like there was a fire?*

He was already late for his meeting and the traffic was shit. He cursed. The traffic was always shit in Bangkok, so what was different now? Other than his thoughts were only partially on the meeting that waited. He grabbed his satchel from the floor of the cab, paid, and shoved his way toward the building. Well, at least now he understood why the guy never showed up for their group lunches or any of the baseball games. He had been brave enough to go after her without him present but not to face him while doing so.

Carter had known Jackson for twenty years, ever since the thought of girls made them puke. Their competiveness had always been a fun part of their friendship. Until now. Now it was so—over. If it weren't for this contact and Jackson's ties, he'd never deal with the man again. Ever. In fact, he'd just—

Carter lifted the phone from his pocket, scrolled through the contacts to Jackson's name, and started to press the Delete key. He hesitated and moved to Abby's. Now he understood why she'd never given him her private number. What an idiot. Still, he couldn't delete the numbers. He told himself it was because his business still had a contract for plant maintenance and Jackson was still a business contact. For now.

He needed to vent and brought up the chat app as he walked. He tripped on the curb with the first keystroke, so stopped and leaned against the wall for a minute.

He typed:

>Hey. I could use a kind word right now. You there?

>She Hearts Dogs: Sure, what's wrong?

Should he really spill his guts to a stranger? He shrugged.

>Just one of those days. Listen, I'm thinking we need to give this meeting thing a shot. After all, we're in the same territory and talk a lot already. It would be shame not to at least have one face-to-face. What d'ya think?

The screen blinked at him as if to say *no, no, no, no.* He waited.

She Hearts Dogs: OK.

He smiled and pulled from the wall, nearly smacking a bicycling woman with a stack of bags on her handlebars. Okay, then.

Fortunate for Carter, he did his best work when angry. The meeting went fantastic. A lot was accomplished, and he was certain another contract was in the works that would up their earnings significantly.

Later that night, he stood at the window of his hotel suite absorbing the twinkle of a busy city. The moon striped a bright sheen across the water beyond, as if to remind him it would be on the other side of the world when he woke up. He shrugged. Maybe he should go out for a while, immerse himself in the local culture and take in one of the night spots. Why not?

From the desk, his computer signaled an incoming Skype call. He frowned and strode to the screen. He hadn't scheduled a meeting tonight. The video chat showed a message.

Carter, are you there?

He pecked a response:

Who is this?

It's Abby. Can we talk?

Should he connect? Hell, he'd already been through this once in the last six months. There was something sick about subjecting yourself to it on a regular basis. He pecked in two letters and strode out of the room to enjoy a little nightlife. The door crashed shut behind him and he was certain it probably woke everyone down the hall—not that he cared.

•••

"For a guy who seemed so much fun in the beginning, he sure gets riled up about stuff." Caroline signed a delivery slip from the cute FedEx guy, gave him a wink, and carried the new package toward the back.

Abby had to appreciate her work ethic. The woman lifted boxes as if they were filled with air and never minded the dirt, labor, or hours. Her outfit was a little quirky sometimes—today particularly: pink leggings with black stripes under a wild green shirt that hung to her hips, with cargo boots. It was a small price for her dependability and support. "I can't exactly fault him for having a problem with his best friend sleeping with the girls he's interested in. That's like me going after one of your boyfriends."

Caroline turned, package in tow, and lowered a brow. "Seriously? I don't think we shop in the same supermarket when it comes to men, girl. I doubt that will ever be an issue."

"Good point."

Caroline shoved through to the back as the door jingled to announce a customer. Abby put on a smile to greet—Roger.

"Hi, Abby." It was the first time he'd spoken her name, and thankfully he didn't do something gross and lecherous like stare at various body parts.

"Hi there! What a surprise."

Caroline returned from the back. "Say, you think we can make requests on who delivers our FedEx packages? That guy was seriously—Oh." She stopped when her eyes locked on Roger.

"Caroline." He nodded and shuffled his feet.

"Dickwad," she acknowledged.

"Hey!" Abby frowned. "Customer talking."

"Sorry." Caroline shrugged and reached under the counter for a pair of scissors.

Roger frowned. "You've changed a lot, Caroline. The years have been good apparently. I didn't even know it was you at first."

"Yeah, well, people usually do when they get older." Caroline snipped some ribbon loose from a roll and started putting together some bows.

Huh, what?

"I didn't say it was *bad*, just different."

Abby's mouth dropped. "You guys know each other?"

Roger nodded. "Sort of. Ask her. We uh, hung out in college a while before Caroline ran off to find herself."

"I didn't *run off* and I certainly wasn't looking for myself in the process. Except for college, I'd never been farther than an hour from here growing up. I wanted to see the world and write about it." She jabbed the newly made disaster-of-a-bow into a pot of ivy and wagged the scissors his way. "I called."

"Yeah, for a while. Then—nothing."

"Well, you were busy becoming Mr. Big Shot Businessman. I was …. We had nothing to talk about."

Roger shook his empty cup of ice and drew a sputtered slurp from the straw. "No kidding. It doesn't seem like the world met your expectations, Caro."

Abby noted the weird nickname and raised a brow. Obviously, there was a lot more to Roger than met the eye. "Caro? As in Karo syrup?"

Caroline threw the scissors on the counter and came around to meet him face to face. "Why are you here, Rog?"

He stepped back into a rack of roses and held up his hands. "God, you're angry. Did your hair start spiking up like that when your personality began bristling too? Or is that something you caught over in Germany or Scotland, kind of like the foot and mouth disease they had in two thousand one?"

That was all it took for Caroline. Her eyes bulged and her face went crimson. She dropped a couple of creative f-bombs before she stormed to the back to unpack the new delivery.

"Soooo, Roger, that was interesting." Abby had no idea what to say next other than, "Can I help you with something?"

He stared at the door as if he expected Caroline to storm through again. She didn't. He blinked and turned her way. "Yeah, um, I noticed something a while back, then last night I got a crazy call from Carter, just before another one came from Jackson. I started digging through my phone messages and voila. He thrust his cell phone in front of her and showed a text. The one where she commented on her physical attributes. As Jackson.

Her skin tingled and heat crept up her neck. "What's that?"

"As if you don't know."

"Okay. You caught me, so what. It's not my fault. He started it. He texted me first. I just didn't have the heart to correct him when he said she dumped him."

"Huh?" He glanced back at the unmoving door then shifted to peer over the plants Abby decided to move between them. For lack of anything else to keep her busy.

"It's a long story."

"I have plenty of time." He leaned against the counter and stuffed his hands in his pockets, awaiting the explanation she'd already botched once. With Jackson and Amanda. Thankfully the door burst open again and a group of teenage boys bustled in.

She grinned and greeted them, thankful for the reprieve. "As you can see, it's a little busy here. Maybe another time?"

"You and I need to talk. Meet me at the coffee shop down the street when you guys close." He was out the door before she could decline. Judging by the exchange with Caroline, she wasn't getting any backup either. The teenagers ordered a round of corsages for an upcoming dance at school. As they left, Abby's cell rang. She answered.

"Well, imagine that. Hello, Abby," Roger drawled. "Surprise."

"How'd you get this number?" She hadn't forwarded the shop phone since she was in it. He'd called her direct.

"Hmmm. I don't know, let's just say—a little text messaging exchange maybe? By the way, it's a beautiful day out ... side. You should come out and play."

Abby whirled around to stare through the window—where Roger waved. *Dang it, and to think I said that guy was shy.*

"I c-can't. I'm working."

He laughed. "Chicken. Seriously, we need to talk. See you after work."

Yikes. "'Kay."

Chapter Twenty-Three

"What's the story with Caroline?" Abby figured if she interrogated Roger first, it might take the focus off her. Judging by the fact Roger had spotted the texting error, she assumed he also knew everything that was said. What she didn't know was whether Jackson had told him about Amanda. Or what Carter may have said either.

"Ask *her*." He swirled some cream into his coffee and lowered into the chair opposite.

"I did. She clammed up like a steel cage, said it was ancient history."

He shrugged. "There you have it. So, Carter thinks you're Jackson. Right?"

Abby took a sip of her latte and cringed when it scalded her tongue. "It seems that way."

"So, why are you pretending? Why haven't you cleared it up?"

"I'm not—I wasn't. He just started texting me out of the blue right after *she* broke up with him. Something about the tickets being a shit idea. Did you see that message too?"

Roger shook his head and rolled the cup in his fingers. "Nope, I've only seen the group messages. I got a laugh out of the one you sent—but I bet he didn't."

She rolled her eyes at the ceiling. "That's not the half of it. Tell me something, what do you know about Jackson?"

"A lot. Why?"

She leaned forward on her elbows. "So you know *everything*?" As in, *he's boinking Amanda and planning to marry her right under Carter's nose?*

"Everything."

"Then why didn't *you* tell him? I mean the guy's a jerk. He was sneaking around with Carter's girl behind his back and telling him to buy her tickets as a gift—a stupid idea, by the way. Don't ever do that. Then I went to Carter's mom's and saw all those pictures of them as kids and—"

Roger's eyes popped. "You did what?"

"He texted me thinking I was Jackson and asked me to go check on Becky—"

"Now you're on a first name basis with his mother? Holy shit."

"She's nice. Carter said her meds had to be refilled before he got back—since he thought I was *him,* what was there to do? I mean, Jackson sure as heck wasn't interested in helping out or he never would have—"

"You don't know that."

Abby snorted. "Where I come from, best friends don't steal each other's girls—or guys—and if they do, well, that's a good way to become an ex-friend real fast. Isn't there a guy code about that too? Or am I living under a rock?"

Roger sipped again from his cup. "I suppose that depends on the guy, but most guys don't go that route. All I know is, she knew Jackson before Carter. They were involved a long time ago and then something happened. Carter brought her to one of our after-work binges and ta-da, old flame reunites—only technically there were two flames."

"She kept stringing Carter along even when Jackson was back in the picture? There's a word for girls like that, you know." Abby took another swig of coffee then cursed and pulled off the lid. She pursed her lips and blew on the steaming liquid.

"Well, in most cases I'd agree with you, but according to Jax, she agonized over it for weeks before she finally had the courage to tell Carter. Apparently there were a lot of issues to work out between her and Jackson as well. Then when she finally told Carter, she didn't have the heart to give him the details. She wanted Jax to do that part."

Abby sighed. "Well, he really screwed that up. No surprise … and no pun intended. Where did I get pulled into all this?"

"You were the first." Roger finished off his coffee and went to put the cup in the trash. When he returned, he checked his phone briefly.

"I most certainly was not the first." She wasn't *that* stupid. Nor was he that, well, inexperienced.

"He saw you first—at the park. He mentioned you a couple of times. Hell, we even followed him to the park once and made bets on—"

Abby held up a hand and shook her head. "Don't tell me. Some things just don't need to be shared."

He grinned. "We made bets on how long it would take him to talk to you. The rest was just a way of goading him into it—making him prove us wrong. No one really thought that."

She furrowed her eyes. "Need I remind you exactly *who* said what? I saw the messages, remember?"

He laughed. "Yeah, well, it worked, didn't it? He finally met you and you guys hit it off, didn't you?"

Did they? Sure, it was fun too. But now? If Carter knew the whole story, he'd hate her even more for spying on him all this time—not to mention she'd completely withheld the business about Jackson and Amanda. Oh, and his mother. The list was growing along with her heavy conscience.

"Yeah, except now he thinks I'm involved with Jackson and won't talk to me."

Roger snorted. "He won't talk to Jackson either. Not that I blame him. Do you think he'd be the same way if he actually knew the truth?"

"Which truth?" It was all getting pretty muddled, but there didn't seem to be any truth left.

"That it was Amanda with Jackson, not you."

She shrugged. "Does it matter? He hates me and I'm not really all that big on him anymore either. I still have to get the shop in the black in the next few months—or at least stop the bleeding."

"You guys looked like you were doing pretty well to me."

"Call me crazy, but from what I could see, you never looked past my partner long enough to see the place was empty. We're getting orders slowly, but it's sporadic."

"It'll turn around."

She wished she had his confidence.

"Give it time."

"Time I have. Money—not so much. So, do you plan to spill the beans to Carter that I've been eavesdropping?" She sipped the coffee, which had finally cooled enough to taste.

"Nah, not yet. I'm saving that for the right time."

"There is a right time to out me? When exactly would that be?"

He laughed. "You'll just have to wait and see, won't you?"

"Uh oh."

He shrugged. "Just because I have a foul mouth doesn't mean I'm a bad guy. Besides, I have my reasons. See ya, Abs." He winked and left.

• • •

The following afternoon the door jangled on opening and Abby's stomach dropped. "Don't come near me." Abby's eyes popped as Jackson entered the store. She searched behind him for the crazy fiancé.

Jackson held up his hands in surrender. "Ease up. I didn't come to cause trouble. I just wanted to clear the air."

"Look, I don't mean to sound skeptical but clarity doesn't seem to be following you around much. In fact, a putrid cloud of confusion would be more the description."

He grinned. "Probably so, but you need to know it's not *all* my fault. You were supposed to meet Carter. It just went to crap thanks to Roger."

Abby hitched a brow and cross her arms. "Seriously? So, you're going to blame this all on him? He's not the one chasing someone else's girlfriend."

Jackson lifted his thin shoulders. "She was actually mine first but skip that for now. Carter and I used to meet at the park Saturday mornings to shoot hoops. Sometimes Roger would show up. As much as he pretended not to, Carter watched you run like you were ice cream. Crazy thing is, he'd never go talk. Said it would be creepy to do so at the park."

Abby grabbed a water spritzer and sprayed the fern at her side. "He's right. If someone approaches me at the park, I usually hit Mach 5 and get out of there."

He grinned again and Abby noted that there actually was a little charm to the guy's smile. Nice face. Sick, quirky morals though. He stepped forward and leaned against the counter. "Right. So, several months ago, I figured I'd help the situation out. I'd seen you talking to his neighbor a few times so I asked about you. I found out where you worked and what you did. Thought I'd try to orchestrate a meeting."

"I didn't work here then." Was this more B.S.?

"I know. You were a project manager for your parents' company. Who just happened to be one of my customers. It was perfect."

She whirled back and the spritzer sent out a cloud between them. "You're the Jackson that was such an ass in that meeting?"

He blinked and looked toward the door. Was he hoping someone would walk in. "Yeah, sorry about that. See, here I was trying to get *you* involved with a project that I could put *him* on and then you'd have to work together for a few months. It seemed perfect."

"Right. Until your mouth overloaded your brain and you went all Neanderthal."

"I know! I know. I couldn't believe I was such an ass ... here I was sitting next to the guy that was with the girl *I* wanted. I needed to get him talking to you and he was all focused on *her*. It was supposed to go totally different and once you and he started meeting in person, it would all work out fine."

Abby pursed her lips and dropped a hand to her hip. "Fine for you to horn in on the girlfriend, you mean. Wow. So pawn him off on me in order to steal his girl. You're even slimier than I thought."

Jackson clenched his fists and turned toward the window to vent. He shook his hands in the air a couple of times then took a deep breath and turned back. "I wasn't pawning him off on you ... I was helping him get out of his own damn way. I just figured if he'd watched you all that time, I'd help him get the first step in. The rest would either work out or not."

"But you'd be working your thing with his girlfriend on the backside at the same time, right?" She clenched her eyes at the use of words.

Jackson let out a growl. "No! Damn it, Amanda and I worked together and knew each other for a long time before they met. It wasn't like that. Forget about her for a minute. You got all pissed off and hung up on the conference call, then next thing I know the company has axed the project and all communication with us. That was to be Carter's big gig. When it tanked, they let him go. He wanted to kill you then."

"Me? I wasn't the one that decided to make derogatory remarks about women in business while talking to the woman I intended to do business with."

"No, that would be me. I'm sorry, but ... I'd just spent hours the night before listening to Carter divulge his 'relationship' with Amanda and ask me for advice. That rant was directed more at *her* than you. She ran out on me a couple of years ago without a word and … seeing her again with him was, well pretty shitty. I'm the one that made that last comment."

"I thought it was both of you. Actually … him."

"Nope. Just me."

Abby cringed. Her stomach clenched. "Uh oh."

He chuckled. "Yeah, you got him fired because of me."

"Why didn't he say something? I mean, he should have … "

"He's my best friend. We've known each other since we were kids. You can't rat out your best friend."

"Sure you can if they … "

"Would lose their job instead of you? Nah, he wouldn't do that."

"He hates me, doesn't he?"

Jackson ran a hand over the counter, clearing off imaginary dust. "Well, he hates a girl named Jennifer Jeffries … he has no idea that's you."

"And now he's texting me thinking I'm you … great!"

"Yeah, that was Roger's stupid idea. He thought if he mixed up the numbers, you guys would work it all out yourselves."

Clarity hit Abby like a freight train. "So, both of you were in on this then?"

"Sort of. See? You were supposed to meet. Kismet. Karma. You know, *fate*."

She frowned and gathered her thoughts. "If that were the case, it would have happened on its own … without all the interference. Which, by the way, has completely screwed all chances. He thinks I'm a lying, manipulative bitch now."

Jackson narrowed his eyes and leaned down. "The chances are only gone if you give up. Sometimes you have to help fate a little."

She thunked the mister on the counter and sent her eyes skyward. "If that were true, we'd all be in different places now, wouldn't we? Besides, sounds like you guys have completely botched the fate thing yourselves. Why don't *you* tell Carter the truth? I don't have time for this. It's already eaten up way too much of my energy and I need to focus on work."

Jackson turned and headed to the door. "I'd tell him but he takes off running when I get within ten feet and won't answer my calls."

"Mine either. Can't say that I blame him."

"Hey, don't say we didn't give it our best shot though."

Abby raised a hand. "Jackson … just so you know … I don't believe in fate."

"Yeah, well I do." He shoved through the door and left.

Chapter Twenty-Four

"How can someone become a habitual liar, impersonate a man, pretend to be a socially and sexually adept player as both, AND have no life whatsoever?" Caroline shook her head in disgust. "You really aren't taking advantage of this, girl."

The man in the corner purveying the roses stilled; obviously his ears were on full alert to whatever came next. He bent toward a bouquet and feathered his fingers over the petals, casting a sideways glance toward Abby. Caroline giggled.

"Thankfully, I don't have to anymore since I won't be talking to him from now on. It was exhausting. Besides, I've met someone else."

"Seriously? Already? Who is it? Carter's brother?"

She dropped her forehead to the counter and bumped up and down. "No."

"Then who?"

Abby flopped an arm over her head and muttered into her elbow. "I don't *actually* know. I meet him tomorrow."

"You're kidding, right?" Caroline slapped a hand to the countertop jolting Abby from her bout of self-pity. She glared toward the roses. "Hey, you buying anything or just eavesdropping?"

The man reached in for a bouquet and carried it to the register. His face turned crimson. "You have anything with yellow roses? My wife loves yellow." He slid another glance toward Abby as he handed over some cash.

Caroline snatched it, punched up the order, and gave him change before Abby could answer. The man disappeared under Caroline's glare.

"You shouldn't run off our customers like that. We need every one we can get."

"If you ask me, he was more interested in your love life than his wife. So, how are you planning to fix this?" Caroline tapped the counter with the new set of dark purple nails she'd gotten on her day off.

"Well, I was hoping you could help me out." Abby grinned sheepishly.

"Ohhhh, no. I'm staying out of this. It has nothing to do with me."

"Are you serious? It has *everything* to do with you. You got me into the entire charade to begin with."

Caroline backed against a plant and tripped over the pot. She attempted to right herself before falling to her knees. When she rose and dusted them off, Abby hitched a brow.

Caroline put her hands up in a mock standoff. "Hey, I had something to do with the Carter thing at first but I had nothing to do with the other ten thousand texts you sent. Or the fact you decided to go check him out at dinner that night, not to mention all the other stunts. That was all *you*, baby. You and your lying, cheating, impersonating, trouble-making ass. BUT, I have nothing at all to do with this new person, whoever it is."

Should Abby tell her about Carter's mother? Probably not. At least not while she was on a tirade. "I met the guy through Justchat. You know, the phone app. Justchat."

Caroline tsked. "Has it really gotten that bad? Geeze, you need a little black book to keep it all straight. I thought *I* had issues. You know I'm beginning to think your mom's way would have been a hell of a lot easier."

Okay, she had a point. Of course, if that was the case, then why hadn't Caroline resolved her outstanding problems? She wasn't exactly living by her rules. "That's preaching to the choir. Why didn't you tell me you knew Roger?"

Caroline rolled her eyes. "There's nothing to tell. We knew each other in college. That's all. I left. He took a fancy job and started his career."

Abby wanted to pry more details. Why had she left? Carter thought he hadn't dated much—was that why? Was there an open wound festering that caused all the derogatory speak? She wanted to ask but, knowing Caroline, she'd just clam up. It'd be impossible to get her cooperation if that happened. She shrugged, "Okay. Your business. I get that."

"Good. Because I thought I handled it pretty well up to this point—like a real professional. I've been pleasant, haven't I?"

"Yep, very."

Caroline put one hand on her hip and grabbed a Coke from the counter with the other. The can had sat there for an hour and had to be lukewarm and fizzed out. She swirled it a couple of times before lifting to sip. "What, you don't think I've behaved? I've overdone it?"

Abby swallowed a grin and kept reeling her in. "I never said that. You've been exceptionally—professional. Stiff as a board. Dull as a post." If there was one thing Caroline hated, it was to be called boring. Abby hadn't really understood it before. The spiked hair and colorful clothes all had an underlying message apparently. One that was beginning to clear up.

Caroline slammed the Coke to the counter; drips erupted from the lid. "I have not!"

"Okaaaay. You haven't, but admit it. You don't exactly act normal when we're at that office, do you?"

She lifted her chin. "I'm a businessperson. I'm not going to go all wacko just because of R—him. You don't like the way I act, say so."

"It's not necessarily actions. I mean, take a look at the way you dress when you go to their office. It's almost like you morph into Lucy Librarian. You never dress like that. I just think—"

"You don't get to think. You don't get to tell me how to act. And you definitely don't get to—"

"Keep throwing flowers at me and I'm going to have to deduct the losses from your half of our earnings. Sounds to me like you're tasting a little of your own medicine, and it's going down like sour grapes. I'll make a deal with you."

Caroline snapped a finger at Abby. "Don't even *think* about asking me to go talk to him. Just because I told you to talk to Carter doesn't mean I need to do the same. It's a totally different situation."

"I wasn't. All I was going to say was this—the next time he talks to you, you could actually talk back. You answer. You have a *discussion* instead of finding the nearest escape route. Deal?"

"I do talk to him. I'm even pleasant."

"I mean about something other than the weather or 'how's business.'"

Skepticism wasn't all that becoming on Caroline. "I'm not going over there. I'm not ... Okay, deal."

Yay. Now all Abby had to do was get them in the same place and make him talk first.

...

While Abby checked them in, Caroline peeked up the stairs. "Why on earth did you guys pick this place?"

Admittedly it was a bit dark but according to Traveling to Survive, it had the aroma of patchouli or incense and served a wonderful assortment of wines and snacks. Plus he had tickets to the concert adjoining the place.

"Well, it's adjacent to the House of Blues and he has tickets for a concert *if* we choose to go. He said it was up to me." Abby inspected her hair in a mirror and ran her tongue over teeth.

The hostess handed each of them a wristband and motioned toward the elevator, "Welcome to the Foundation Room." She pressed the button for them and Caroline seemed relieved that the stairs were not an option. Abby entered and surveyed the walls, padded in swatches of burgundy velvet, silk, and brocade. As if someone had cut up a lot of Victorian clothes and stapled them to the walls. Interesting.

When the doors slid closed, Caroline turned. "So, how should we do this? Should I go first and walk the room, then come back and let you know before you get off the elevator? Or should we both get off at the same time and pretend to be meeting someone then check around for him?"

The hostess pursed her lips in confusion, but Abby ignored her. "Well, if we can enter without being seen, I'd rather you look. I'm chicken. What if he's a dog … or old. Oh my God, I never thought to ask his age. That was stupid. Still, he didn't talk old. He likes the same music I like and seems youngish."

The hostess cleared her throat. "So, you're meeting someone for the first time here?"

"Uh, yeah. Dumb right?"

"No, it's cute. And don't worry, the elevator opens to an empty hall so you can wait there." The doors slid open as if to confirm and she held them while they exited.

"Whew. That helps a little." Caroline looked at Abby. "You look amazing, by the way. No matter what he looks like, you're the hottest woman in the place and he'll be lucky to have you as a date."

Abby smiled. "Thanks. You're the best. So, go look." She gave a playful push.

Caroline disappeared around the corner. There was a hum of voices in the room and Abby could only guess at the size of the crowd. Still, it couldn't be too hard to find a guy with an Astros cap on his head in this kind of place, right? Most guys probably wouldn't be wearing a hat at all.

When Caroline returned, she was carrying a bloody mary and munching on celery. "Wow, they make really great drinks here."

Abby stomped a foot. "Well?"

"Um, well he's tall. Dark hair. Nice eyes."

"I like tall and dark. Sounds good. Is he good looking? Oh, why do I care? It doesn't really matter. He's a nice guy, right?" Abby wrenches her fingers together. "Great! Thanks for checking, I'll go on now. You can take the car and I'll catch a cab." She handed the keys over.

Caroline grabbed the keys and clenched her fingers in the process. "Um, question."

"What is it? What's with him? Come on … spill."

"No, nothing's wrong. It's just that—he looks kind of like—Carter. You think Carter's good looking, right?"

"Carter's history. An over-complicated ass that I hope to God I don't see again in this lifetime. By the way, I meant to tell you that you're going solo on that contract from now on." Abby pulled a brush from her purse and ran it through her hair.

"Weeellll that might be a problem."

"Why?"

"Look, it wasn't his fault you know. All the complications, those were actually just a part of all the miscommunication. He's …"

"History. Look, I'm going in. I'll call you later."

"No. Wait. Abby!"

"What?" Abby hit the brakes and checked her friend's harried expression.

"It's him. It's Carter. He's in there with a friend and he's the only guy in a baseball cap. An Astros baseball cap."

Abby's gut felt like a vise had tightened over it. "Yeah right. Ha. Ha. That's not *even* funny."

172

Caroline put a hand on her arm. "I'm not kidding, honey. It's really him."

Abby stepped out and peeked around the corner. Yep. "No fricking way! How the hell does that happen? Is this a joke? Did you send him here? Or Roger?"

Caroline gulped her bloody mary and shook her spiked head. "No, really. I didn't know."

Abby yanked her phone out of her purse and looked at the Justchat app. How the hell could she join an app that was *supposed* to be anonymous and end up with him out of all the people in the entire city? "That's crazy. Why would I get stuck with him? I'm calling their customer support. Hang on."

She dialed the number she found in fine print on their support page. After pressing several more keys and going through a selection process, she finally ended up with a real person on the line. "You want to tell me how you guys choose who sees our chat messages? I mean isn't it supposed to be anonymous? *Totally* anonymous?"

The attendant on the other side sounded confident and soothing. "Yes, ma'am. All of our members are anonymous. No real names are used, nor divulged. Nor are addresses, or other personal information. However, if the person wishes to give out information they can. We also go through a series of questions upon setting up the account ... all optional, of course ... which are used to determine like personalities. If you answer them, then we will use those to distribute your chat messages to people with similar interests. However, you are welcome to skip all the questions if you choose."

Damn. Wish I'd known that up front. "So, if a person happens to answer all the questions, including locale related ones ... you use that as sort of a matching thing?"

"Yes, ma'am. It's intended to put like personalities together in a situation where they can take it to the next level if they wish."

Abby pulled the phone from her head and stared at the screen as if the woman had lost her mind. Not knowing what to say, she simply clicked end on the call and shook her head. "I don't believe this. Is the whole world out to get us? I mean me?"

Caroline lifted a brow and leaned in while sipping her drink. Abby could smell the tomato juice and pepper as she opened her mouth. "So, what'd they say?"

"You wouldn't believe it if I told you. Look, I'm not going in there. Give me the keys back and let's leave."

"But I'm not done yet. And besides you can't just leave him there. That's even meaner than everything else you've already done."

"Is it? The guy dumped a trash can on my head. I think he's gotten his payback. Besides I can assure you he won't want me to be the date." She punched the button on the elevator repeatedly.

"Jennifer Abigail Jeffries, you get your ass in there and talk to that man! Stop playing around. Think about it, woman. There has to be a reason all this stuff keeps happening—"

"Yeah, I am too chicken to tell the truth and we both have some very meddlesome friends who just can't seem to butt out of our lives."

Caroline quirked a brow. "Hey, none of us had anything to do with you using that app to meet him. I don't even know what Justchat is. You did that completely on your own."

"Yeah, but the rest ... "

"The rest was karma, honey. Nature's way of trying to beat into your thick skulls that the two of you need each other."

"Right. Like a pitcher needs a broken arm."

Caroline thumped a palm to her head, "Geeze you're a pain. Come on." She grabbed her hand and dragged her out of the hallway and into the bar.

・・・

Carter took a drag on his beer and slid a glance around the room. She should show any time now. He wished he'd asked what *she* looked like. He just mentioned the cap because in truth, he didn't really care. He liked her voice—or at least her written voice—and it hadn't even occurred to him to ask for descriptors. Not like him to do that. Actually not like any guy. He was losing his touch.

Oh shit. He whirled around and faced the bar. *What the hell is Abby doing here?* With her ditzy partner even. He focused on the screen above the bar and the game. Maybe they wouldn't see him and leave. There were a lot of people around. None of them wearing a stupid Astros cap. He yanked it off and stuffed it in his back pocket.

"Well, if it isn't my partner in crime and trash buddy." *Great.* So much for not being seen.

"Oh, hey." He put the beer to his lips and ignored her. "What are you doing here? Seeking another victim?"

Abby lifted her head and grabbed the refill beer the bartender brought him. She drank two gulps then wiped her mouth with her hand. "Mmm. Modelo. One of my favorites." She dropped the glass back in front of him.

Carter shoved it her way. "Feel free to drink the rest then. Preferably on the other side of the room if you don't mind. Out in the parking lot would work too."

Abby twisted her nose at the fizz from the lime. Guess he should have told her he'd pushed one into the bottle. Although if he'd actually intended her to drink it, he probably wouldn't have done so. She puckered her lips. "Ooh. Ooh. Aren't we a little grumpy tonight? What's a matter? Had a bad day?"

Was she tipsy? Or just feeling extra nasty for some reason? "My day was great actually. Getting better by the minute. But I kinda have a date so why don't you and your friend go somewhere else?"

"A date? Lucky you." Abby peeked around his backside then smiled into his eyes. Dammit he hated when she did that—he immediately felt the heat and his dick started to betray him. He couldn't stave off the reaction as much as he wished he could. He watched her glossy lips move. "You forgot to bring the trashcan though. Want me to go get it for you so you can dump it on her too?"

Carter rolled his eyes and took another drink, glancing in the mirror at the entrance. "Real funny. Tell me something, Abby. Or should I call you Jennifer? Who'd you manage to get fired this month? Or who else are you stringing along like he matters?"

Her mouth fell open. Thank God he'd finally found a way to silence the sarcasm. Now if he could just get rid of her before his date showed. He glanced at the entrance again as a couple entered. Nope.

Abby winced and followed his gaze. "Well, I guess I'll let you get on with your date then. Bye now." She wiggled her fingers and walked away. He hated himself for watching too. Her hips always had this natural sway that showed off the tightness of her butt and legs. All that running certainly did the trick. Too bad the rest of her was so hard to deal with. Except in bed.

He closed his eyes tight, trying to dispel the image.

Chapter Twenty-Five

Saturday afternoons were the best. Everyone that came in the shop had a celebration to attend, therefore moods were always good, and it was the day before Abby's upcoming relaxation break. Sundays were her day off, just as Fridays belonged to Caroline. Both of them worked Saturday since the day tended to be busy and they often had a lot of deliveries beyond just normal store activities.

Two hours to closing. Then she'd be at home with a Netflix movie, some microwave popcorn, and much-needed peace and quiet. The phone rang and Abby picked it up, acknowledging her mind had already left. Until the voice on the other end spoke.

"Um, hi, this is Becky Coben's pharmacist. Do you have a minute?"

She stared at the display as if it had reached out and slapped her. How did they get her number? Why *her* and not Carter?

"Is everything okay? Does Becky need something?"

"No, that's not it. Um, we sort of made a mistake here and we need to check on her, make sure she's doing well. One of those meds is new here and she hasn't taken it before. Apparently there are a few known drug interactions with something she's already taking and well, we just want to make sure you're aware."

Holy crap. If they called to check, then it had to be fairly serious. Thoughts of Becky lying out in the tall grass behind her house flitted through Abby's head. "What kind of interactions?"

Hesitation made the crackle on the phone sound explosive. "Well, there are a few things she needs to watch out for. Dizziness, high blood pressure, loss of appetite, frequent urination, nausea—"

"You've *got* to be kidding me! All that and you didn't even think to mention it?"

"Well, she already knows about the others and normally her son is here and reads through everything and asks us. Someone else picked them up this time. Our girl didn't think to check it because she usually has a lengthy visit with Carter."

Yeah, I'll bet she does. A lengthy visit, huh? So, when it's just some unknown girl from out of town, who cares about the health and safety of the patient? Abby thrust her hand under the counter and yanked out her purse. It caught on the edge, spilling the contents on the floor. She shifted the phone between her shoulder and ear, using both hands to scoop the mess into the bag.

"Have you told Carter all this?"

"We called but it kept cutting out. He said he was out of the country and gave us this number to call. Said it was … "

"Jackson's. Yeah, I'll go check on her. What else do I need to know and how can I reach you if there's an issue?"

She should just call Roger and tell him to go. Still, she felt responsible. Besides, Becky was nice. The voice on the other side scrambled off several other minor things and she noted everything, asking for a repeat while she penned it onto a pad then ended the call.

"Caroline, I have to run out. I know it's early, but I have a little problem. Sorry. I've already forwarded the phone to my cell for the night so it should be quiet."

Caroline just waved her off.

There was no way in hell she intended to be responsible for anything happening to Carter's mother even if she was on his shit list.

The drive to the farm was agonizing, but she made the trip without once consulting her GPS or Google maps. When she rolled to a stop behind the house, Becky wasn't in the yard as before. The house was still. With the sun behind the roof, long shadows engulfed her as she tromped up the steps and knocked on the door. No answer. She stepped to the window, framed her eyes, and peered through the glass. With dusk encroaching, it was too dark to make anything out. Her stomach growled a reminder of the time, but the deeper sting of fear was more threatening than hunger.

She hated to intrude. Circumstances being what they were, it was probably best. A quick jiggle of the doorknob showed it was unlocked. She stuck her head in and called, "Becky, it's Jackson's friend Abby, are you here?" She also cringed at calling herself *Jackson's friend.* It was definitely more an insult than a compliment to be on that list of friends.

The silence was oppressing. No car noises, sirens, people—just big chasms of—nothingness. She clenched her jaw and stepped inside. No lights were on, and her fear heightened. What if she'd had a dizzy spell and passed out? *Please don't let her have fallen and knocked her head on something.* Worse, what if her blood pressure spiked and she had—NO, stop thinking that way.

Abby strode through the main areas then started toward the back. Like many old houses, this one had a lengthy passageway to traverse in order to reach the bedrooms. She opened a closed door and cringed. Steps filtered down to a basement. No. She thrust aside the thought of Becky falling into the darkness. She rushed to another door. An empty bedroom decorated in lavender and green—a girl's room. Then she heard it.

A faint moan followed by a stronger one. Oh no. She trudged toward the sound and threw open another door. Becky screamed and jolted upright. Along with a strange person beside her—a strange *male* person.

"Oh my God. Becky, are you okay?" Abby wanted to melt into the carpet. This woman wasn't dying or hurt, if her eyes served her right. In fact, just the opposite.

"Abby, is that you? What the heck are you doing here this late? It's nearly dark outside. Did Jackson come too? Or Carter? Is he home now? He said he was coming home." The woman pulled a robe from the end of the bed, drew it around her, and dropped her tiny feet to the carpet.

"I'm so sorry. The pharmacy called and said—interactions—someone needed—I came to check on you. Um, I'll go in the other room." Her feet came unglued from the floor and she rushed out.

In the kitchen, Abby shook her head and clamped a hand over her mouth. Well, if Becky's blood pressure was elevated, Abby was fairly certain it had little to do with the prescriptions. She stifled a giggle. Did Carter have any idea his mother had a boyfriend? Did she? Did women have flings at that age? She frowned at her stupidity. Why not, there was nothing wrong with—

"Well, I guess you came at a very awkward time, didn't you?" Becky's voice was strong. She walked into the room without the walker she'd used on the prior visit. Her shoulders were straight and her back stiff, though her hair could use a comb.

Abby straightened. "I didn't mean to scare you. It's just the pharmacy called and said they made a mistake on your prescriptions and there might be some drug interactions. When they started naming everything off, I panicked."

Becky raised a brow and shuffled to the counter. She flicked on a light and ran some water into a pot. "You could have just sent Jackson, or had him call. You didn't need to run all the way out here, honey. You want some tea? I'll heat the pot up."

"You're fine." Abby stated the obvious.

Becky clutched the robe tight and nodded. "Of course I'm fine."

Abby shook her head and tilted her head toward Becky's bare feet. "No, I mean you're better than fine. You're walking around."

The older lady's face went six shades of pink before she sighed and set the pot on the stove. "Okay, you caught me. I'm not really sick. Haven't been for over a year. I get around fine. I take the walker outside for safety, but that's all."

Abby laughed. It was hilarious if she thought it through. This old woman, who had them all thinking she was under the weather and needed constant supervision and visits, had played them all. Her story was the biggest ruse *ever*, far surpassing anything Abby had done.

"Why the big farce then? You have everyone worried sick."

The teapot hissed. Becky poured two cups then added the bags. She carried them to her dining table and set one down before moving to another spot and settling herself. "I know. I know. It was awful. Sit and get comfortable. I shouldn't have kept it going like I did. It's just that after Carter's sister left us, he barely spoke. We never heard a peep. It broke my heart how little he'd seen his father before we lost him too. Then it was just me, here all day, talking to myself. Sometimes a neighbor came by. The doc stopped in once in a while, being a good friend of the family, but other than that, it was—miserable."

Abby sipped the hot liquid. Her eyes watered a bit and she wasn't sure whether it was from the heat or knowing this woman was so—alone.

"When I got sick and they called Carter, it was like a new start for me. Us. He kept coming by and we talked. A lot. The doctor came out and checked on me too, so I didn't really need Carter to be here, but I wanted him. I knew if he didn't believe me ill, he probably wouldn't take the time. What with his work and all. Not to mention he still can't seem to cope with what happened."

What exactly had happened? Abby lifted her cup and blew on the steam before taking a sip. She slid her gaze out the window. Fireflies hovered over the darkness of a barely visible manicured lawn. Someone was taking great care of it. Was that someone Carter or the man in the back? Or Becky?

"Ahem." A somewhat throaty voice surprised Abby and she turned. The man had the good nature to appear embarrassed as he waved. "Hi."

"Abby, this is Gavin Bernard. Doctor Bernard."

Abby made sure not to give away any surprise. *Oh.* So the doctor wasn't just being nice. He had a vested interest in Carter's mom. Eeeuw. She glanced at his ring finger, not caring that he noticed.

"My wife died eight years ago. We were great friends, the four of us. We had to be, it was a horrible thing to lose your child before she even had a chance to live. It was the only way we could get through it."

Obviously, there was a lot more to *that* story and Abby cringed at the thought of hearing it. It was too late at night and she'd already caused enough trouble for one day. Hell, for one year. Still, her curiosity about the length of the relationship was piqued. How long had they been involved? Had Carter known?

"You were—" She looked from one wrinkled face to the other.

Becky throttled her head from side to side. "No! Of course not. I loved Carter's dad and Gavin loved Maggie too. It wasn't like that. In fact, we spoke very little until my husband went into the hospital with cancer. Gavin came to check on me a lot after I brought him home; we kept up. All of us. We'd been through a lot over the years and … "

Dr. Bernard joined her at the table and placed a hand on her shoulder. Abby was unsure what to do. She hardly knew these people and certainly wasn't on the best footing with Carter, yet they'd just divulged something not even he knew. Too much information, actually.

"You don't need to explain to me. It's none of my business." Abby stood, set the half-empty cup by the sink and turned. "I'd better get going. I guess I don't need to tell you what the pharmacist said, do I?"

Becky glanced at Dr. Bernard and laughed with hesitation. "No, but it's comforting to know you cared enough to come out.

It's also just past sunset and way too late to make a drive back to the city. You'll stay in Carter's room."

Huh? What? *No way.* After several attempts at refusal, Dr. Bernard managed to wrestle her purse and keys away. Before she knew what hit her, Abby was wrapped up in navy sheets with basketballs on them and smelling something that drove her crazy. *Him.* Odd because he'd been overseas for a month. What did he do—plaster his DNA into the fabric along with the accompanying detergent scent?

Chapter Twenty-Six

The light of day always seemed to bring clarity to the worst of problems. Abby had not only created the biggest farce of a personality by continuing to communicate with Carter after she knew who he thought her to be, but also by deceiving his mother. And now the doctor too. Today she'd come clean. To everyone: Becky, the doctor, and even Carter if she could track him down and get him to answer her. She'd start with his mom.

Abby was disappointed when she walked into their kitchen. Her hope to have a good talk with the couple was dashed. The room smelled of cinnamon and toast, yet it was empty. A note sat on the counter by a coffee cup.

Good morning! We forgot to tell you we were leaving early this morning to attend a craft fair in Fort Bend County. Make yourself comfortable. There should be plenty of things to eat in the fridge and there's coffee in the pot. We'll be back this afternoon—hope you can stay long enough to visit then.

—B

So much for that talk. Abby picked up the note and ran through it again as if it might change in the re-read. Hmmm. She wasn't about to snoop through Becky's fridge but the coffee smelled good. She poured a cup then padded barefoot to the bathroom. A quick wash up and she'd head home. She looked in the mirror and grimaced at the reflection staring back. Frazzled hair, smudged eyes, and wrinkled clothes. Ugh. Why had she decided to drive like a bat out of hell to see a woman she barely knew who parented a guy that now hated her?

She pulled open a drawer and rummaged for a toothbrush and toothpaste. Thankfully there was a new set waiting there and she took advantage of it.

"You want to tell me why you're in my bathroom using a toothbrush—in my mother's house?"

Abby jolted around and screamed. Carter leaned against the doorjamb, hand on his hip, staring at her.

The toothbrush in her mouth fell to the floor. *Clank.* Toothpaste oozed onto her chin. She couldn't answer.

"Well?"

"Um, you told the pharmacy to call me to check on her."

He grabbed a towel from the rod and tossed it at her. "No. I told them to call Jackson. Are you telling me he sent *you*?"

Wow, that was harsh. Abby wiped the toothpaste from her chin, leaned over, and slurped water then swirled and spit. She needed a few seconds. What should she say *this* time? The truth was getting more and more complicated. Would he believe it? Did it even matter? As much as she enjoyed their time together, this was more convoluted than her life needed to be at the moment. It wasn't worth the strain. Fortunately, she didn't have to go into details because his mother swooped in behind and grinned.

"Carter? I'm so glad you're here! And you're still here too, Abby. That's great. We made it into town and decided to come back and see if you wanted to go with us. I mean, you probably have to get back and all but still, it would be nice."

Carter's eyes darted between his mother, Abby, and the red-faced Doctor Bernard standing in the hallway. "Mom, you're walking?"

She grinned sheepishly. "Uh, yeah, I am. Quite well in fact. You remember Gavin Bernard, don't you?"

Carter raised a brow and stepped from the bathroom, nodding. He didn't speak but offered a hand.

"He's been kind of helping me get around and well, I'm doing great. See?" Becky held out her hands and displayed her newfound balance. "So, you two want to go with us to the craft fair? Did Jackson come too?" She glanced around.

"I don't know, Mom." Carter smirked at Abby. "Did he?"

Becky slapped his arm lightly. "Well, he didn't come with her. I know that much. She rolled in last night and scared the bejeezus out of us." She clamped a hand over her mouth. "I mean me."

Carter was dumbfounded. "Last night? Exactly why are you here, Abs?"

Becky grabbed him in a big hug. "She was checking in on me. Isn't that sweet? Who cares? Let her clean up and join us. Then we'll head into town. I'm so glad you came. What time did your flight get in?"

Carter responded as he was pushed through the doorway and away from Abby. Good. She needed to collect her thoughts and speak calmly as she unraveled the multitudes of mistaken conversations and identities. Something she had no intention of doing with his mother and her boyfriend present. It was embarrassing enough.

Abby was hoodwinked into a craft fair along with Carter. Fortunately for him, Dr. Bernard chose to make a beeline for the concession stand after thirty minutes. Abby stifled a smile when Carter said he'd better accompany him in case he needed anything. Yeah, right. She only wished she'd thought of it first. Her feet started to ache after an hour of following Becky around. What was she thinking when she assumed the woman was feeble? There was nothing weak about this lady if she could handle a crowded fairground.

After admiring more quilts than she could stand, she excused herself for a drink of water and to sit. She managed to scope out a quiet and dark corner under a tree and sighed with relief as she rubbed the arch of her left foot.

"Need some help with that? Or does Jackson take care of it for you? Or maybe some other dumb guy."

She squinted at Carter standing over her. "I imagine you'd rather cut it off right now."

"You got that right. There's a dart board in the game room at home—don't plan on standing too close to it."

"Nice. Look, this whole thing is just a big mix-up. I made a mistake." She lifted a hand and pulled on his arm. "Sit down. My neck can't crane that far up and the sun is blinding me."

"So, my mom is dating the doctor apparently. And *your* boyfriend sent you here instead of coming himself. Does your boyfriend know about me, about us?"

...

Her phone buzzed on the surface between them and he knew he shouldn't have checked but he glanced to see the display. Unfortunately it was facing down. She ignored it.

"Speak of the devil. You're not going to answer that?"

She shrugged. "I don't want to talk to him at the moment."

Jesus, she played a lot of games. Here with him while Jackson called looking for her? How many others were being strung along? The phone rang again and he reached out and snatched it, hitting the button to answer before he got it to his ear.

"Stop." She bolted both hands to grab it, but he turned away and listened for a familiar male voice.

"Hey, Jackson." He narrowed his eyes on her face as she shook her head.

The *unfamiliar* voice on the other side startled him. "Uh, hi—Who is this?"

Oops. Not who he thought—he lifted the handset away and looked at the name—her—dad? "Um, I'm Carter—a friend."

"Of Abigail's? I didn't know she was seeing anyone. How long has *that* been going on?" Wow, that was pretty condemning.

"We're not—" The phone was yanked from his hand before he finished. He mouthed the words *your dad?* Panic mixed with anger as she nodded.

"What do you want, Dad?" She strode away with the phone, spoke a few words, then put her phone away.

Carter dragged a foot across the ground and shoved his hands into pockets. "Sorry—I thought it was—"

She darted her eyes skyward. "I know who you thought it was. You know, you should try trusting me. Maybe I'm not really as bad as you think."

"Trust isn't something I do very well."

"Yeah, I gathered that."

"You could have talked more. I wouldn't have minded."

"Well, I mind. My dad is a pain in the ass right now, right behind my mom. Every time I call, there's always *something* I haven't done or at least haven't done right. I keep telling myself they have good intentions, but right now, I need a lot more than that. I need—"

"Some confidence?"

She shrugged. "From them? That's asking more than they know. Not happening."

"They're just trying to protect you."

"Maybe." She leveled her eyes on his. "I could use someone to have a thread of faith in me right now. You know, faith I can do this. I want to be successful so bad I can taste it. Maybe I don't need a rich boyfriend to survive, even though they struggle to believe it. I mean I'm smart. Capable. Can't they see that?"

Wow, were her parents really that backward thinking? It never occurred to him her family wasn't in her corner, rooting for her success.

"Trust is a hard thing for most people." He wasn't referring to her parents either—he was as guilty in that respect as they were. His adult life had been riddled with women and friends that said one thing and did another—people that hid the simplest of things rather than expose themselves to potential pain.

• • •

Abby's heart toasted her insides a bit. He sat, beer in hand, and drank in silence, watching the crowd move around them. She was worn out from all the confusion but even tired, she wanted to wrap her arms around his neck. Which really pissed her off. She should have never gone to Sotby's that night and she definitely shouldn't have answered the texts. Or let Caroline do it on her behalf.

"Look, I haven't got a clue what you're doing here, but it's wrong." His voice was more a growl than words. So much for the warmth she'd briefly felt.

A popping noise caught her attention and she shifted to look behind. "How are you with a shotgun, Carter?"

"Huh?"

She hooked a thumb at the toy gun booth. Sure, it was set up so kids had entertainment while their parents shopped, but why not? "Want to take a little target practice? We can pretend the targets are each other. Winner has to spill their guts. You up for it?"

"Spill their guts? As in what?"

"Honesty. Tell something totally honest about themselves. Think you can handle it?"

"You're serious? I'd think that was way too close to the fire for you."

"What's that supposed to mean?" She lifted a brow and had the familiar urge to touch him.

Carter shrugged. "Honesty doesn't seem to be your thing, but I'm game if you are." He rose and strode toward the small counter. A row of pop-guns sat waiting for takers, each with a small rope anchoring it to a makeshift tripod.

A comment like that should have burned because she always thought herself incredibly honest. Under the circumstances, she had little defense. How could she blame him for his thinking? Still, she'd set him straight and give him a chance to vent in the process.

The entire exchange was destined to be indelibly imprinted on her mind; the monotonous carnival music chorded as a set of fake birds flitted across the backdrop. They disappeared, only to return seconds later and repeat their route. She had been preoccupied, thinking of the right way to say what she'd so completely botched before. Over and over. Now, studying his clenched muscles, she had to admit—he was hot, in multiple ways. His anger, the humid day, and just watching him made her temperature spike.

When Carter bent to aim the pop-gun, his back hip taunted her with memories of being locked against that hip. His T-shirt stretched up and bared the indention of his lower spine just above the waist of his shorts that hung loose on those delicious hips. She wanted to reach out and touch that spot, stroke a circle around the slight hollow, then follow it to other even hotter spots. She bit her lip, clenched her fist then started—to—reach.

Pop. Pop. Pop. Pop.

The sound jolted her from the daydream as each pop was followed by a ting sound. He turned and grinned. "I hope you brought your A-game. You'd better get started—I'm already up by two hundred points." He swung the gun barrel at his score, displayed in red lights on the wall above the birds under the words *Player A.* Then he proceeded to lightly pummel the trigger until he'd sprayed the targets and drove his score up higher.

She let out a sigh and laughed. "Oh, I brought it, all right. Prepare to be blistered into submission."

He darted a raised brow at her over the barrel then, without turning back, flipped the trigger three more times. Hitting something each time. Should she be intimidated? Not unless she was concerned about winning, which she wasn't. In fact, she planned to lose.

Abby plunked two quarters into the slot and picked up the pop-gun. She leaned over at the waist, knowing her shirt had dipped as his did and revealed even more skin. She hoped it affected him as much.

He sucked in air. "I am sooo going to whip your ass, Abs. So, do I get to pick the subject of this honesty exposure or are there certain things off-limits?"

She pulled the trigger five times, speaking as the two targets flopped down. "No limits."

He kept shooting right along with her. She missed. He hit. She hit. He hit. Seconds ticked along until his rapid-fire trigger clicked, signaling the end of his turn. He set the gun down and came up behind her. Leaning over her back, Carter's entire body weighed against her, hard and warm. "Don't choke," he whispered in her ear.

Abby choked. But not because she couldn't shoot.

She squinted into the sight, tried calming her jangled nerves, and sprayed the remaining shots across the terrain of targets. When her gun clicked, she set it down. The score glared at them in red lights. Player A: 1150, Player B: 650

"You cheated." She feigned a protest.

"How can you cheat at pop-guns?"

His body pressed into hers and she swore she felt him breathe. "You're distracting me. How am I supposed to hit anything when you plaster yourself against me every time I pull the trigger?"

He chuckled. "All's fair in hate and war. You said no rules."

"You misquoted that, didn't you?" She pushed a hip back and forced him off her.

"I said what I meant. Exactly how are we going to do this honesty thing?"

She ignored his remark and turned to lean against the counter. Crossing her arms, she considered that question. *Haven't really thought that far ahead.* "I want a rematch."

Mimicking her, he crossed his arms and rolled his eyes. "I think I should probably tell you I used to hunt a lot with my dad. We also spent a lot of time at the gun range and, in case you didn't notice, that score is pretty near perfect." He pointed at the red light.

Yeah, she'd noticed. That and more.

"I think I should tell you I have a concealed handgun license." Not that she ever used a handgun. She owned one and went to the range about once or twice a year, mainly because her father insisted.

He grimaced. "I should have known you'd welch."

Okay, maybe baiting him when he was already angry probably wasn't wise. "Okay, I was kidding—I meant it. Ask me whatever you want."

He surveyed their surroundings. "Here? Now?"

She rolled her eyes. "Yeah. Unless you want to delay the agony?"

"Agony where you're concerned sounds pretty good to me. So, it's my choice? We can do this right here or whenever, wherever I want?" He looked surprised.

"I guess so, but why wait? Let's get this over with." She was ready. Apparently, he wasn't.

He dropped his arms and slipped his hands into the pockets of his frayed shorts. "I'm trying to think which question to ask."

He was making this ridiculously difficult. "You have that many? Why don't I start then?"

"Hey, I won. Not you. *You* don't get to ask anything."

"What are you afraid of? I might ask something personal? Get under your skin?"

He shrugged. "Already did that, remember? Under my skin, on top of it, wrapped in it—you name it."

Her face flushed when the booth attendant leaned over and pulled the shotgun from under her behind and handed it to a kid, apologizing. "Oh, sorry. We'll move."

The guy grinned. "I was enjoying it, but we're kinda busy."

Abby strode back toward the tables they'd vacated. "So, ask. Or lose your turn. This isn't going on forever. There's an expiration date."

"On honesty? So there *are* rules now? Figures. Okay, here you go." He grabbed her arms, spun her around, and dipped his head dangerously close.

Damned if his smell didn't make her want to close the gap. If it weren't for the red hot anger flaring in his eyes, she would have. Most likely an incredibly stupid move. He might have pushed her away.

He was driving her crazy. His chest grazed hers and, for a second, his wall of fury seemed to waver. He glanced down as her chest heaved with the breathing that came in gasps. Mainly because there was little more than a hair between them. "Do you think about me when you're in bed with Jackson?"

"*What?* Are you serious?" She glanced around at the throng of people within earshot—at least three glanced their way. One of which was—Dr. Bernard. *Gulp.*

"As a heart attack." His nostrils flared and he leaned closer, seemingly unaware of their audience.

She bent backward as he loomed above, his hands clenching her arms. What a stupid thing to ask. In order for her to say yes, which apparently he wanted to hear, she would have had to been in bed with Jackson at some point. So, while she'd sworn honesty—she had to say … "No."

He released her arms and she fell backward. Right on her butt. The gravel dug into her hip. *That'll leave a bruise.* He turned and stomped toward the cars.

"Wait! Let me finish." She crawled to her knees then lifted up. He was fifty feet past before she caught up.

He'd stopped abruptly at one of the craft booths and stared. "Abby, you ever wear one of those?" He pointed to something in a costume booth complete with ornate outfits from every century, cartoon, movie, or character.

What? She focused, trying to understand the sudden change. "Huh?"

He pointed at the camera booth behind the outfits. "Let's do it. Get a picture. What do you say? I'll pick yours, you pick mine."

First, he was mad and leaving, then he wanted a *picture?* What the hell?

"Have you lost your mind?"

Carter shook the hair surrounding that lost mind fervently. "Nope, but I thought it might be fun to see you wearing this." He reached into a rack full of clothing and yanked out the dress on the end then turned it for her to see. A pilgrim-like dress of drab colors with a bright red A in cursive emblazoned on the chest. *The Scarlet Letter.* Seriously? He raised a brow, mocking her.

"Oh. Yeah, I bet you would. Let me see. I'll wear it, if you wear that one. She pointed at a hanger covered in bulky green bumps. It was shoved in the back, but she knew what it was right from the start. There was no way he'd wear that. Not ever. The big green machine? The Hulk? Not him. He was too seriously pissed off.

"Okay." He shoved the hanger against her chest.

She rubbed where a bruise was sure to appear. "Seriously?"

"Afraid?"

Her? Afraid? Nope. "Not me, but once you get that on, I have to see it. No, I want a picture." She walked to the green bumps, pulled them from the rack, and held it forward.

He chuckled. "No worries. I can rock this thing."

Abby doubted that. No one looked good in green bulges. "Just curious—why'd you cave?"

"Nothing would make me happier than to see you in the costume that fits your true nature at the moment. You can probably wear the scarlet letter better than little Hester did. Too bad we can't go back in time."

Yikes. He wants to see me hang?

She stepped into a changing booth while Carter slipped the photographer some cash. She stepped out of her clothes and hung them on a hook then slipped into the dress. She smirked at the look. As she remembered, the girl in the book had a very high-necked, Colonial style dress. The dress in the mirror was nothing close. The dipped neckline exposed a fairly large amount of cleavage with the large red A strategically placed to point right to the darkness of the cleavage shadow. The back had a lace-up corset-style she hadn't bothered to tie. Ridiculous. She shrugged and stepped out.

Plunk. Her face smashed against the largest mass of green fabric muscles *ever*. Carter wrapped the fake bulges around her and squeezed so hard, she saw nothing but darkness. Green, dusty smelling, darkness.

"How's that for muscle, Abs? Nothing like the Hulk. Man, I loved those movies when I was a kid. Check it out." He stepped back—or rather waddled back—in the massive thunder thighs covered in a tiny pair of ripped jeans shorts. She couldn't help but giggle. Carter held his hands out and flexed with gritted teeth.

"You look like a giant Brussels sprout."

"Hey! Don't hate the muscles. Look at my six-pack." He thumped the over-inflated chest of the costume.

She wasn't going to tell him the real one was better.

He frowned. "You look like—I expected."

A girl in a barmaid costume patted him on the back. "Your face, sweetie." She held out a tub of green goo. "Just wipe it on. It washes off."

"Nah, this is good enough." He held his palms up and tried to step backward but the giant nubs of his fake feet tangled and he fell flat. On his back.

Abby grabbed the tub and dove on top, sprawled eagle. "Oh, you'll wear it, all right. I'll put it on you myself. If you're going to make me wear this, you have to do the full get-up." She swiped his forehead and cheeks then smudged it around until his face was completely green.

Carter tried to put an arm around her but the bulging fabric muscles kept getting in his way. He was stuck flat on his back. "Think you could help me up?"

Abby rose and reached a hand out for his. He held up a green boulder-like paw and she pulled—the hand off. "Oh my God! Here, give me your hand. The real one." She dropped the green glove and grasped his skinned fingers. She tried to pull him to his feet. No go. She straddled one of the green legs, bent her knees, reared back, and pulled with both hands. Then fell flat onto him again.

"Geez, that thing must weigh a ton." Her over-exposed bosom smashed against his slimed-green cheeks. The slickness left a swath of green makeup up the side of her neck. Gross.

Abby tried to lift up. The bubbled fabric worked like pillows or rather wedges—to push down until her chest was planted across his—nose.

"Abby?"

"I know. I know. I'm trying. It's just—those stupid muscles are like a fabric slide. I can't move."

His voice was muffled and hot against her breastplate. "Here, let me roll over."

She put a hand to his shoulder, but it only slipped and dropped her right back into place. "Oomph. Sorry."

"Hold still." He murmured. "I can't breathe."

"'Kay."

A loud roar ensued behind them. Abby assumed there was a show starting. She peered over a green boulder. Yep. There was a show, all right. The massive lace petticoat of her dress was hoisted up like a tent above her. She could only image what her blue and pink hearted panties looked like under all that lace as she flailed to get a balance on the green bulk of Carter's costume. *Yikes.* Her face flushed.

"Um, Carter?" She felt a cool breeze on her backside.

"I've almost got it. Rock with me, okay?" He rolled to the right then shifted and rolled back. They started to tip over then fell back. *Thud.*

Abby was certain her entire chest was now slathered in green gooey makeup. "Carter, my ass is showing."

He snorted into her cleavage. "It wouldn't be the first time. Wish I could help you but I'm a little stuck. Rock again." He grabbed her back with his exposed hand—only with the petticoat above her head there was only skin and panties. He clutched tight as they lurched to the side.

A scolding glare was wasted since his face was stuck underneath. She grasped the shoulders of the green costume and leaned hard to the right. Thankfully, they tipped enough to flip over.

Only she ended up under a big green cushion with dirt and grass in the crack of her butt.

Roars of laughter surrounded them. Seconds later, Carter was whisked off by some bystanders, and she looked up to blue skies and white puffy clouds. Abby blinked then wiped the green smudge from her eyes.

She glared at him, recognizing the fact his face was only green down one side—meaning she was also green down one side. "You happy now?"

He smirked, attempting to stifle the laughter. The green bulges rumbled. Then Carter lifted the remaining boulder-sized hand and slapped the green muscled leg. His body—correction, costume—rocked as he belted out a laugh equal to the size of the costume. He started to clutch his stomach, but the movement overbalanced him. He stepped back. "You look hilarious. Your face is green. Your chest is green. That petticoat thing under your dress is splayed out like a halo. And there's—"

"I get the gist. Shut up." She rose to a sitting position then pushed forward until she could get her feet under her. "Stupid idea."

The crowd around them roared and … oh my God, took pictures.

"Everyone here has pictures of my underwear and butt. Thanks. You're enjoying this waaay too much."

There were tears in his eyes when he pulled off the green glove and rubbed them. "I'm sorry, Abs. Really. Okay, maybe not. Here, let me help you." He grabbed a piece of fabric from the shelf and started wiping her face and neck. "Wait, I can't move in this thing. Hold on."

Carter stepped back, unzipped the side, and let the green bulk drop to his waist. Dammit. Just like that, heat surged through Abby. He stood naked from head to navel in front of her. Albeit, he had a stupid-looking green Hulk-like costume around his hips. But above it—above it was real muscle, real skin, and damned if it didn't make her want him. Even with green makeup smeared all over his neck and face. How pathetic.

Abby took a piece of the fabric and started wiping him as well. He locked on her eyes as he cleared grass, makeup, and dirt from her forehead.

Her heart pounded like thunder as he rubbed the green from her chest, dragging the cloth against her skin as she gulped in air. He leaned forward and brushed his lips lightly across hers. His index finger clutched into the bodice of her dress and he stroked it against the skin underneath. Carter attempted to step back. A burst of need went straight through Abby and she reached a hand up and pulled him in before he stepped too far. "Don't." She met his mouth and opened to kiss him hard.

"Don't?" He spoke against her mouth.

"Yeah, don't go." She kept his mouth to hers, stroking tongue against tongue. Screams, whistles, and applause brought her back solidly to the present. Wolf-whistles.

Carter wrapped an arm around her and waved. "Okay. Show's over, folks. Go buy some quilts or something."

Abby was thankful her face was buried in his shoulder where the crowd couldn't see. Maybe they wouldn't recognize her once she'd put her clothes back on.

"About that picture ... "

He snickered. "Let's just skip it, okay? Get dressed, Abs. Just curious—weren't there some sort of knickers or undergarment to go under that outfit?"

"I didn't think I'd need them. Can we get out of here? I sure hope your mom doesn't know any of these people."

"Don't worry. I doubt she'll want to claim us after that. To answer the question—she's lived here most of her life so, yes, she knows them. Just about all of them. And they know me too. I doubt I'll live down the big green suit any time soon. Nor the makeup."

Abby sighed and rushed into the makeshift dressing room. "Great."

Chapter Twenty-Seven

He probably should have given the *Scarlet Letter* costume a little more thought. That was a bad decision. He clenched his fist, the warmth of her skin and the silk of the panties fresh on his fingers. He grinned. Okay, maybe it was only half-bad. The green hulk costume was hot, itchy, and stupid, and he'd allowed her to talk him into it to soothe his spitefulness. That part was more than half-bad.

The booth owner had yelled at them initially, until the crowd gathered and she saw the potential for business. When they finally removed the green makeup and returned to street clothes, she offered them a coupon to visit her store in town. Carter excused his way past the line of people looking for costumes or waiting for pictures, to find Abby. It hadn't escaped him that *all* of them shot several glances his way as he searched for her hair, face, and normal clothes among the gawkers.

It wouldn't surprise him if she'd ditched him. It had been ugly to suggest the dress. He deserved it. Pure childish jealousy as green as the dumb costume she put him in. He frowned. He had no idea why the green monster had settled in. That wasn't a normal feeling. So what if she was already involved when he'd met her? That happened all the time, and he had to admit he'd sampled the market himself more than a few times. She hadn't seemed the type, though, which had been a plus. But she hadn't just been with anyone. Jackson. She'd had a one-night stand with Carter as well. She perfected the C in casual, even more so than most of the guys he knew. Yeah, she'd probably bolted. He shrugged as if to dismiss her.

Only she hadn't.

Abby stood in front of a booth, her back to him. Handmade bags, skirts, and tops hung before her, a myriad of colorful creations by one very creative seamstress.

"Carter!"

He turned to his mother's call.

"We have to go." By the way she rushed toward him, her health must have mended quite some time ago. Why had she lied about it? He started to ask then hesitated. No, not here. Not in front of the entire town. They'd already caused enough excitement for one day.

"You don't have to tell me twice. Okay, I'm ready." Carter turned to Abby. "What about you?"

His mom thrust a hand out. "No. Not you! Us." She gestured between herself and Doctor Bernard. "Gavin was called to the clinic. Some sort of emergency."

Good. Carter was ready to leave anyway. Actually, he'd been ready for a couple hours. He shrugged. "That's fine. I don't mind."

Becky waggled her head and shifted a glance at Gavin, who cleared his throat and spoke. "You stay. I, um, have a ride already. Here are my keys. Just leave them at Becky's. We'll pick it up later."

Carter lifted a brow. "Mom? You don't want us to take you back? It may be a while."

"Oh, for crying out loud, just take the damn car, okay? I'm going to visit one of the girls from church. She had surgery a couple days ago and is still recovering. Besides, the two of you need to talk. Preferably *not* in front of the entire town in green paint while airing your underwear. *Capisce?*"

Carter grunted and returned his mother's glare. "Yeah, and you and I need to do a little talking too, before I go back. Seems like someone's been holding out on me."

Becky grabbed the doc's arm and rushed toward a waiting car. "We'll talk later. Go have fun. You know you need it—you've been working too much anyway. We'll see you back at the house later. Much later."

Just like that, they were alone. In a crowded craft fair.

Fortunately, Abby was as ready to leave as he was, so coercing her into the car wasn't necessary. Coercing her *out* of the car when it ran out of gas eight miles from home was another story. She stared at him as if he was lying out his ass. He cursed Doctor Bernard—for the gas, and for his relationship with his mom.

Abby opened her mouth then closed it. A couple seconds ticked by before she spoke. "You really think I'm that stupid? That's the oldest line in the book. No one ever runs out of gas anymore. Come on."

He cursed again and stepped out of the car, slamming the door. "Yeah, well, it's not my car so give me a break, okay?"

"Doesn't it have one of those signals that shows it's low?"

Carter glanced at the red light above the gauge. The car was old—maybe ten years or so. The letters by the light had long since rubbed away. "If that red light with a black dot next to it is supposed to mean something, then sure, but how the hell am I supposed to know? Besides, it's too late now. The gas station is fifteen miles one way and the house is eight in the other."

"We're going for gas?" She'd stepped from the car and followed him into the road. There were no signs of traffic. Not even a dust cloud.

"Hell, no. I'm going to the house … it's closer. He can get the gas when they come home. If you want to go, feel free."

His shoes crunched as he marched away from the stranded car. A quick glance at his phone showed the time and he added another curse. He'd intended on spending a couple of hours or so with his mother, taking care of her meds and checking out the house, and then getting an early start home.

"Where you rushing off to?" Abby's voice was way too cheerful. "Work?"

"No, it's late. I was hoping to leave earlier than this. I haven't been home in—"

"Three weeks and four days."

She noticed? "Yeah. Something like that. Listen, Abs. I'm tired and I shouldn't have acted like that earlier, okay? It's just—"

She interrupted. "How close are you to Jackson? I mean, do you call him a *best* friend? Or just a so-so friend?"

He shrugged. When they were younger, it would have been best. Now? He had no idea. They hadn't kept in touch very much in college. Then, when they both ended up in the same city after graduation, it had been easy to catch up. He'd seen Jackson's status on Facebook and shot him a note. "We were best friends as kids. Now? I don't know. You tell me."

Abby's eyes shot skyward. "Leave me out of this for now. This had—has—nothing to do with me. Let's say you were in a bind and needed help. Like now, for instance. Let's say you were stranded fifty miles from home instead of eight. Would you call him? Would he be there for you? Despite anything else?"

Hmmm. Good question. He considered it. A cardinal flew across the road in front of them, lighted on a fencepost and flicked its tail up and down. Abby grabbed his arm to stop his steps. It opened its wings and flitted away. "Yeah, probably."

"Do you think he'd call you?"

"I have no idea. Why does it matter?" Aware her hand still clutched his bicep, he backed away.

She released him.

"What's your point?"

"I don't know. I ... just wondered. I wanted to make sense of it. I mean, why would he—"

"Why would he? Are you serious? Look at yourself, Abs. Anyone can see why *he* did what he did. What about you? Why him?"

"It wasn't him."

"Then why me?"

"It was never him. Where's your phone, Carter?" She stopped walking and settled her hands across her chest.

"In my pocket, why?"

"Can I see it?" Her voice was soft. He drew the phone out and handed it over when she snapped her fingers.

She opened his contacts, found Jackson's name, and pressed Dial.

"You're calling him? From my phone? What kind of game is this? You answer his phone when I call *him*? Now you call him from mine? You are seriously deranged."

She groaned. "Dammit. No signal. Seriously? Where are we, Mayberry?"

He laughed. "Yeah, pretty much. So, why check in with my phone? Why not call him on yours?"

Abby ignored him and walked in silence for thirty long-as-hell minutes. The silence was killing her. "What happened to your sister?"

"She died." His standard answer when people asked came easily. It was a good way of saying leave it alone.

"I *know* that. How? Or is that off limits?"

Off limits? No. Too close for comfort? Maybe. It happened so long ago, he really had no desire to dwell on it. Enough. "I thought I was the one that earned the right to ask the hard questions. I won, remember? All you've done is hammer me with one question after another since I showed up. Tell you what, let's just leave it alone. I won't ask anything of you, and you don't ask anything of me either. Sound good?"

"Ooooh, sounds like someone has some pent-up issues."

They crested a hill, then another, and his mother's house came into view in the valley below. Thank God. "Finally."

"Aw, a reprieve from the hard questions. Aren't you lucky."

"And aren't you catty."

Abby thrust a hand out and dug her nails into his bicep. Again. "Give me your phone again."

"Use your own to call him. No signal, remember?" He tried to shake her loose.

"Give it to me." She held out her other hand and snapped her fingers.

"No."

"Okay, fine. You call him then. Right now." She tightened her already vice-like grip.

"No."

"Then text him. Send him a message. Tell him to go to hell. I don't care. Say something."

"You're really obsessed with this threesome thing we have going on, aren't you? You play him when you're with me and you play me when you're with—" The fingernails sank in and hell if she hadn't drawn blood. "Hey!"

"Don't say it. Not about me. It's not true about me. *I* am not with Jackson," Abby hissed.

Holy shit, was water pooling in her eyes? She extracted her claws from his arm and nearly ran down the hill. Damned if he knew what her problem was. Other than being certifiably crazy. So she wanted him to call Jackson? Okay. Fine.

He dialed.

• • •

Abby was breathless and almost made it to the long driveway when her cell burst into action. Why the hell couldn't it have done that earlier? Why had this po-dunk country place chosen to lose the signal right when she needed one? What sort of crazy fate made stupid things happen the way they did? She glanced at the display and stopped running. She stopped walking as well.

In fact, she stood dumbfounded, staring at the display for two seconds. Then she hit the button to answer.

"It's about time you called."

She turned and looked up the hill at an equally dumbfounded but extremely sexy man. Who had just been hit by a brick wall.

"You?"

"Yeah."

"How?"

"How am I supposed to know? You're the one that started it. You sent me a message."

He trudged toward her down the hill. She retraced her steps up.

"I sent you a message?"

"I believe your exact words were … 'she broke up with me, you idiot. The tickets were a shit idea.'"

Seconds ticked before he spoke again. "I called information for Jackson's number but you can't get a cell number there, so I asked Roger to give me his number along with several others of our friends. He must have written it down wrong. Or I … "

"You got it. Your friend Roger gave you my number instead."

"Why would he do that?" There was less than fifteen feet between them and he closed it in three steps.

"You need to ask him that question but according to Jackson—"

"So, you are involved with Ja—"

Abby threw a finger up. "No! He wanted me to understand what happened in that meeting. He came by the store to explain it but that was after you'd already quit talking."

"Uh, sorry. So, all this time I've been texting and e-mailing Jackson—it was you?"

She nodded. "Pretty much."

"And you never said a word? You let me think you were him? Why?"

Uh, oh. Well, that was the question. She had no idea.

"I didn't intend to. You just … kept going. And things got more and more messy. Then … " She hadn't a clue how to tell the story in full. There was too much to tell.

"Then?"

"We met and I didn't know you were the same guy sending the messages *or* the same guy that I had fired. Not at first." Abby kicked a rock and it tumbled down the road as they ambled toward Becky's drive.

"Wait. So, you knew it was me when I was at Sotby's? You were there intentionally?" His frown deepened.

"No. I went to Sotby's because I was going to meet … " Who? What should she say?

"Me." He clenched his lips together and stopped walking. "This whole thing was a game, wasn't it?"

"What? Of course not. I went to Sotby's because this random guy that was texting me thought he was meeting the person on the other side of the conversation. So, technically I was invited. After all he'd been through, it seemed wrong to let him sit alone."

"There was no blind date?"

Abby grimaced. "Ugh. No. I never go on blind dates. Way too complicated."

Carter leaned over, picked up a rock from the road, and stood to toss it into the trees. "No, you just date friends of friends. And pretend to be someone else. And kiss one guy when you're sleeping with another. Or maybe it's more of a booty-call one night here, one night there thing? Yeah, nothing complicated about that. Simple as hell."

Abby growled and stomped a foot. Dust flew from below her shoe. "Look. I haven't done any of those things. I was just trying to be nice."

His eyes popped. "Nice! You've *got* to be shitting me. That's nice? Which part? Damn, you really have a skewed sense of etiquette."

"I didn't want to be the one to tell you about Jackson. It wasn't my place to do that."

"Right. Who am I to want to know the girl in my bed was in his the day before? Why should that matter?"

"I wasn't in his bed the day before. Or the day after. Or any day. Ever! I don't even know Jackson. Other than the day I doused him with water and the day he came into the store for the wedding ..."

"Wedding?"

Abby threw a hand to her mouth. What an idiot thing to say! Hadn't she already complicated it enough? Now, there was *that*? No. More. Lies. "Yes, he's going to be in a wedding and we're doing the arrangements." Okay, it wasn't perfect but still accurate.

She stomped to Becky's porch and tried the door, hoping to escape his scrutiny. It was locked, so she dropped to the step and stretched her legs in front. It was time. "Carter, I've lied to you since I met you. Well, technically, since right *after* I met you because you texted me the same day you ran over me with Ruckus. You thought I was Jackson and I never told you—you just kept sending messages. At first, I tried to stop it. Then, after that day in the park ... well, you were talking about me. Then you said how much you hated dishonesty and I knew you'd never forgive me. I thought maybe once we had a little more time, it would be easier. I was—"

"Spying."

She shrugged, unable to look at him. "Sort of, but it wasn't intentional."

Carter stepped up to the porch and dropped next to her. "How do you figure that?"

She shook her head. "It doesn't matter. In fact, none of that matters. Here's the thing. Whatever you think I have or haven't done, it's probably not true. The key part being that you *think* it, you don't *know* it. Everything that's happened between us in person, not through messages, that was real. You *know* that. I *know* that." She put a hand over his as it rested on his thigh. "Trust that. It's the real part ... the truth. Okay?"

He squinted and leveled his gaze on her mouth. "Is it? Was it?"

Abby looked away then slapped her hands to her thighs and stood. "You'll have to decide. I have to go home now. I only came because I thought Becky was in trouble. I need to get back. I have to work tomorrow."

"Your keys are inside on the counter, remember?"

She had forgotten to pick her keys up when Becky rushed them out. She tugged hard on the doorknob. "Dammit. I feel like I'm being held hostage."

"You are. She slid your keys to the side of the counter when you weren't looking. I noticed but it didn't really register until now. That's how my mother resolves things. She's always been like that, which is why I chose not to come home after Carley died."

"Carley was your sister?"

"Yeah. My mom's good at expressing herself. She's big on communication. That was her way of getting past the loss. She *talked* about it. All the time, in fact. I hated it. Every time I came home, everything we said and did revolved around Carley. It was like a mosque in this house."

"I bet that was stifling for you. You felt unimportant." How sad his parents had been so swept up in their grief, they forgot to love their remaining child.

"No, that wasn't it." He picked a twig from his pants and tossed it in the grass. "It was like we were all supposed to want to stop living simply because she did."

What? Abby swiveled and stared at the back of his head. Had his sister committed suicide? Was that what haunted him? "What are you saying? She wanted to die? She did it on purpose?"

His shoulders were stiff and the hair flitted over his head, tossing the strands around at will. "No. People don't do what she did on purpose. It just happened."

"What exactly did she do?" This was why the texting had turned into such a fiasco—he spoke in riddles and innuendo. *Yeah, right. Dump the blame on him.*

Carter shoved off the steps and trudged toward the backyard, ending the conversation before it became too intense. "I think Mom used to hide a key on the back step. Let me check."

Abby saw no choice but to follow. She hopped to the ground and jogged to catch him. "You didn't answer my—" She rounded the corner.

He tiptoed to retrieve something from the overhang of the door.

"Wow, there's some great security."

He slipped the key in the lock and turned—or at least attempted to. It didn't budge. He tried again with no success, then removed it and returned it the hiding spot. "I guess she changed the locks."

"When was the last time that key was used?"

Carter shrugged. "I don't know, maybe eight years ago?"

"If it doesn't work, why did you put it back?"

"Good point." He left it and hopped to the ground, slipping his hands in his pockets.

Abby did a one-eighty of the yard. "So, any other possible places to look for a key? A secret stash somewhere?" A group of ducks bolted to the air behind the shed where Abby had first seen Becky. "Look!" She raised a finger toward the birds.

"We get a lot of them out here. Mostly green heads."

"So, that hunting you did with your dad, was it here? In the fields behind the house?" She imagined a young boy that spent his days running through the fields in the summer and hunting ducks in the fall. It must have been a paradise for a child explorer.

"Sometimes. When I was younger, we went out there." He pointed past the barn. "But after Carley was gone, we went on hunting trips. I always thought Dad had to get away from it just as badly as Mom wanted to memorialize it."

"How old were you when she died?"

"Fifteen. I had almost finished my freshman year. She was eighteen months older, a sophomore."

"Oh, I thought she was—"

"Little? Nah, she'd just gotten her driver's license a few months earlier. She wasn't one of those who rushed to get it, mainly because she had no need. There's not a whole lot to do here."

"Tell me about her." Abby half-expected a snarling comment. He simply walked away, toward the barn.

With his hands still in his pockets, Carter strode softly across the thick grass. "Why don't I walk you around the place while we're waiting? Feel like seeing farm life up close?"

Hmmm. They had just walked eight miles to get to the house. Wasn't that close enough? The wind whipped his hair away from his face as he turned in profile. Okay, up close with *that* might be nice.

"Sure." Besides, there wasn't anything else to do and she obviously made him uncomfortable with the questions. So uncomfortable he had no desire to sit and talk any further.

They walked in silence toward the shed, veering to the right on an almost hidden footpath, and made their way toward the field beyond.

When they cleared the structure, her breath caught in her throat. "Oh my God, you had *this* in your backyard and can't understand the allure of flowers?"

They stood at the crest of a hill looking toward a meadow that was ringed by trees. The entire area was carpeted with bluebonnets, starting just below their feet. The only break in the sea of blue was real water, as in a small pond with a dock jutting into it. The darker greenish blue of the pond seemed dismal compared to the vibrant color of the flowers. Abby sucked in the scent. She didn't bother to stifle a moan of pleasure.

Carter shrugged. "It's a little overwhelming, isn't it?"

"That isn't exactly the word that comes to my mind. More like beautiful, amazing, or something straight out of a Hallmark card. I don't understand. How can you see this day in and day out for weeks every year and not find it the most exotic and enticing thing ever? I could pitch a tent out here and stay for days."

He snickered. "Not unless you want to get stung by a hundred bees ... or worse, mosquitos." He trudged forward into the tall sea of blue, unconcerned for the survival of the beautiful stalks.

"Watch out, you'll trample them." She reached for his arm, attempting to hold him back.

He walked straight over the state flower with no concern. Wasn't there a law against that?

"Aren't they protected or something?"

He turned with a humorous glint in his eyes. "People always think that. They also think you can't pick them. It's not true. Sure, you're not supposed to dig them up or go tailgating through them doing figure eights in a car but it's not illegal. Someone might get pissed and beat you up, but other than that, it doesn't matter. It's okay to pick them and it's okay to occasionally *step* on one or two."

Carter's glance dropped to the hand on his arm, which she withdrew. Damn, if that hadn't sent a spark through her—*again*.

"No, it's wrong to pick them. They're the state flower. I know that's not—" She stopped when he plucked a handful of the stalks then stepped toward her.

"Here. Turn me in if you want, but no one cares. This is private property and the flowers are only protected in the manner that private property is."

The clump of flowers he thrust to her sent a burst of the most heavenly scent through her brain. When he jiggled the bunch again so she'd reach up, she didn't. He stepped closer and bent to her face. Waiting.

She shook her head. "I can't."

"Are you seriously telling me you don't want them? Come on. Aren't you the girl who told me about the aphrodisiac qualities of flowers in general? This has got to be right up your alley. Besides, don't you trust me? Surely, you've broken worse rules than that in your lifetime?"

Okay, he had her there. Especially if one took into account the past weeks. She'd broken a lot of rules in her communication with him, but none of those were illegal. She glanced toward the house, fully expecting the town sheriff to roll up and handcuff them both.

Carter threw his head back and laughed. It wasn't much of a laugh, but still more than she'd seen in a long time. "I don't know what's funnier, seeing you splayed on the ground with your panties in full view for the town or you standing there thinking you'll get arrested for taking a few flowers from me. Abby, trust me on this. It's okay."

He tucked the flowers into the opening of her neckline, patted it, and turned back to the hill to continue stomping through the plants with little regard for their beauty. The dainty scent filled her nostrils and she lifted them from her blouse, wishing she had water to store them safely.

It was difficult to match his steps, but she tried hard to keep her shorter footprints well within his, in order to minimize their destructive path. Even if it *was* okay, it didn't seem appropriate. They moved down the hill toward the pond. Again, she imagined a small boy running through the fields and stopping to throw a hook in the water.

"Are there fish in the pond?"

"There used to be. We haven't used it much in the past fifteen years or so. Dad stocked it when I was little and we pulled a few catfish out."

There was a large yellow and white boat tied to the dock. It was anchored by a small grouping of faded plastic flowers. A shrine? A tribute? Oh, shit. *No.*

When Carter's footsteps suddenly veered away from the dock and toward the trees, her gut turned over in pain. "Carter, was that for Carley? I know you don't want to talk about it, but it's nice someone took the time to leave something for her."

He shrugged and kept trudging, not appearing to care whether she followed. "I imagine that was Jennifer Seely. She used to come down a lot and sit and talk to the water as if they were down there. She started seeing a shrink after her parents caught her out here in the dark one night. Mom said she still comes out every two or three years when she visits her parents. They live a few miles down the road."

Abby's stomach turned. She hesitated to ask. "Jennifer was a friend of your sister's?"

He stopped suddenly. Abby slammed into his back. His scent shot through her as her face smashed against his shirt. He turned, steadied her, and held her forearms—in a death grip. His knuckles were tense and white. "She was Carley's best friend. She was with them when they drowned."

Drowned? No wonder he avoided the area, but—did he say *they?* More than just his sister? Her curiosity was piqued and she bit her desire to ask. Would she have wanted to talk about it in his shoes? Crap.

"I'm sorry, Carter. So sorry. I didn't know. I don't really know what else to say."

"There's nothing *to* say—and no need to apologize. It's not your fault. And despite what Mom wants to think, it's not hers either. Carley did it to herself. She wasn't supposed to be there. She lied. To all of us. So, when things went wrong, there wasn't anyone around to help."

Abby noticed the tic in his jaw. Anger? He was angry at her for dying? "Even if she had told you, would you have been able to save her—them?" Abby searched his face.

"She wouldn't have been there. I'd have told. Or stopped them." He released her arms and lowered himself to the grass that sloped gently toward the water. Carter lifted a knee and rested his forearm across it then pulled a dandelion from the ground and started plucking the yellow flower apart, piece by piece.

Abby squatted next to him and wrapped her legs under her. "Which is why she didn't tell you."

He closed his eyes, while lifting his head toward the sky. "Abs … she'd be alive today if she hadn't been lying to all of us over and over again about where she went, what she did, and who she was with. She was such a—"

"Teenager. She was a teenager, doing normal things a lot of teens have done. Was she a good swimmer?"

"Swim team six years. That wasn't the problem."

"Then … "

"She and Jennifer had been doing these sunbathing and swimming outings for weeks. They even skipped school on occasion … and that day too. They wanted to get tanned so they could look good when they went to the lake with Jennifer's parents the week after school let out. I don't get why that's such a big deal with women. Deanna, the doc's daughter, heard them talk about it and bribed them to take her with them—she was going to tell if they didn't take her. Her dad knew nothing until the sheriff came by his office just as he left for the night."

Abby stood silent while a bee buzzed her head. She wanted to jolt away or swat it, but moving might break the mood and she wanted to hear—whatever needed telling. The golden body and silky wings flitted around her arm then up toward her face. The buzz rang out between them until Carter moved closer and swatted on her behalf.

"Deanna neglected to tell them she couldn't swim. At all. I mean, what kind of parent doesn't teach their child to swim? That's a basic thing, for God's sake, and he's a doctor. Hadn't he ever considered the danger? When Carley and Jennifer decided to jump in and cool off, Carley thought it was funny to push Deanna off the dock." He pointed at the end of the wood planks. "Into ten foot deep water."

"Oh my God, Carter."

"I know. Carley had no idea because she jumped in too and swam to the dock. She and Jenn panicked when Deanna never came up. They could see her hair floating and jumped in. Or at least that's what Jennifer said. They tried to pull her up, but Deanna lost it and started squeezing and clinging to Carley. She tried to grapple with Jennifer too, but she pulled free and swam."

"She didn't try to get them out? Or call for help?"

He nodded. "She screamed and screamed, but everyone was either at school or work. She ran up to the shed and got a rope then dove down and tied it to them and pulled them in—but it was too late."

"You were angry." She stated it matter-of-fact. The pain in his eyes flashed and he squeezed them tight. Did his lip quiver?

"It was an accident. She tried to save both of them but couldn't. I wish—it's amazing how much can change in just a few minutes—and no matter whether a person wants to go back and do it again, you can't. It's not like playing a game where you get a do-over."

"You wish she'd told you they were going."

"I—Yeah, like I said, I could have stopped her. Or at least been the one trying to help. I was bigger even then. She was such a liar. Why? I mean, we were close growing up. She had no need to keep secrets from me."

Abby hated to state the obvious, but he was her little brother. "You said yourself you would have told. You really think a teenage girl's going to skip school to sunbathe and let her little brother in on it?" How many times had her brother and sisters been caught doing similar things? She had no idea. She only knew what she heard her mother and father fighting over. That had been a lot.

The only times she was ever informed was when her older sister wanted to use her as an excuse to go somewhere. "Are you telling me you never did anything like that?"

His gaze bored holes in hers. "I've done a lot of things, but nothing that could have killed someone."

"Oh, come on. I doubt she even considered that at the time. They were just getting a tan."

He shrugged and reclined into the grass, resting his head on intertwined fingers. "Who cares what was going through her head. All I know? She lied and she died."

Abby's stomach sunk. That made what she'd done even worse. It wasn't just a lie—it was a lack of trust. A whole series of them, in fact. Was he projecting what happened with his sister onto the stories she, herself, had told? Her throat suddenly closed up. *She lied. I lied. We both weren't who you thought. Who you hoped.* Who could be?

Abby lowered back onto the grass at his side and closed her eyes also. What was there to say? Obviously he thought, had he known, his sister would have lived. That he could have prevented it. That her dishonesty killed her. What had Abby done? She'd lied also—about even worse things. There was no way this could possibly end well, and damned if she hadn't wanted it to. All the mistakes she made were done to, what? Protect him? Or maybe just cover her ass? *Shit.*

The wind brushed gently against Abby's face and carried footsteps on wood. Soft steps along weathered-gray slats above the water.

She rose to her elbows. A figure stood at the water's edge. A young woman in scrubs? Recognition wafted over her—the pharmacist.

"Jennifer?" Abby started at Carter's voice just as the woman spun around and saw them. She wiped her face and forced a smile. From where they were, Abby had no idea whether the woman's eyes joined the smile or sparkled with tears. She imagined the latter.

"Hi there." Jennifer waved and strode up the bank to stand over them, blocking the sun. "Your mother said you were here. I thought I'd stop by. When you didn't answer, I came to see—"

Carter swept a hand around him, motioning at the flowered hillside. "Can you believe how they've grown? Who would have thought two little packets of seeds would do all this?"

Jennifer swiveled a head up the hill and back. "Nice, isn't it?"

He nodded. "She'd have loved it."

Jennifer's eyes misted and she crossed her arms over her chest, looking up to the house behind them. "I suppose."

Abby was lost to some extent and lifted a hand to shade her eyes. "You planted the bluebonnets?"

She nodded. "It was a tribute to them. I had to do something. I'd already tried everything else—drinking myself into a stupor, nearly flunking out of school, drugs—you name it. Then I decided if I hadn't already killed myself, maybe I wasn't supposed to die that day. Maybe none of us were, but at least I had a chance to do *something*. So I planted these and told myself if they grew, then that meant my friends were in a beautiful place."

Carter leaned back again and closed his eyes tight. A sting of water puddled in Abby's lids. She stroked a hand over his stomach without thought. He caught her fingers and strung his into them. She stared at his hand clutched to hers as if draining some strength—or maybe comfort from the touch. With his eyes still closed, he spoke. "Well, this is certainly a beautiful place."

A bee zipped over Jennifer's head and she waved it away. "No—not here. I meant, I come out here and talk to them sometimes. When I planted the flowers, I remember saying ... " Her voice drifted, quiet.

Abby turned. "Go ahead. It's okay."

Jennifer squared her shoulders and dropped a hand to play with the hem of her shirt. "I told them I was sorry. That I tried but I wasn't strong enough. I wished I had been—every time I think back, I wish I'd stayed down there with Carley and been able to get Deanna calmed down enough to bring her up. When she kicked and scratched, I got scared and just saved myself. Carley stayed with her. I didn't."

She stopped speaking for a few minutes and Abby couldn't look up, just kept her hand clutched with Carter's while he lay silent.

Abby swallowed the lump in her throat. "You would have died too."

"Maybe I should have."

Carter bolted up, his hands clenching Abby's tight enough to cause a painful gasp. "No. It was an accident, Jennifer. It wasn't your fault. You tried your best."

Jennifer's eyes met Carter's. "When I planted the bluebonnets, I said, Carley, if they die, I'm going with you. If they don't live, then maybe I shouldn't either."

Carter cursed. "That's crazy."

Jennifer's head wagged back and forth. "Maybe so, but look." She held out both hands and did a three-sixty turn to admire the sea of blue flowers. "The first year, there was only about a ten foot patch of them. Every year, there are more and more. I figure that's her way of telling me I have to keep going. I have to do all the things we used to talk about because—"

Abby's voice was soft as she finished the sentence. "Because she can't?"

Jennifer closed her eyes and nodded.

Carter stood and pulled Jennifer into a hug that probably sucked the breath out of both of them. "It was an accident, Jennifer. It was just a bad accident, but these flowers are an amazing tribute. Thanks. You can't blame yourself. You know it wasn't your fault."

Abby now understood why the local pharmacist had such a thing for Carter. It had nothing to do with a crush, but a driving need for forgiveness. Only he never thought of forgiving her, did he? No, of course not. He never blamed her because he was too busy blaming himself. "You're right, Carter."

Her words broke their comforting embrace and tore them apart. "Huh?"

"You're right. It was an accident. No one's fault. Not hers and not yours either."

"I never thought it—"

"Sure you did. You thought if she trusted you enough to tell you, you could have prevented it. That was just another way of trying to accept the guilt—trying to find an explanation for something that's unexplainable. It happened. That's all."

He walked back to her and slipped his arms around her, his eyes filled with sorrow. "I wish it were that easy."

"I blamed myself too." Dr. Bernard's knees gave as he approached from above. In the distance, Becky waved from the hill above. "I should have taken the time to put Deanna in swimming lessons. I should have signed her up for soccer and softball—all that stuff. All I did was work every waking hour … all the time. If I'd been a decent dad, I'd have done those things and Deanna would have been able to save herself. They both would be alive."

In her gut, Abby knew his burden had been the hardest to bear. Mainly because there was truth to his words. Guilt was the worst of internal adversaries. It ate a person up from the inside out. While Abby barely knew the man, he had probably lived with a massive amount of guilt. It must have been unbearable at times.

While her eyes rained down cheeks that most likely were blotched as well as wet, she had to stop the massive amount of finger pointing, all of which were pointed inward by each of them.

"Stop. All of you." Her voice cracked on the last word. She sucked in air, rattling on wet lungs. "It was my fault. If I'd known them then, I would have saved all of them. I mean, I was a damned lifeguard for four years. I was trained in CPR—I knew what to do." She whirled on Carter, hoping her tactic worked and didn't piss him off. "Why the hell didn't you meet me when you were in high school? I mean, I only lived what—three hours from here. What was your problem?"

Three mouths dropped open and six eyes stared as if she'd lost her mind. Uh-oh, maybe that had been a bad plan. Seconds ticked past.

Carter's mouth hitched at the corner and he blinked. Then he smiled.

Jennifer let out a giggle then clamped her hand over her mouth and darted a look to her side.

Dr. Bernard was the only one who didn't appear to see the humor, but he stayed silent.

"You were a lifeguard?" Carter asked. "Seriously?"

"Yep. Damn straight."

He huffed. "I wish I'd seen *that*. Well then—you're right. I guess we'll blame you. This pity party is officially over. We have a scapegoat."

Abby let the weight of fear roll off her shoulders. It had been a gamble to try such a bold move, but what else was she going to do? Sit around and listen while they all tried to take the blame for something that couldn't be changed, even if they tried? What point was there in that? Thankfully, Carter hadn't gone off the deep end and lost his temper. He hadn't yelled at her for making light of a very not-light situation.

No, instead he stepped right into her and wrapped those big warm hands around her waist. He dropped his head to her shoulder and kissed lightly against the line of her collarbone. Right there in front of all of them. "Thanks, Abs. What else can we blame you for now?"

Chapter Twenty-Eight

When Carter followed Abby into the kitchen a short time later, he registered the significance of what had transpired. Admittedly, she'd made light of his past but still, the weight on all of them was the heaviest blanket he'd been under. Making sense of something that had no sense had never worked.

"You feel like a glass of iced tea?" His chest squeezed when her eyes softened. How had she known what to say to get them over that moment of self-loathing? If he were honest, it was one of many that haunted him over the years. He imagined it was worse for Jennifer and the doc.

She nodded, obviously uncomfortable with what she'd discovered. He dug a pitcher from his mother's cabinets and filled it with ice cubes. The pot for brewing tea bags was in its familiar spot and he filled it then started the brew. "People used to tell me I was lucky I hadn't been there that day. It pissed me off."

There had been nothing lucky about arriving by bus at your home to a slew of police cars and an ambulance. His father had greeted him at the gate in silence. The heaviness in his expression had never been forgotten. At the funeral, Carter overheard his dad tell a friend, "No one ever expects to bury their children when they come into the world. It should have been the other way around. This isn't natural."

It wasn't natural. Neither were all the years that followed where they each chose a different way to deal.

"They meant well." She ran a hand up his arm and squeezed the knot at the base of his neck.

He hadn't given a shit what they meant at the time. There was nothing lucky about losing a sister in such a stupid way. He shrugged.

Carter turned toward the window and stared at the barn that acted as a barrier between the house and all the pain in that field. He loathed what lay beyond. The very existence of the building shielded them from seeing it every day.

He closed his eyes. He wasn't sure how long they stood there—her hand on his back with the dim light from outside peeking through.

The sizzle of water bubbling over the pot broke the silence and he whisked it from the stove. Pulling the steeping bags out, he dumped the tea over the ice and added water. He was thankful for a task that kept his hands and mind moving.

"Good intentions don't change much, do they, Abby?"

Abby's jaw tensed as he handed her the tea. She took a sip.

As much as he appreciated the way she'd broken the mood earlier, the full weight of Abby's betrayal still felt like a fist around his heart. She hadn't trusted him with the truth either. Why should he have expected her to? "Don't you have to get home?"

She pulled another long sip from the glass then tipped it over the sink and dumped the contents. The plastic glass clinked against the counter where she left it before striding to the door.

He flinched when the door banged behind her. Her car starting and crunching on the gravel was the final straw. The floodgate opened on years of disappointment.

He cried.

Not the loud, moaning sobs his mom had done—or the handkerchief hidden sniffles of his dad. He stood at the sink listening to the whir of her car disappear into the wind, and the tears slid down his cheeks. Just a couple. Nothing earth shattering. That wasn't happening. Hell if it hadn't hurt worse to give up on her than it had to let go of Carley.

Abby hunched over the steering wheel like an eighty-year-old woman headed to church. An hour later, her neck started to ache and she readjusted in the seat. She'd darted about five glances at the rearview mirror, hoping Carter might follow. He hadn't. Why should he?

Even if he had, there wasn't any mechanism to explain her deceit. Funny, it seemed plausible at the time. Before she knew him. Before she cared—and she did. The knot in her chest tightened. Why? She had no need for a relationship at the moment. Her business was drowning her. There was no time to devote to anyone else. He understood that better than anyone.

Then it hit her. She thunked a palm to her forehead. That was the reason. It mattered that he believed in her, simply because *he believed in her*. Her entire family doubted her ability to sustain a business and chided her to be sensible. He did the opposite. He had applauded her entrepreneurial spirit—admired and encouraged her.

Her phone blinked on the seat and she glanced at the screen. A chat message. Great.

> Traveling To Survive: You there? I could really use someone to talk to right now.

A cold rock of guilt settled deep in her stomach. Not doing this anymore. He had to know the truth. All of it.

Still, she couldn't abandon him. Not after what just happened. Abby whipped the car into a parking lot, put it in park, and lifted the phone.

> She Hearts Dogs: I'm here, friend. What do you need?

Traveling To Survive: I just spent half a day with the most horrible person. One of those people that you can't decide whether you want to strangle or ...

What did the dots mean? She cringed and typed.

She Hearts Dogs: Sorry you had to deal with that.

Traveling To Survive: Where were you? Weren't we supposed to meet the other night? I waited for a while. Then this horrible woman I knew showed up with some friends and I, well, I wasn't going to deal with that too.

Abby clicked in a response with tears sliding down her cheeks.

There's a really funny reason why I couldn't be there and I'll have to tell you. When we meet next time.

She stared at the words, then backed them out and started over.

She Hearts Dogs: I'm sorry about that. I did show up and I looked around but didn't see anyone in an Astros hat. I talked for a while with someone and then left.

Traveling To Survive: You were there? Really? Oh crap! I took the hat off but only for a few minutes.

She stared at the blinking cursor, knowing he had a million things flying through his head at the moment. Right about now he was cursing her for showing up and ruining his good time. Again. What would he say if he knew that truth also?

She Hearts Dogs: Whew, so should we try again?

Maybe all the support he'd given was just to get in her pants, but damn if she hadn't needed that desperately. A huge slice of support pie served up by a gorgeous man who made her toes curl. That was exactly what she wanted, though she'd never realized it.

What had he wanted? Underneath everything else, what had he hoped for from her? She had thought maybe just a fling. Nope. Something that she'd been unable to give.

Honesty.

Chapter Twenty-Nine

Roger's presence at Carter's house two weeks later should have seemed peculiar. They hardly ever visited each other, though they met for beer or lunch during the week. Sometimes they played golf. Yet, before Carter opened the door, he knew the man by the banging. Roger always rapped four times, loud and hard, with the last one delayed a tick.

"What?" Carter scruffed a hand over his face in an effort to brush the sleep away. He hadn't bothered to dress or shower, nor had he planned to. It was Saturday morning. He peered at the widescreen, which had been blaring all night while he lounged on the couch.

Roger stepped past and drew in a breath. "Shit. I thought *I* was a pig. Want to tell me what's going on with you?" He picked up a half-eaten piece of pizza from the open box on the floor and sniffed it, then lifted a brow before tossing it back.

"Nothing. I'm just taking advantage of my time off. Haven't had any in a long time." Carter scratched his naked chest over the top of gray sweats he'd cut into shorts long ago, when he wore a hole in the knee. "You need something? Is there a problem at work?"

Roger tripped over a pillow cast to the floor the night before and teetered toward the philodendron. Carter lunged at his arm and steadied the man. The plant was none the worse, still as green as ever. Still trailing along the floor and curling into his life.

"It looks good. One of Abby's?"

"Yeah, you want it?"

"I suck at plants, but that's why I came. Have you seen their new blog for the store?" Roger leaned to whisk the pillow and toss it back home on the couch. "Got any beer?"

"At this time of morning?"

Roger had a rule about drinking before noon. Or maybe it was one o'clock?

Roger hitched a brow and gave the *you-have-to-be-shitting-me* look before tapping his watch twice. "It's not morning where I come from." He strode to the kitchen, grabbed a beer from the fridge, then paused to pull a trash bag from a cabinet before returning. After popping the top, he tossed the bottle cap into the bag. He slugged a drink then set down the beer. "Go get your laptop and take a look. They've been advertising like crazy on their blog. All sorts of crazy shit. You need to see it."

"No thanks. I'm a little capped out right now on rambling technology conversations. Blogging. Texting. Tweeting. All that shit. People can say and do whatever they feel like and hide behind a mask of anonymity, or worse, false identities. What are you doing?"

Roger scooped the pizza box, a half dozen plastic cups and paper plates, and some wadded paper towels into the trash bag. "I'm cleaning up, man. Someone better before the landlord comes in to fumigate the place. It's gross. You're gross."

"That matters to you why?"

"If you don't get your shit together, and fast, we're going to lose this job. You've been sulking around for days, and we have a deadline coming. If you don't get your head straight, we're toast."

"Don't you mean I'm toast?"

The plastic bag rumpled as he wadded it and thrust it into the bin near his sink. "Yeah, and since I'm tied to you like a sail because I jumped on your bandwagon when you sold it, I'm toast too. What the hell is wrong with you? You've never lasted more than a few months with any other girl. Why'd you expect it to be different this time?"

Well, shit. If he put it like that, Roger was right. Too right. Carter never lasted because he never wanted to. Never trusted anyone. Which had been pointed out so many times, he'd lost count. Yet, he'd tried with Amanda, and then Abby.

"She lied to me."

"Waaa-waaa. Get over it. You lied too."

Carter jolted his eyes at the silhouette against his window and squinted when the drapes ripped open to reveal the blinding sun. "I did not."

"Sure you did. The day you met her."

What the hell was he talking about? "At the park or the restaurant?"

"When you ran over her with the damn dog. Remember. You said she had big brown dirt spots on her ass and you never told her."

Seriously? "Big deal. I wouldn't exactly call that lying—"

Roger strode close and leaned up, attempting to gather enough height to intimidate. It hadn't worked, though Carter dared not snicker. "You didn't tell her. Lying by omission is still lying. Weren't you the guy that said just the other day that *not* telling something is as untruthful as an outright lie?"

"It was just dirt. How the hell does that compare to—"

"Yeah, it was just dirt. On her ass. And those messages were just texts. Go back and look at them. With the exception of the one about her body, what had she meant by it all?"

"She pretended that Jackson—"

Roger waved a hand. "I know. I know. But hell, we'd just insulted her, and you have to admit it was funny."

Carter frowned. "No, it wasn't."

"Yeah, it was. Go get your computer. I want to show you her blog. You aren't going to believe—"

Bang. Bang. Bang. Someone was at the door. Carter peered through the glass. What the hell? Flowers? He yanked it open.

A man in a blue shirt and jeans held out a bouquet of white roses. "Delivery for C. Coben. Is she here?"

"I'm Coben ... Carter Coben."

"Oh, uh, that's weird." The man shot a glance at Roger then grinned. "Can you sign for them?"

After dashing his signature on the pad, Carter closed the door and carried the flowers to the kitchen. Who the hell would send him roses?

"There's a card." Roger nodded and plucked it from the ribbon, tossing it toward Carter.

The tiny white envelope landed on the tile and hissed across the surface. Carter snatched it just before it could tumble over the edge. He slid out the message and read.

My favorites are the white roses—if you strip the petals and scatter them around (especially in the bedroom), they're like silk to step or lay on. And they smell like heaven.

--Gene in OK

"What the hell does that mean? I don't even know anyone in Oklahoma. These have to be for someone else." Carter tossed the card back.

Before Roger could read the note, the door summoned again. Roger chuckled. Another delivery, which didn't seem to surprise Roger one bit. "Go ahead. Open the door."

Carter signed for another bouquet. This time it was some frilly white and purple things that frothed like waves of ribbon, surrounded in a bunch of green leaves. With another card:

> My wife, God rest her soul, always loved orchids. I bought them for her every anniversary. She died of cancer two years ago and I can't walk by them now without thinking of the good times. We had a lot.
>
> Dan, in Seattle

He dropped a hand to his hip as he held up the words to Roger. "You want to tell me what this is about?"

Before Roger answered, there was another bang at the door. Carter wasn't surprised to see another delivery person. However, when he glanced over the man's shoulder and counted no less than five floral vans crowding the street, he was caught off guard. Plant- or flower-laden people clamored out of each and lined up on the sidewalk.

When he finally thunked the door shut several minutes later, the entire kitchen and living room disappeared behind floral arrangements. All sorts of bright and colorful creations, each with a note. His throat closed up and his lungs tightened. He opened each of the living room windows to vent the smell. "God, I hate flowers. Should I repeat myself—what's this all about?"

Roger still had a Cheshire-cat grin as he shrugged. "Read the notes then go get your computer."

"Just tell me, asshole. And help me get rid of these."

Roger shook his head in denial and sipped the remainder of the now warm beer. He tossed the bottle in the trash and deposited himself on the couch with Carter's television remote. "I think the Astros are in New York this weekend."

Obviously, Carter wasn't getting an explanation so he pulled each of the cards from their plastic harness and sat to read. One by one.

> I wanted to send peonies, but the florist didn't have them so I sent carnations instead. For my girl, Liz, it's peonies. We have some in the backyard and, well, one of our children was conceived near that bush. Grin.

Carter swore. "Unbelievable. Random strangers are sending flowers to tell me where they did the deed with their wife or girlfriend? Seriously?"

Roger laughed. "Nope. That's not at all what it's about. Keep reading."

"Open the door. It's claustrophobic in here. I think I'm going to—"

"Sneeze?" Roger knew he wasn't allergic. It would have been an easier thing to say if it were true. It wasn't.

"No, puke. These things reek. I think I'll toss them out."

"Don't you dare! Read the damn messages, idiot. These people went to a lot of trouble to send them, the least you can do is give a little damn respect and time. Besides, you have that plant there and haven't thrown it out. What's the problem with flowers?"

Carter swore the man baited him. *What's the problem with flowers? They smell. Reek, in fact. Like a damned … funeral.* "The plant doesn't smell."

Roger lifted a hand at the notes in Carter's fingers. "Read the messages. I want to hear the rest."

So he did. "This one just says 'Passion. Red roses are for passion, lots of it.'"

Roger thrust his hand in the open potato chip bag resting at his side and chomped on a chip. "Yeah, passion is good. I could use some of that right now. What else?"

"How about, 'Lavender. We love to spray the sheets with lavender. It's hard to find sometimes but damned if it doesn't make my heart turn over.' It's from some guy named Bruce. How can a guy with a big name like Bruce say something that sappy?"

"Which one was that on?" Roger surveyed the room until his eyes landed on the purple clump. "Ah, there they are. Wow, they're live too. He sent you a live lavender plant. Cool."

Carter growled, "No, not cool. Who needs a fricking lavender plant? I don't want to—"

Roger held up a hand. "I get it. The question is—do you?"

Carter flicked his eyes over the other notes, each one alluding to how the guy that sent them worshipped his girl. He wondered if *those* women were also lying, cheating—

He tossed the notecards on the floor, scattering them like a deck of playing cards. He clenched his eyes shut and leaned back in his overstuffed easy chair. "Sure, I get that I can't stand the smell."

Roger's feet hit the carpet and retreated. He hoped the man was on his way out. As soon as the door shut, he'd gather all the vases and toss them. To his disappointment, the footsteps returned.

Carter opened his eyes as Roger shoved his leg. "Here's your laptop. Log into it and I'll show you."

"I'm really not following, Rog. You're saying this is all about me? Impossible. I don't even *like* flowers."

Roger held up a hand and darted a glance at the ceiling, "Yeah, yeah. I know. You've already said that way too many times. We all know you don't like flowers. We even know why. You just need to—"

"The why is easy—there's no purpose in them. They have no value." He leaned over and typed his credentials into the screen and waited while Roger brought up the browser and typed in a website address.

Roger hitched a finger at Carter in a gunshot-like gesture. "Now, you're getting somewhere. Here, read." He swiveled the laptop and returned to mainlining potato chips.

He had no desire to read anything more about Jennifer Abigail Jeffries, the woman who'd been anything but honest with him from the day they met. When the banner for Abby's shop popped on the screen and a picture of her and her partner filled the corner, his interest changed.

Caroline was a lot more witty and interesting than he originally thought. Obviously, quite talented too, by the way she'd designed their site. He grabbed a pen from the table and started tapping next to the keyboard. Or at least it appeared that way until he started reading the second blog post entitled "Fear of Florists—It's Real."

An ailment that apparently comes from an undetermined source and hides itself behind a veil of apathy or other emotions. Remember the guy I told you about in prior posts that had a thing for our boss? Or maybe it was the other way around. Who knows.

Anyhoo—as it turns out, she finally came clean. Thanks, boss. I had completely run out of excuses for all her personality aliases. She had become the Sybil of texting. Why? He was a nice guy and seemed to like her. Why not just 'bare all' ... grin.

Unfortunately, when she came clean, there were a few skeletons in the closet ... or should I say pond?

Yeah, right. He slammed the pen down. Not fricking funny. "Are you kidding me?"

Roger jolted and scanned from the game he'd been watching to Carter. He stopped chewing and hitched a brow. "What? You got a problem, bro?"

"Don't you think it's a little macabre for a florist shop to write that shit?" It was even more so for him to read—he'd already lived it and wasn't interested in a rewind.

Roger shrugged. "You obviously quit before you got to the good part, keep reading."

You see, this guy that apparently rocked her world hates flowers. Even though he's been in the shop and hired her to do his plants—he can't stand the smell. It also seems he has difficulty looking at them, though he won't admit it. She said he's one of those guys that hasn't got a thoughtful bone in his body so the basic idea of flowers doesn't make sense. She also mentioned he had a huge hang-up about lying.

Don't we all?

No, THIS GUY seems to have the market cornered. See, apparently when he was a freshman in high school, his sister drowned. She lied to everyone about her whereabouts and skipped school with some friends to sunbathe. Near a pond. I know. I know. You're going to ask why someone would sunbathe if they couldn't swim. That's it—she COULD. In fact, according to my basic research, she was expected to go to state finals in freestyle as a junior. She had competed since childhood. So why would she drown?

Because she's a kind and decent person, like him (contrary to HER opinion). Her friend couldn't swim and ended up in the pond through a lark. Her efforts to save the girl took them both down. As in forever. It must have been sad and devastating for his entire family.

What happened after was amazing. They lived in the country. The girl apparently often grabbed a flower from the weeds and tucked it into her hair on the way to school. It was sort of her signature. When she died, the entire town came to the funeral with flowers in their hair. That was in addition to the flowers that filled the church. For weeks, it was common to find a bouquet tied to the mailbox or fencepost.

The girl's best friend planted her deceased friend's favorites, lantana and bluebonnets, near the pond where the two girls died. The community support was uplifting.

For everyone but our texting guy. See, he hated them. The flowers, not the people. He ripped them down from the fence or mailbox almost as quickly as they went up.

Why? He said he hated the smell. When his father passed a few years later, that increased his animosity. Perhaps there were other losses before that?

Now, I'm no psychologist, but I call bull on that.

Personally, I'd say it's more an issue of association. Ivan Pavlov is famous for the theory of Behaviorism. He proved that if a bell is rung at the time of feeding for a dog, said animal will salivate at the sound of the bell. Over time, the dog will salivate at the sound regardless of food delivery.

I say our man has associated pain, discomfort, and sadness with the very presence of flowers.

Sooooo, if life forced him to make that association—why can't the community around him force a better association? Pavlov did it with dogs and a bell, right?

I challenge you, the reader, to help. Show this man flowers can celebrate love, joy, happiness, or perhaps even gratitude. Hasn't he had enough of the other things?

Here's his address:

Oh, and lastly—you may think this is a gimmick to get you to order flowers from us—absolutely not. In fact, whatever you do, DON'T order from Jeffries Florist.

Why? Because if you order from us, the delivery will come from HER—my boss, the texting god. Hence, the association might continue. It has to come from random acts of kind, nice people who want to share happy events.

Carter was speechless. He strode to the kitchen, grabbed the milk from the fridge, and downed half a gallon. *Un-fucking-believable.*

He'd become an advertising gimmick. Was that really what people thought of him? He was a wounded sap?

Roger's voice further annoyed. "So, what d'ya think? Pretty awesome, right?"

Carter turned. "What the hell is awesome about being the town's pity case? She made me out as some sort of scarred, fragile moron. It's not about the flowers—it never was. I'm a guy—guys don't give a crap about flowers. That was the most ridiculous marketing prank I've seen."

Carter slammed the milk jug back into the fridge and thrust the door shut. A knock at the door stopped further ranting. He hitched a brow at Roger. "And now I'm being plagued by sentimental fools trying to prove a point. Not happening, *bro*. You can answer the damn door from now on. I'm going for a run." He escaped to his room and changed into shorts and a T-shirt. He pulled socks and shoes from the closet and headed for the door.

"Hey, it's a kid." Roger caught him before he stepped out.

"I don't care if it's the pope. I don't want or need any more flowers and dumb stories to accompany them." He yanked the knob, ready to send the kid running with a growl.

Brown eyes the size of quarters blinked over a handful of weeds. The kid's scruffy hair and torn socks were a fitting match for the dirt on one knee and Band-Aid that hung from his chin.

"Hi, I'm Trent. I brought you these."

"Uh, thanks, kid. That's nice, but—"

"Is it your birthday?"

"No."

"Oh, well—maybe tomorrow?"

"No."

The boy shifted from one foot to another and ran a hand across his nose. The dirt on his fingers attested to the freshness of the weeds in his hand. "These are daisies. We give them to each other whenever there's a birthday."

"We? As in you and your girlfriend?"

The kid rolled his eyes. "Gross. I hate girls. Kinda like you hate flowers. Or at least that's what my mom said this morning." He pointed down the street. "I live there. There are five of us. I'm the second youngest. I have a baby sister. My oldest sister is in college at U of H. We give flowers every birthday for each of us. Mom said you needed some."

Carter shot his eyes skyward as the kid had. "I don't really need them, but—thanks." He took the wilted mass of green, white, and yellow. He silently cursed the sentimental mom down the street.

The kid wiped his hands on his shorts, leaving a trail of brown dust. Mom probably wasn't going to like the look. "So, what do you do?"

"Huh? I work at a—"

"No, not what kind of job. What do you do for birthdays? How do you make someone feel special?"

Carter squinted at the brown eyes starting to look like they belonged to a miniature Yoda. Kids. They asked simple questions that just weren't so damned simple. Not simple because the truth was he had no idea how to make someone feel special—or feel anything. He'd tried and failed miserably. "Um, I don't really. I mean there isn't anyone to do that with. My mom is kind of far away and my—"

"But you go see her, right? You could take her flowers. She'd like that. They're cheerful."

No, they're not. He wasn't going to debate the subject with a ten-year-old. Was he even ten? The kid was a shrimp. "I suppose I could, but we don't do that."

"Why not?"

"I don't know. We just don't." Carter thought for a moment. "I don't have them growing in my yard like you do." He chose not to mention the weeds in his hand weren't exactly a desired flower and Carter had gotten rid of them a long time ago. Nor did he mention there were at least ten dozen flowers in his living room at the moment.

The kid's eyes flashed and he grinned. "Oh! Well, I'll get you some. I'll be right back!" The kid hopped off the step and ran away before Carter could stop him. *Shit.*

Chapter Thirty

Abby stared at the computer screen. It glared her budget's bottom line as if to say "I told you so" in her mother's voice. A failure. She was officially a failure—at business—and basic life in general.

If those numbers were an indication, her parents would gloat for years over her fantasy of business-ownership. Which is exactly what it would be in a couple more months—a fantasy that was over. Caroline's efforts to advertise had helped but only served to prolong the slow bleed. They just hadn't found enough customers to sustain the expenses and two salaries.

She'd have to break the news soon so Caroline could start job searching before they closed the doors. God, she hated to let her friend down. How could she hurt the only person to stand by her during the trip down fantasy-lane?

Correction, Carter had been somewhat supportive. He needed to work out his issues though—and they seemed larger than hers, or at least deeper. She sighed. Yet another sign of how miserably she'd managed to this point. Ruckus let out a sympathetic whimper at her side and she dropped a hand to pat his head.

"You're kind of lost too, aren't you, bud? Why'd Maddie have to get all sick and leave you with me, right? Sorry, boy. It doesn't look like I'm too good at taking care of much right now. A business, a friendship, a guy—or a dog. She wanted to leave you with Carter, but he's gone a lot right now so you're stuck with me. I promise I won't let you down though. I may not be able to keep the shop running, but don't you worry. You're going to be okay."

She turned back to the computer and focused on her nonexistent cash flow.

Whoosh. The stockroom door blew open. Ruckus blurted a short bark at the interruption.

"You want to come take a look at something?" Caroline asked.

Abby waved without turning focus away from the dismal numbers. "Can't. Busy."

"Yeah, well, so am I, dammit. Get your ass out here and help some of these people." The door clamored closed behind Caroline.

People? As in more than one? Maybe two? Why couldn't she handle a couple of customers on her own? Jesus, had they been slow so long two people in the store constituted a rush?

The wheels on Abby's chair screeched as she slid the chair back and looked through the glass.

At no less than twenty people.

She blinked.

The crowd hadn't disappeared.

She rubbed her eyes.

Yep. Still there.

Holy cow.

More than two or three customers? Was there something going on outside that brought them in? She attempted to see to the street for a commotion but damned if the crowd blocked her view. She grinned and followed Caroline's order.

A nice-looking man in a business suit caught her before she was three steps from the door. "Hi, I'd like to do the BFB. Is there a sign up form? Do you have a catalog or a brochure I can choose from?" He seemed incredibly tense and impatient. Perhaps a control-freak not interested in waiting his turn? Abby could relate if she had a clue what he meant.

Huh, what? BFB?

Caroline overheard from the counter. "I can get that for you. We don't have a catalogue yet—still working on that. We have samples throughout the store and can make just about anything. Basically, what you do is give us the kind of things you think she'd like and we keep track. You pick the dates you need them and tell us whether you want them delivered by us or you. If you want to deliver them, we can take them to you at the location of your choice if necessary ... or you can pick them up in the store. How does that sound?" The smile on Caroline's face transformed her.

Abby needed to know what this BFB thing was and how to make it—especially if it had the potential to be in big demand. Had she sold something else Abby couldn't provide, like the catering?

The man returned Caroline's smile and the tension in his shoulders seemed to settle. "Sounds great." He joined her at the counter and she pulled out an order slip to write down information.

Another customer caught Abby with questions about plants and within a few minutes, she had sold three and carried them to her car. Shortly after they worked out a system—Caroline manned the counter while Abby flitted around the store answering questions and carrying items to her for tallying.

Then two other customers requested the apparently famous BFB package, which she still didn't understand and confusion overcame the short-term business success. She sidled up to Caroline after another young man left with a receipt. "Enlighten me, what exactly is a BFB package?"

Caroline slipped the paper in a manila folder along with the other orders, closed the flap, and leveled eyes to Abby. "Best Flower Budget. It's on our blog. Basically, a guy—or girl—comes in and tells us their budget for the year. Then we schedule a series of arrangements so they're delivered on the right dates for that person. You know, anniversary, birthday, Valentine's. Then we give the customer three to four more. Those are the special ones to be used for the 'just because' days. Or maybe an 'I'm sorry' day. They pay a one-time fee and we take care of it all. It's in the blog. I had no idea people would think it a big deal."

"So, basically, it's a subscription service for flowers? They pay for us to deliver throughout the year, right?"

Caroline winked. "Brilliant, huh? Pay for it now ... and the flowers keep showing up for your loved one for months. She gets the special treatment and he stays out of the dog house and never forgets. We just have to stay on top of the schedule, which should be no problem since you're kind of anal about organization."

"Wow, you thought that up?" Abby threw her arms around Caroline and hugged her. "You are—amazing. I don't know what I'd do without you."

She shrugged out of the squeeze. "If you keep strangling me, you'll find out real quick."

Abby dropped her arms and stepped away. The knot around her stomach loosened a bit and she pivoted to help more customers, relieved there were more. A subscription service! What a fabulous idea! In fact, she knew exactly what types of things she'd recommend. Her mind churned out a few of her favorite arrangements. They needed a catalogue, of course. She had a high definition camera at home. She'd start making up samples when things slowed down.

Caroline could post the pictures on their website or blog—or wherever she'd done her magic. Which led to another question. What else had she put out there that might lead to more customers—or more problems? Abby shook that thought away. She wasn't ready to burst the bubble at the moment. Plenty of time for that later.

By the time Abby turned the sign on the door to closed and reached to set the bolt, she was exhausted. There had been a steady stream of customers the entire afternoon and, while the business was a godsend, her stamina and energy were waning. She missed her evening runs through the park.

"Ahem." A deep voice startled her and she searched the room. Had they missed a customer? With the lights dimmed, she searched the room. Nothing.

"Caroline?"

No sign of the recognizable spikes over the shelves.

"It's me, Roger. Had you forgotten I was coming by?"

Cripes. She practically jumped out of her skin when he stepped from the darkness of the shelves. And yes, dammit, she'd forgotten all about asking him to stop in before closing for his *sit-down* with Caroline. She darted a glance toward the lights that seeped from the door of the stockroom. After their tiresome day, was her friend up to a confrontation?

Duh, stupid thought. Caroline was *always* up for that.

"Hey, Gandhi!" she called out. "You have another customer."

Caroline's voice responded with masked impatience. "Would you mind taking care of it? I'm trying to get that last shipment unboxed."

Abby swallowed her mirth, knowing if she knew who waited, the pleasantries would have disappeared.

"I'll take the boxes for you. This one asked for you by name." She swung the door open and held it wide. Making a sweep of her arm toward the darkened store, Abby waited for Caroline to exit before stepping to finish her task.

As much as she wanted to spy on the two when she was done, she escaped out the back door. Good for them. They were talking. About what was the big question. Oh, yeah. They had history—she wondered if that meant one of them would be teaching the other a history lesson before the night was over.

Chapter Thirty-One

"A true test of a man's character is what he does when no one was watching." Wasn't that what Dad said over and over during Carter's teen years? It was a quote from someone famous but he didn't know who.

He looked out the airplane window as the pilot started their descent. The sun blinded him over the horizon. Nice outside and thanks to the time change, he arrived mid-morning. He was ready to get home. Should he make a trip out to his mom's before Monday? Since she was obviously mobile, it wasn't necessary. Besides, she had the good doctor now. There had been a time when he couldn't picture his mom ever getting involved with a man other than his father. He'd thought it would bother him, but it hadn't. Just the opposite. In fact, it was a comfort to know she wasn't alone and had someone to keep tabs on her health daily. Maybe he shouldn't go.

He had a pile of work in his briefcase that would take hours to sort out.

On the other hand, the bluebonnets were probably still in bloom. God, that had been a sight to see, all that blue laid out over the hillside like a carpet. *Yeah, just like that mish-mash of color that blanketed my living room two weeks ago.*

Then there was the smell. Abby had given it the kind word of scent—to him it was more of a stench. Still, she'd looked like a movie star sitting amongst them. Shit, it had been cute the way she tried to avoid smashing the blooming weeds.

The wheels of the plane hit the tarmac and the thrusters sucked the plane slowly to a roll. He shot a look skyward, appreciating that this pilot had made a smooth landing. No bumps, just a soft touch and roll. He hated it when they hit hard. Or bounced.

Should he call Roger and let him know he was on the ground? Nah, he was having "a talk" with Abby's friend Caroline. No need to interrupt a brewing volcano.

Speaking of Caroline, had she posted anything new on that famous blog of theirs? He could have slapped those spikes right out of her hair had he seen her before he left. Good thing he wasn't there when she showed for the weekly maintenance. What a nosy-Nancy, splashing his business all over the Internet for the *entire world* to see. Jesus. Had she known what happened after? The only people that *hadn't* shown up at his door were news crews. Thank God. Maybe he should send her a cleaning bill for the time it had taken to get rid of the damn things and clean all the petals and leaves from the floor.

Okay, maybe not *all* of them. He had decided to keep the lavender since it was still alive. Maybe. He'd been gone a while. Hopefully it hadn't died from neglect. Then there were the daisies Trent put into a jar and tied a string around. How could he throw that away when the kid showed up all smiles and snivels? Shit, it had been sweet the way he beamed at his effort to create the perfect bouquet for Carter's mom.

Crap.

Had he killed the daisies? The kid would be hurt if he didn't deliver them. Thirty minutes later Carter crammed his luggage in the backseat of his car and slid onto the driver's seat. He'd have to be quick, but he wasn't letting Trent down. He'd run through the driveway, stop at his place, and grab the weeds—even if they were half-dead—and deliver them.

The entire plan hit a huge speed bump when Trent rolled up on a bicycle the minute he drove up.

"So, what did she say when you gave 'em to her? She liked them, right? My mom says they're the most beautiful daisies in the state. And she loves the string—makes it even more special. Your mom liked them, didn't she?"

Carter hadn't even stepped out of the car yet. The Band-Aid that had hung from Trent's chin a while back was gone, replaced with something red and wet. Kool-Aid drips? No, parents didn't do that anymore—not healthy. It was likely some sort of juice. Carter reached out with his thumb and flicked it away. A new bandage was wrapped around the back of Trent's elbow—from a bike spill? Judging by the number of dents, yep.

Telling him he hadn't done it yet would crush the boy and, for some reason, those wide eyes just didn't deserve to be crushed yet. That would come in time, very likely from his first girlfriend. Not today.

"She thought they were awesome. And you were right about that jar and the ribbon you tied around them. Nice touch. In fact, she told me to bring more next time." Okay, so calling the dirty string a ribbon was a stretch, but it sounded good.

Trent's eyes crinkled into a big grin. Holy shit, he'd lost a tooth while Carter was gone! Damned if that didn't warm him further. The boy held up a finger. "Don't go anywhere. I'll be right back. I can't take too many though, 'cause Mom said I'll kill it if I don't leave some. Right back, okay?"

Carter nodded. "Right back." Perfect. Now he wouldn't have to deliver the dead ones at all. Sure, he'd lied to the kid about delivering them but only to keep from upsetting him. The fresh ones would be delivered as promised, and all would be well. He stopped four feet from the door. A pile of mail the size of a basketball lay below the box, obviously the ones that wouldn't fit. The box was stuffed to the rim. Various envelopes in random sizes and colors were mixed in with the normal junk mail. Cards?

He hated cards about as much as he hated flowers.

"Just great."

His mother greeted him at her back door. Her face broke into a grin as he approached with the jar of daisy stalks, and she dropped a hand to her hip. "Well that sure brings back some ancient memories. The last time I saw something like that, you were in grade school."

"Well, these are from a kid down the street from me. He wanted you to have them." He thrust the jar her way and dropped a peck on her cheek. "He picked them himself."

"Now that's a sweet thing to do. Why?"

"Because he said he always gives them to his mom on her birthday and said I should do that."

Carter followed her into the house as she deposited them in the window over the sink.

"It's not my birthday."

"I know, but when he asked if we did that, I told him no because I didn't have any. Being the helpful little guy he was, he rounded me up a bunch. Who was I to let him down by not delivering?"

That sparked a good laugh. After a couple hours of stilted conversation, a nice dinner she prepared while they talked, and a glass of tea on the back porch, Carter was ready to go back to the city.

"Wait. Here. Take these with you." She shoved a vase his way—stuffed full of no less than twenty stalks of bluebonnets. "They won't last long, but Abby will love them. Wait! Why don't we pick some more and you can take some to the kid. He can give them to *his* mom and return the favor. That'd be nice, right?"

His throat went dry. *You mean go out there and pick them? By the dock? Carley's dock?* Hell, no. No, not nice at all.

He balked. "No time, Mom."

"Take the time. It's a nice thing to do and cheerful. He'll appreciate it and so will Abby. How is she, by the way?" She didn't wait for an answer but strode toward the door and worked her way down the stairs. While she was moving well, stairs appeared to be more difficult.

"I haven't seen her in a while. Not since we were here last."

"Why not?"

He shrugged. *Because she deceived me from day one.* "No reason. Mom. We're not ... together."

"Not now maybe, but don't tell me you weren't at some point. I may be old, but I'm not stupid. That look on your face was pretty transparent."

What look? "I got her confused with Jackson and it was all a mistake."

She hitched a brow. "You trying to convince me of that? Or yourself? I seriously doubt you confused her with that beanpole friend of yours. I know you're not that dense."

She had a point there because he actually hadn't *missed* Jackson. Abby, on the other hand, had been torturing his thoughts. He hated unfinished business. What the hell had Roger said about her partner? It was like reading a book and stopping on the next to the last page. It burned in your head until you completed whatever needed completion. You needed to close the book.

"Mom, just leave it. Okay?"

"Okay, but maybe you need to just let go of the past and live the life you have now. Things work out on their own if you let them."

Carter helped her pick the damned bluebonnets and even tied some crazy lacy ribbon around it from her sewing kit before he slid behind the wheel of his car. He returned home to an empty apartment, after leaving the flowers at Trent's doorstep. Like a kid would do. He chatted for three hours with *She Hearts Dogs* before he fell asleep.

Chapter Thirty-Two

You can bullshit the rest of the world, but there isn't any B or S in family. Jason had used that phrase frequently when they were teenagers as a reminder he was always one step behind her, or ahead, depending on the issue. Why was she surprised when her brother walked in the shop door on a Tuesday morning?

"I thought you said you were too busy to drive all the way into the city," she admonished when he approached her side.

He scratched the scruffy facial hair lining his chin. "I am, but you're making quite a commotion on the Internet and I wanted to see for myself." He darted a glance around the crowded shop. Abby was thankful Caroline's marketing gimmicks had created a steady flow of customers. "I thought I'd warn you the rest of our clan is coming this weekend. They wanted to surprise you, and I know how you hate family surprises."

Great. Just what she needed—more lectures from her parents. "Crap, why?"

He tapped a finger against his chin. "Hmmm, I don't know … maybe because you haven't answered your phone in weeks?" He came up behind her and put a hand on her shoulder, rubbing the knot she hadn't noticed. "Everything okay, Abs? Everybody's a little worried. I'm worried."

"Don't be. I'm fine. Just busy. The shop's open every day, so I don't have a lot of spare time. Besides, the last thing I want is another 'why would you want to do that' lecture from Dad. Or a 'you know it would be easier if you just let me fix you up with Scott Crankston' from Mom. Between the two of them, one would think I don't have enough brain cells to take care of myself *or* find my own social life." Which was true, though she'd not admit any such comment.

He snickered, but the look on his face was agreement mixed with amusement. Still, he apparently knew not to poke the bear. "Have you been following the Astros this year?"

They spent the next half hour chitchatting between customers as he followed her around the shop. When a lull in business quieted the room, Jason suggested they meet for lunch and left. Why had he driven so far just to check on her?

They met for lunch at the nearby café.

"So, what gives? I know you didn't just happen my way. Something's up."

Jason glanced toward the door, a dead give-away she'd delved into deep water. He shrugged. "Nothing. Just wanted to stop in and see how the new business is doing. And tell you I'm proud of you."

Huh, what? She gulped. Proud of her? No one in her family had ever said that. Was he sick or did he need something? "Need I repeat myself? What gives?"

He grinned. "Honestly? A friend of yours made it very clear we've been less than supportive of you on something that's real important to you. Come on, don't say you haven't seen it."

"Seen what?"

"Your blog. You've got quite a following."

"Do I look like I have time for blogging and social media? Besides, whatever is there was put up by Caroline for advertising purposes. It's worked well, so I've left it to her literary skills since she's the one with the background in that. Are you telling me she's posting my personal business there too? I've had enough miscommunication via electronics for one lifetime. Don't need any more."

"She's good. And judging by the number of people that came through the shop today, effective. Listen, remember when we went over to Europe and Dad nearly panicked when he couldn't get in touch?"

"I didn't know he panicked, but I do remember about ten different missed calls in two hours while we were on the bicycle trip in the vineyards. It was one of the greatest experiences *ever*. Why?"

"Well, he called me at least *twenty* times. Then he left a message at the hotel desk and when I called, he screamed. I mean like never before. I heard words I didn't know he could even say … or knew. Bottom line, he was worried sick I'd led you down a path of danger and destruction. That I'd corrupted you. He was about five minutes away from jumping a plane when I called him back. He worries about you, Abs."

"All parents worry about their kids. That's normal."

"There's nothing normal about us. You know that. I mean, look at Jerrick. He's living on some farm in Montana and looks like a frickin' mountain man."

"He's developing a new strain of hybrid wheat to feed three times what a normal crop will. He's a genius."

"He's a hippie. And a genius. And me, I don't exactly fit the mold of perfect kid."

"You're kidding, right? The best tight end in the state as a junior. College football star. You graduated in four years with honors and have a job with the company making three times my annual budget for this shop. How much more perfect do you want to be? I used to roll my eyes when I followed you around Europe and the French girls trailed after your ass." She feigned an accent. "Oh, Jason, you have the sexiest voice. Your hair is so—soft." She reached up and thrust her fingers through his curls with no attempt at gentleness. Okay, maybe they were a little kinder. "I wasn't sure if you were *traveling* across Europe or *screwing* across it."

He grinned. "It *was* kinda fun, wasn't it? Still, you were the one they worried about the most. You always took on more than you could handle and expected too much. You never said a word about it when things got hard and we all wondered when you'd crack."

"That's ridiculous. No one even noticed what I did. Mom and Dad never had a kind word of support in anything. I doubt they even … "

"Knew or cared? Hell, you should have heard the phone call from Dad then. If you ever thought they didn't care, that would have cleared it up permanently."

"I'm in the middle. No one notices or fawns over the middle kid. They're not the first or the last."

"Which is why they're usually the sanest."

"Not really."

"Look. I know we don't say the things you want to hear much—"

"Like never."

He reached out and squeezed her arm. "But everyone cares. You know that, right?"

She let a couple seconds tick away as she let his words sink in. Sure they did. They were family. Still, they could have been a tiny bit supportive once in a while. "You know, I remember going to one of your games and sitting behind the cheerleaders. Dad came up to the gate as the team ran on the field as he always did. You stopped long enough for him to give you a huge hug and tell you he was proud of you … and to kick some ass."

"He did that every game."

Abby blinked back the sting in her eyes. "That's my point. Not once did I ever get that. Not once."

Jason brought the other arm up and wrapped her in a hug. "You didn't play football. He had no idea how to relate."

"He should have tried."

Jason dropped his arms and pulled back. "Think back. He said it in a different way. You never let him close enough to talk like he did with me. He was different with each of us. It took me a long time to understand it. Abby, you're the only one of us that can stand completely on your own two feet. No one has to tell you how proud we are because the only one you seem to have trouble pleasing is you, sis."

"That's ridiculous." But it was true. She never let herself think she was as good as they were. She always thought herself insignificant. He was right. Still, a few hugs and atta-girls would have been nice. "So, why did you come, really?"

He sighed. "You're holding out on us. Who's this guy you're seeing?"

Chapter Thirty-Three

Carter stared at the computer screen and cursed. The entire thing with Abby had been his fault from the beginning. Why hadn't he done this before?

A two-minute comparison of the paper from Roger that documented their most used numbers would have cleared the entire fiasco. He ran an Internet search on LinkedIn for Abby, then for Jackson. Roger had written the number down wrong. Ironically, the number Carter blocked weeks ago because he thought it was a telemarketer was the right one. If he simply had answered the phone instead of blocking it, the entire mess wouldn't have continued. He stared at Roger's list. Had he done that by accident?

There had to be karma in that, right?

Crap. He was starting to sound like Jackson … or his mom.

Carter picked up the phone and dialed the *right* number.

"We need to talk. Feel like lunch?"

• • •

There was something very satisfying about seeing his friend from childhood with no less than twenty extra pounds. Jackson's Johnson Murphy shoes were shined to perfection, but the designer shirt stretched across a small basketball that rolled over the top of his perfectly pressed designer khakis.

Carter smiled but didn't get up from his seat. "You're fat."

Jackson squeezed his tall, not-so-lanky physique into the seat across, and the shirt stretched further. Was it going to pop a button? He patted the roll above his belt lovingly. "What can I say? Life is good."

Is it? Carter frowned. He wanted to make it short. Admit his texting snafu and get it over with before walking away from Jax permanently. "So, tell me about your relationship with Abby."

Jackson's face screwed up in a look that Carter had known for years. "Who's Abby?" He didn't look away nor flinch. He was telling the truth.

"You know, running chick."

He nodded and opened his mouth. "Ooohhh, the crazy flower girl? Why the hell does everyone think I know her?"

For the first time in a couple of months, the baseball in the pit of Carter's stomach dislodged. "You don't?"

"Never seen her until she poured a gallon of water in my crotch. Wait, is she the one responsible for getting you into a green hulk suit in makeup at the craft fair?" He burst out laughing and slapped a hand to his knee. "My mother told me about the whole thing. In fact, I think there are some pictures floating around town somewhere. Another one of your historically big stunts the town will talk about for years. Look out, they may end up on Facebook."

Carter pounded a hand to the table, jolting Jackson's mirth away. "You said you met her first."

Jackson's humor wavered then disappeared. He adjusted in his chair.

A waiter arrived to take their order, which included a scotch and water for the overweight ex-bean pole and ex-friend. It hadn't helped the guy that the sun shone right on his midsection through the restaurant floor-to-ceiling windows. He was uncomfortable. Good.

"I was talking about Amanda. I met Amanda first. Several years before you, actually. We were friends in college. Then she landed an internship with Dad's office."

"You work together?"

"Not now. Only for a year. We did several projects together. She's damn smart and worked on a lot of the company contracts for jobs I sold. Then, without warning, she quit after a year. I never knew why."

"Are you telling me you were seeing Amanda when you introduced her to me? What the hell?"

The man's eyes collided back to Carter. "Hell, no. I hadn't seen her until that party. You and I both met her that night. Only, it was the *first* time for you. For me, it was like finding my high school sweetheart. I had no idea I'd missed her. We'd been such great friends, it never occurred to me there was more."

"So, you guys got back together."

"Not at first. You asked her out, remember? Here I was telling you it was time to trust again. To make an effort at a relationship and you picked the one damn woman that—"

"Don't shit me. You always wanted the ones I dated."

"That's ironic. I thought it was the other way around."

Carter cursed, but the baseball was gone from his gut. He should be completely pissed about Amanda, but the only emotion he felt was relief. It wasn't Abby. It never was. He grabbed his fork and cut a big slice of the enchilada on his plate. With a mouthful, he shook his head. "You and Amanda, that's crazy. I should beat the shit out of you, you know."

Jackson grinned. "Not near as crazy as you and the plant lady."

Not funny.

"You could have told me about Amanda from the start and saved us both a lot of trouble." He took another bite then washed it down with the drink he'd sent the waiter back for. He knew it was taboo during lunch, but one wouldn't be a big deal, would it? He needed something to keep him calm.

"Well, I hadn't even talked to her when you first met. The night we all went out for drinks to celebrate you landing the new assignment, I decided to ask her why she quit her job. Why she ran out without a word. She'd had a lot to drink, and while you were outside on the phone with some client from across the world, we talked. A lot. Turns out she left because of me. Anyway, one thing led to another and when you said you had to go to work, I took her home." Jackson looked away. He took her *home*.

"That was the week before she ditched me. You guys—"

"I know. She was tied in knots for days before we talked it out and decided we had to stay together. Then it was figuring out how to tell you. I was standing around the corner in case it got ugly. I told her it wouldn't, but she didn't believe me. I know you, man—I knew you weren't in it for the long haul, no matter how much you pretended. I saw the way you drooled over that runner in the park."

The light came on. Blaringly bright. Carter shook his head, gulped the last of the beer, and absorbed what he'd learned. What more could be said? All those years as kids, sparring and competing for kicks—and this?

He should be pissed, but the only thing that seemed to surface was relief. In truth, Amanda was more his style anyway. "Consider yourself off the hook, man. Why did you talk me into the baseball tickets? What was the point in that?"

"Don't you remember? You were going to buy her some expensive bracelet. The price tag alone was gonna set you back a week's pay. She'd never wear it and if you got it back, it'd be a total waste. At least with the tickets, you had something for yourself out of it. Something you could use."

"You weren't doing it for yourself?"

Jackson had the courtesy to look down. "I kinda hoped I'd go too. Once in a while. But I wasn't sure how things would turn out. I expected it to take a while to get past this. At least we're talking again though. That's good."

"I'd better get back to work." He tugged his wallet out and dropped some bills on the table. "Here's my part. We'll talk later."

Much later. He still needed to digest the screw-ups he'd started when he sent the first text to Abby. And the last text to Jackson.

Jackson reached out and held his arm. "Wait. There's one more thing you need to know."

Carter shrugged his hand away and scowled. "I think I can handle this one from here, Jax. I can be civil about Amanda because—well, it doesn't matter now, and Abby's history. But you're not going to screw up anything else in my life. Sorry."

"Don't *do* that to yourself, man. Listen to me. If you don't, you're gonna regret it."

That caught Carter's attention. *He seriously thinks I can make a bigger mess than he's already made?* What a complete ass. "Listen to you? Are you kidding me? What's happened to you, man? Do you get a sick pleasure out of screwing up the good parts of my life?" *Screech.* His chair legs were like fingers on a chalkboard as he jolted up. The chair toppled and the entire restaurant glanced his way. Carter ignored them. "Not this time, Jax. I've known you all my life and until now, I hadn't realized what an asshole you are. I appreciate you getting me in the door with the Asians, but … "

Jackson's voice remained calm. "That's exactly why I'm here. I did the intro—and I can't let this go down the way—"

"It's not up to you."

"Look, you're pissed at me about Amanda. I get that. This is different. This is your career."

Carter yanked a fistful of Jackson's shirt up and leaned lower. "And you want me to fail. Why? Is this competition we've had since high school really that big of a deal to you? Jesus, Jax, get over it. Nobody cares anymore."

Jackson darted a glance around the room over the cloth that was under his nose. He sighed and held up his hands in a surrendering gesture. "You're right. No one cares. Not even then, but think about it, Carter. I've known you since you were a snot-nosed kid that took showers once a week and hated girls. We built forts in the trees and fished in your pond. You changed. When Carley died, you caved in, man. My best friend … tanked. How the hell was I supposed to get you back? Guys don't hug and kiss and talk shit out. We—compete."

Carter rolled his eyes. "So all this is just therapy for me? Yeah, right."

"Not for you, idiot. For me. You want to know why my parents moved to that po-dunk town? Because I was a shit-ass kid destined to either be in gang fights, on drugs or dealing them. I had a temper a mile long and nowhere to vent it. They planted me in that little town to get me away from trouble. *You* were *my* therapy, dumbass. The only siblings I had were you and Carley. You made me stop hating and start being a kid. I lost both of you when she dove into that water. So, yeah, I started throwing challenges at you. Every chance I got. It was the only way to get my brother back. You didn't seem to respond to anything else."

Carter winced. He pulled in a breath and clamped his eyes shut. Not once in all these years had he given a thought as to how his family trauma had affected Jackson. It never occurred to him it had. His stomach churned as if he'd been sucker-punched. He opened his mouth to speak but couldn't.

Jackson clamped a fist over Carter's fingers on his shirt. "You made me a better man, bro. I'm not going to let some half-assed investor who can't manage his money take you down. I don't intend to let you walk away from someone you want … or need … either. Nor am I going to let Roger's slip-up on the number ruin our friendship forever. That was an idiot trick and I told him at the time. My mouth-fart in that meeting didn't help either. Here I was, my best friend planning a serious relationship with a girl that had abandoned me. I just … went off. That wasn't how it was supposed to go. Look, we messed up all the crap with Abby because we care. Roger bumbled the numbers intentionally. Maybe it wasn't the right way to do it, but he knew just like I did that she's right. Carter, sometimes you just can't let the fences down long enough to see what's waiting for you. Carley never wanted you to be alone, never trusting anyone. What kind of life is that?"

Carter's mouth dropped.

...

Her family made the effort to come to visit and decided to go to the—Astros game? Seriously? It wasn't a bad thing because she loved her team, but certainly unexpected. Not to mention they'd come from so many different places to see her and there was catching up to do.

Surely they'd change their minds? Apparently not. Jason had bought tickets on the third base line, right next to the dugout, so he could make a valiant effort at heckling the opposing team. Abby rolled her eyes when he started the first round of insults before a single pitch had crossed the plate. It had been his mode of operation since Little League. She'd hated it then and now. As a teen, she made sure to sit as far from him as possible, hoping no one knew they were blood. Fat chance. Tonight, she'd grin and bear it with pride because her entire family was visiting for the first time ever. Who knows? Maybe the Astros would win too— they were certainly due. It had been a rough season.

Besides, this week she'd decided to finally clear the air with Carter and her conscience would be clean and clear for the first time in months. She'd call him tomorrow. Her shoulders had knots the size of boulders and she couldn't wait to get rid of the tension. Her family would be her support system.

Abby surveyed the empty seats flanking her. Except they'd all disappeared and left her—alone again. *Great. The national anthem hasn't even begun and they all ran off.* She shrugged. Probably to shop or load up on beer and hotdogs.

The two-story-sized speakers crackled above then burst into action. "Ladies and gentlemen, we have a special program for you tonight. As you know, the Astros have entered the social media arena and our marketing group heavily searches for ways to improve our branding and offer you a better baseball experience. We also love finding local businesses that portray the spirit and entrepreneurial attitude that makes Houston a great place to live. Lisa, in marketing, happened onto one such business recently and tweeted out a link."

"All of you responded in force and gave amazing support—not just to the business, but to the people affected by the business. Soooo, one gentleman whom you all decided to adopt and—let's say—show the way, wanted to return the favor. Everyone, give a hand for—"

"Excuse me, ma'am. Can you come with me please?" Abigail rotated to a stadium employee with a security badge.

Huh? Is something wrong? Did Jason do something stupid like attempt to run out on the field? Dammit! He did. Her brother was standing next to another security staffer. Right next to the rest of her family ... *on the field.* What the hell?

"What have they done? Am I in trouble? I had nothing to do with whatever it is, okay?"

Her family had been in town less than a few hours and already made their presence known in front of the biggest crowd ever. She wanted to run into the bathroom and hide, but the security person slipped his fingers around her arm and motioned her to the steps then to an elevator that required a special key. "You're not in trouble. Right this way, ma'am."

She might not be in trouble, but whatever they'd planned was going to be *serious* trouble when they made it back to her place. Maybe the lack of family involvement the past few years was a plus. How many times had she been publicly humiliated before?

None. Okay, except for baring her undies at a craft fair, but that was her own fault.

Holy crap, the entire baseball team was standing in front of her and this guy was leading her—to them? He opened a gate and motioned for her to step onto the grass.

This was surreal—her pseudo-bodyguard led her down the third base line then across to second. She shook hands with each of the baseball players and they handed her—roses? It wasn't Valentine's Day, or her birthday. There were no holidays nearby. She smiled and thanked each of them. *God, it would be nice to think up something witty. If I could swallow my tongue long enough to do so. And if I knew what the hell this was about. Has the anthem been sung yet? I am NOT singing. No way.* She shook her head as another rose was thrust her way.

"You don't want it?" *Bo Porter, the Astros manager is talking to me? Someone prop me up before I pass out.*

"Oh, uh, yes. Thank you. By the way—I've been watching your son. Think he'll match your record?"

The man winked and laughed. "I've been watching him too—and if genetics has anything to do with it, we'll see."

Yay. The end of the line. Now what? Her stomach churned. What was the entire stadium about to witness, and why did her family stand there waiting? *With flowers.* Good grief. She worked with flowers all day. It wasn't a big deal.

They all had daisies, her favorite—second to orchids, of course. Orchids were too high maintenance. Aw, that had to be Jason's idea—he was the only one she'd told.

"Step aside, old man."

She *knew* that voice. Intimately. Carter?

A hand slipped out and shoved Bo just before *he* stepped out. "Hi, there."

Uh-oh—her gut was quaking. Her knees started to buckle.

He grabbed her hand to stabilize her. "You okay?" *Damn that smile.*

She could stare at him all day. In fact, she probably was staring.

"Uh, I think so. You did all this?" She waved at the crowd. Holy shit they were standing. For her? Her ears were ringing and dark circles clouded her vision. "I think I'm going to pass out. Carter, look—I told you I'm sorry. I really never meant—" She grabbed his bicep to keep her knees from buckling.

He was going to do this right here in front of an entire stadium full of people? He grinned. "I know you never meant to hurt me. You never wanted to cause all the commotion. And you never meant to lie. Basically, you meant to stand in the background, but that didn't work. Here, I brought you flowers."

She stared at the froth of color he handed her. Orchids. "But you hate flowers."

"I had a phobia about them, yes—which some of these people pointed out over and over again. I'm working on it."

"I love orchids." Abby peered deeper at the colors. "And daisies."

He stepped in so close she smelled him. "Your brother told me. About the daisies. Caroline mentioned the orchids." He pointed behind her and she swerved to see ... Caroline? Yep, and Roger. Hmmm, and the two exes? As in ex-girlfriend and ex-best friend?

Abby brought her gaze back to Carter, knowing he was the only thing that kept her from fainting into the plastic cushion of second base. "You want to tell me what this is all about?"

"Sure, it's about you. I have a question to ask."

She vaguely heard the crowd cheer and an announcer's voice. The signs across the top of the stadium blared in bright white lights: "Will she?" Uh-oh. The clamminess of her skin took over and her eyes went completely black. *Thump.* She smelled the dirt just before her face planted into it over the mound of second base. Then she saw nothing. Voices around her clamored.

She had no idea how long she lay there. Passed out on the Astros baseball field. Before an entire stadium of people. When her eyes finally cooperated and she was able to open them, Carter was right in front of her. And he was smiling. Geez, she wished he'd stop that. Or maybe not. It was the only thing that had kept her from passing out earlier and the one thing she could focus on now. The thunder of the fans yelling, whistling, and cheering roared around them.

And he laughed!

She furrowed her brows. "Knock it off. This isn't the least bit funny. I just passed out in front of a baseball stadium of people, my family, *and* the entire Astros team. You brought me here for this? I mean I know I … "

"Abby, I just want to ask you a very easy question."

She held up a finger to stop him and shook her head. "No! I don't even know you. I mean we weren't even … okay, maybe I do know you *that* way … but not this way."

He grabbed her face with both hands and she stopped talking when he leaned in and pressed his forehead to hers. "Not *that* question, babe. Neither one of us is ready for that yet. Abs, you said you always wanted to do this with someone that you cared about."

Her face burned. "Eventually most people want to…"

"Would you kisscam me?"

Huh, what? Kisscam? Not … "Oh. Uh, you did all this just for—the kisscam?" She looked up and saw the two of them on every camera in the stadium. Yikes. She had dirt in her hair and plastered to her neck. And white chalk from the baseline!

Carter shook his head. "I didn't." He waved at the people down the first base line, which included his family, the exes, Caroline, and a few strangers. "They did. Well, actually *we* did. They had to beat it into my head about the flowers and then I made them pay for it by showing up here. I told them I got the message, but I wasn't going to believe it unless you did."

"Believe what?"

"That being the center of attention with flowers—or cameras—or the media can be good if there's love and affection behind it. No matter what the situation. You really should read your blog someday. Caroline has really done a number on both of us. So, all these people are tired of waiting to find out."

She blinked because her eyes had stayed open and were dry. "Find out what?"

"If you're going to kiss me so we can get this game started."

Holy shit. He had done all this just to get her out here for something that she'd mentioned in passing. And the flowers. They were splayed around her like spilled cards. A carpet of color and scents. She slid her hands up his shirt and wrapped the collar tight in her fingers. Then she yanked him in. Yep. She kissed him on the kisscam in front of the world. The roar of the crowd around them was nothing compared to the thunder of her heart thumping.

When they finally separated, she sighed. "I'm sorry I wasn't Jackson and I answered your messages."

"I'm not."

She let her weight sink into him. That was good. Maybe she wasn't sorry, either. But … there was still one more thing—

"Oh, and Abs, Caroline told me about your *other* identity."

Her eyes popped up. "So you know I'm 'She Hearts Dogs.' You're not mad?"

"I was at first, then I realized something. That was the *real* us. The way things *should have happened* if meddling friends and family hadn't gotten involved. See, no matter how hard we fight this thing, you and I will just keep getting thrown together until we stick."

Her insides heated. "You think so?" He wanted them to stick? She liked the sound of that.

Epilogue

Eight months, one week, and two days later …

Carter scooted his barstool to the table and held up a hand to the bartender to order a beer. Jackson and Roger sat opposite and two other newbies from the office flanked him. "Sorry I'm late, guys. What's the score?" They'd all agreed to watch the game at the sports bar by the office, since time was short.

"Five to three, good guys." Jackson drew from his glass. "What took you so long?"

"I had to make a pit stop. Check this out." Carter pulled the box from his pocket and set it on the table. The entire group did a double-take.

"Whoa," Roger said. "Is that what I think it is?"

Carter popped the lid open to display the diamond nestled in the white silk lining. "Yep, sure is. What d'ya think?" He grinned.

Jackson leaned forward. "So, she's seriously the model you want to buy, bro? You sure about that, mister short-term lease? I mean, she's nice and all, but that's … big."

Carter punched him in the arm, enjoying the pain as his friend attempted to rub it away. "You're one to talk. You're biting the bullet in what … two weeks?"

Jackson relaxed back. "Good point. Still, you guys have only been together a year. What's the rush?"

"It's almost two years if you count all the time we were dodging each other because of you, asshole."

Jackson held up his hands. "Hey, I had nothing to do with that … uh … okay, well, maybe a little, but not with Abby. That was all your mess. So, what makes you think she'll say yes?"

The scent caught his attention before her voice, but he knew Abby was behind him when Roger blurted out a curse and looked past his shoulder.

"What makes you think she won't?" she said.

Carter whirled in his chair.

Abby dropped both hands to her hips and challenged Jackson. "Hmmm?"

Dammit, this wasn't right. *Jackson.* He furrowed his brow and growled at the man across from him. "Dammit, Jackson—do you have to screw up *everything* for me?"

Carter wrapped his arms around and drew Abby into a kiss so long his friends turned to the game and Roger muttered, "Get a room."

When they broke free, her eyes had water puddled in them and they glittered like stars. He put his forehead to hers. "So, um, this wasn't exactly what I had planned. Pretend you didn't see that."

She untangled an arm from his chest and pulled the box from the table then slipped the ring into place. "We promised each other honesty, remember? Pretending would be a lie. Besides, I honestly want to wear it and—the answer is yes."

"I'm sorry. I meant to ask you at dinner later with candles and wine. And flowers. I love you, Abs. As in foreverness."

She giggled and pulled him back in for a kiss. "I love you as in foreverness too."

He gave Jackson another scolding glare, though it was lost on the man as he lifted his drink to toast them.

Carter snorted. "Remind me to make your life as miserable as you've made mine someday."

Amanda approached in her perfectly starched business suit and Jackson pulled her in tight. "You'll get your chance in two weeks, best man."

"Huh, what? I thought Roger was the best man." Best man? In Jackson and Amanda's wedding? It was ironic if he stopped to think.

"I wasn't sure you'd want it so I asked him first—but you know I'd never really want anyone else. Sorry, Roger."

Roger nodded and stuck a finger in the air. "You guys all make me sick anyway." Still, he winked at Abby.

Was Carter ready to write off all that happened? He wasn't sure. Then Abby gave him that damned smile that killed him during the seventh inning stretch. Yeah, he guessed so.

"Okay, I'll be your damn best man, but you need to know—paybacks are hell."

About the Author

A little about me … I grew up on a farm near a small town called Peculiar, which is just south of Kansas City. I'm a graduate of Oklahoma State University with additional post-graduate studies at OSU and University of Wyoming in Casper. I married my college sweetheart while still an undergraduate, and we have three kids.

I've had a long and prosperous career in technology and still actively work as a technology consultant. A few years ago, I chose to go back to my first love of writing and have enjoyed every word. I hope you will too.

More from This Author

(From *The Designated Drivers' Club* by Shelley K. Wall)

The wind shoved Jenny Madison through the bar door into the mass of noise and people. A paper sign taped to the window fluttered next to her, an advertisement for the play Home is Love. A clever patron had crossed the word home and penned DRINKING over.

Jenny concentrated on the prior word and squelched a desire to go there.

"Yeah, and you'll be locked out of it if you don't get busy," she muttered. Her boss' words rang heavily, scratch that, ex-boss'. He had fired her because her attitude didn't fit their work environment. A stack of bills pended disaster if she didn't forge ahead.

Jenny walked with faked confidence into the crowded club. She carried business cards, monogrammed notepads, and refrigerator magnets with her new business name. This was her fourth stop of the evening. She adjusted her denim skirt down over her legs and tugged the lapels of her black jacket forward. Admittedly, it wasn't as professional as she wanted but it sufficed. She had not worn heels in a month and now that she donned a pair, her feet complained.

"The Designated Driver's Club." A petite brunette with studs in her eyebrow read from the business card. "What does that mean?"

"It's a membership thing. You pay either annually or monthly. We pick you up anywhere you want and take you home, then back to your car the next day—or we deliver it if preferred. Our drivers are safe, alcohol-free, have good driving records, and we guarantee you won't get a DUI." Jenny mustered up her best cheerful smile. "And all for a price that's less than the cost of a ticket."

"You'll pick up anywhere in the city?" The girl's stud lifted along with the brow attached to it.

"Yes. Anywhere."

"Wow. Great idea."

"Thanks. You can sign up on the website listed on the card, or call that number there." Jenny ran her finger along the print. "We take all major credit cards. Oh, and we don't lecture anyone or give them a hard time. Our drivers are courteous and confidential. We recognize everyone needs to have a good time once in a while—we just want it to end well, too."

She flashed a final smile at the table, ran her tongue over her teeth and moved on. Her cheeks ached and her lips cracked from forced cheerfulness. A few more tables and she would step back outside and teeter her heeled feet to the car.

"Hey!" A tall twenty-something guy with shaggy dark hair called after her. "How many drivers do you have?"

"Enough," she answered with fake assurance. Okay, a little white lie—but she doubted it would matter. If, by chance, she had more calls than she could handle, she could recruit a few friends to help. Or—even better—hire someone. Her own staff. That sounded impressive.

Jenny whipped around to get the final tables just in time to meet a cocktail waitress head-on. The waitress was quick and evaded the collision. Jenny wasn't as speedy. Her hand full of cards and goodies fluttered to the floor, spreading out in a small carpet of paper. Footsteps threatened to trample her stash. She let out a curse, bent, gathered them quickly and rose with a huff.

"Nice." A male voice admired from behind her. She turned, catching blue twinkling eyes focused on her backside. Her face reddened as she remembered her denim skirt had "bite me" emblazoned on the pocket. She had a black jacket over it and thought it would cover everything enough to look professional but casual. Ignoring his chuckle, she plopped a few business cards and notepads on the table. The men with him picked up the cards and read.

"Check this out, Buzz." A man with highlighted brown hair and a torn handkerchief around his neck flipped a card in front of the blue eyes.

"Hmmm." He lifted the card with long, slender fingers. "So … bite me girl, what's this about?"

Jenny launched into her monologue, consciously aware of the blue eyes boring into hers as she spoke. When she finished, he lazily glanced down to her hands, then back up.

Mr. Highlights and handkerchief leaned over, both elbows on the table, and grinned. "Do you have a quota on how many times a person can call?" he asked. The other two guys with them laughed. "See, Buzz here, has a tendency to overdo it—a lot. You know, brokenhearted, luckless guy … drowning his sorrows. If it weren't for me, he'd use a service like this almost every night."

Buzz Blue Eyes shot him a murderous glare. "John, you know you'd be lonely if I didn't call you. You can't stand to stay home every night anyway." He tapped the business card up and down on the table. "I'm David."

"Not Buzz?"

"Nickname. Thanks to these idiots." He jerked a thumb at the group flanking him and introduced them one by one. "John, Kevin, and Grady."

"I'm Jenny … and a membership allows you two pickups a month. Anything more has a minimal charge attached." She forced the smile and held out her hand. She made it up on the fly, but they wouldn't know that.

"Yeah." David lifted the card. "Jenny Madison. The girl with two first names." Observant guy.

"And bite me on her bum," Grady chirped in a British accent.

Jenny glanced at the Paul McCartney wannabe and said, "You're British?"

"No, Grady's from Kansas City. He just does that to attract chicks," David clarified.

"What do you expect?" John laughed, "Look at him—if you look like that you better have a gimmick."

Okay, they're somewhat funny, in a brother-trying-to-be-bad-boy way, she thought. "Well, nice talking to you gentlemen." She tossed a wave at them, dropped some cards at the next table and headed for the door. Cory, the bartender, nodded once in acknowledgement.

Jenny glanced back over a shoulder briefly before shoving out the heavy wooden door. Buzz Blue Eyes waved before turning to the redhead that had slipped into the booth next to him.

• • •

Jenny patted the hood of her black Mercedes. "Maybe I'll get to keep you after all. Let's cross our fingers and hope." The car had been a splurge last year. She had driven an almost-antique Toyota until that point. When the heat went out on it, the cost to repair was more than the Blue Book value. A trail of repair costs had haunted her so long; she finally gave into her friends' urging for a replacement when she got the pittance of trust money from her dad. Had she predicted the current outcome, perhaps she'd have chosen a small, used Chevy at the time.

• • •

Three weeks later, Jenny happily set up an automatic pay schedule for her car payment and rent. A monumental step from the scrimping and saving she was used to. Steady income was not to be overrated. She decided to celebrate and meet the girls at Foxy's, their normal bar. She would not drink this time—just in case a call came in.

Presently, there were forty clients signed up for her service and a steady stream of calls for pickup. Her work schedule had completely flip-flopped from the old office job. Now she usually started around six P.M. and received calls as late as three or four in the morning. Sleep came during the day, rather than night. Her new forced wake-up time was noon. Mainly because she had to get out and enjoy the daylight or she would go crazy. The nocturnal vampire lifestyle was interesting but wearing.

The stuttered tone of her new hands-free phone interrupted her thoughts. She looked at the display—a work call. "Great," she muttered. She had just pulled into the lot at Foxy's.

A customer pickup at the cliffs was a novelty—one that piqued her interest and drew fear at the same time. Jenny hadn't been there since high school. Still, her service guaranteed a pickup anywhere. The absence of streetlights would have been creepy but for the full moon lighting the way. Regardless, when a rabbit jumped into the road and bounded for the trees she freaked and let out a squeal, then giggled nervously at her skittishness. A subtle noise motivated her to roll down the window despite her fear. She heard … singing. A lilting, strong, male voice belted it out somewhere ahead. Her headlights shone on the frame of a man sitting on the ground at the edge of the cliffs, his head back, and his mouth open. Singing.

Jenny got out of the car. Saying anything at all might send the person over the edge, so she eased up next to him and sat too. A comfortable distance initiated between them. No way was she going to dangle her legs like that. It was too far to fall; she just let her feet hang slightly over.

"Scared of heights, Jenny Madison?" the man asked. She peered into the shadows caused by the headlights on his back.

"David, right?"

"Yeah. Thanks for coming. I didn't know you also did the driving."

"Uh, we're a little short-handed tonight." And every other night too.

"Isn't this place great? I love the natural acoustics."

Over his shoulder, fireflies blinked a scattered dance in the dark sky. He leaned back in the dirt and put his hands behind his bushy hair.

"You okay?" she asked.

"Good enough. We had a bad night tonight. The fans were flat." Fans? She knew he couldn't see her look at him, but she lifted an eyebrow anyway.

"What constitutes a bad night?"

"I'm in a band. We play small gigs around the city." He said it nonchalantly, as if she should have known.

"That's cool. What's the name of your band?"

"Blind Optimism."

"Hmmm. I don't think I know it." Funny name.

He laughed. "We played at the Jazz House tonight. We sucked."

"Is that why you're here?" She leaned back and laced her hands behind her head too, staring up at the stars and fireflies.

"I guess. I like to come up here and try a tune out occasionally—without all the back—up music. It gives me a chance to listen to the voice and the words on their own."

"Makes sense. It sounded good when I walked up. Was that one of your songs?"

He chuckled. "The one they hated."

"Oh, well—it sounded good to me. Maybe the backup was the problem and not the song. So, the guys with you last month were your band?"

"Mmm hmmm," he acknowledged, his eyes starting to close.

"Well, David—the rock star—Buzz. Let's get you home." She lifted up and pulled on his arm to move him away from the cliff and get him to his feet. Jenny noticed the pile of bottles on the ground behind him when they walked into the headlights' glare.

She punched in the destination on her GPS and turned the car around. A few minutes later, his head was laid back against the headrest, eyes closed. The open mouth and soft huffing told her he was asleep. His head rolled to the side when they pulled into a clean but aging subdivision. From the rearview mirror, she thought his eyes registered their location.

David adjusted his lanky frame to a sitting position. "Are you from here, Jenny Madison?"

"No, Texas." She met his eyes briefly.

"Me, too. Where in Texas?"

"Wayward. You know it?" She glanced again.

"I've been through it once or twice. Near Austin, isn't it?" She nodded. He laughed. Not a loud boisterous laugh—just a lyrical expression of humor.

"What?"

"I just wondered what the parents of the small town girl with two first names ... and bite me on her ass, felt about her being this far from home."

"They always told me that Wayward fit me great but I didn't necessarily fit it."

"That sounds like a riddle. What the hell is it supposed to mean?"

She laughed this time. It startled her to hear it. "I think that's a very polite way of calling me a misfit." She turned off the engine in front of the house. "Do you need help in the door?"

"Is that part of the service?" His eyes widened as he spoke.

"Don't start getting ideas, Band Boy. We just make sure you get inside, we don't go in."

"I didn't mean ... No, I'm good. Thanks!" He got out. With hands in his pockets, he strolled slowly up the drive and into the house. Jenny went home and looked up Blind Optimism on the Internet. She downloaded and listened to the videos. Not bad. A little too cheerful for her, but they had talent. Or at least he did.

•••

Two months later her business had grown to seventy members. Out of boredom Katy agreed to help part-time. David was now officially a regular. He called every two weeks, mostly from the cliffs. Once, she was summoned from the bar where she met him. Each time, he was alone when she arrived. He never really seemed like he needed a ride home.

She wondered if it would be rude to start giving clients sobriety tests. It would kill her to admit it but she looked forward to his calls. He was nice to talk to. At the cliffs, she had listened to him for hours. She had even bared her soul a little too.

Now that Katy was helping, she decided to take her first night off in three months. It was Sunday and Katy had mocked her. They rarely got more than one call on a Sunday anyway so it almost didn't count as a day off.

The doorbell to her apartment chimed. She peeked through the small hole. A delivery. Why would anyone deliver on Sunday?

"Ms. Madison?"

"That's me."

"I have your tickets here. Can you please sign right on that line there?" The man pointed to a dotted line.

"I didn't order tickets."

"There's a note." He handed her an envelope. "Have a good time," he said as he turned to leave. She opened the envelope. One ticket to Rock Fest in the Canyon. The note read:

Jenny,

You were never meant to fit in.

In Wayward or anywhere else.

You were born to stand out.

David Keith

A man with two first names sent her concert tickets? No. She looked at the lone paper addressed to her business, which was also her home address. Correction. Concert ticket. Singular. The list of bands on the ticket included his. The time was—today. He wanted her there.

• • •

It took her two hours to talk herself into going. She hated going solo to public places. It was so awkward to be alone in a crowd of people. She voiced her concerns outwardly, as she shoved her way through the crowd to her seat. Blind Optimism was the opening act. Jenny practiced a response should his earlier evaluation of their talent be accurate. Listening to him berate his group was one thing, but if he gave her the ticket in order to see a supportive face in the crowd—well, she hoped she didn't have to lie. She prayed her own evaluation was more accurate than his.

He waved when he walked on stage. He looked right at her when he sang … and the other ten thousand people in the park, of course. With all the lights, she doubted he received more than a glimpse of her. Yet, she imagined otherwise. The idea that he harmonized only for her breezed cheerfully through her head along with the tune they performed. She was rewarded between songs. He sent her drinks with a note. I am the designated driver today. Charming. She raised a glass to him in thanks. The drinks waited on the floor as she rose with the rest of the crowd and danced to the music. His voice could charm the chrome off a car. The glare of the lights enhanced the sparkling color in his blue eyes as he serenaded her and the thousands of people around her. She thrilled at his success and could see he mirrored the feeling.

"What do you think of them?" the man sitting next to her asked. She turned to a middle-aged, friendly faced black man with a bit too much fashion sense.

"I like them! They were pretty upbeat, don't you think?"

"I guess," he answered.

"You didn't like them?"

"The bigger question is ... would you buy their music?" Strange question from a random stranger. Jenny looked past him to see a man with dark waves talking to someone on his other side.

"Of course I would! The guy's got a great voice, a happy smile, the kind that makes you want to ... "

"Yes! That's the answer I wanted." The guy gave her a quick smile. He patted Jenny's arm and turned back to his company. "Let's go." The man and the two sitting with him rose and left, without even seeing the headliner.

Fifteen minutes after David's band cleared the stage, a man plopped into the empty seat next to Jenny. Apparently, this guy only cared about the main act. She mused that he missed a pretty good show by arriving late. She watched the band warming up onstage. The man's leg rubbed hers. Jenny edged away and frowned. The nerve! His fingers tickled her side. Now, that was too much.

"Hey buster!" she spat, knotting her fingers into a fist. Then she turned. Her mouth dropped. It seemed laughter and blue eyes were a very sexy mix.

"Hi, Jenny Madison." David's voice was melodic, even when saying her name. "What did you think?"

He had changed shirts and wore a hat to cover his hair. He smelled good. Spicy. He had showered. She stared for a second, and then cleared her throat. "Your drummer gets too loud, and your backup singer was off key on the second song for a short while.

He laughed and touched his lips lightly with hers. She didn't hit him but thought about it.

"And I see you're happy to be here," he responded.

"Some guy has been plying me with alcohol," she quipped. "Here, have one. I have three." She waved a hand over three glasses, one empty, and two full.

"What a creep." A slow grin crossed his face. "I'll pass."

"Since when?"

"Since two months ago."

"But I've driven you home four times."

"Yeah. I wanted to make sure I got my money's worth, even if I didn't need it anymore. Besides, how else was I going to see you?" His lips turned up again. "Devious, aren't I?"

"Absolutely sinful." She tried to keep her mouth straight but couldn't. The corners lifted and she let her teeth show.

"Did that hurt?"

"What?"

"The smile. I haven't seen it much since you dropped your business card on our table." He laced his fingers into hers. "It looks good on you."

"Well, don't get used to it."

"I'd like to." He turned to face her. "Isn't this fantastic?" Excitement in those blue eyes was even sexier. He continued, "I mean—look at us—I'm opening for a major band. Your business is soaring." He fell back into his seat. The look of pure pleasure on his face was refreshing.

"Yeah, I guess it is fantastic." She would have never believed it herself four months earlier.

"Jenny Madison from Wayward?"

"Hmmm?"

"I think you're my good luck charm, can I be your designated driver tonight?"

She thought for a minute. "Okay, but only because the service I use is short-staffed." She giggled.

"This is going to sound cliché but … I like you, Jenny. You make me laugh, and it really jazzes me when you laugh."

"Well, don't get used to that, either."

"What? Liking you?"

"No. Me laughing," she stated. "I don't do it much."

"We'll have to work on that."

• • •

Grant Tucker had noticed the girl in the seat next to Hodge when she sat down. Brown waves, big chocolate-colored eyes, long legs, and a smile that filled her face. She was entranced by the music and alone. A groupie for this little unknown band? Surely not. They're not that good. Why else would she come alone though? He watched her for a while and found it interesting the way she tried to contain the smile that hinted at dimples. As if she enjoyed the music but wanted not to. Or maybe she just had trouble enjoying herself period?

When Hodge asked her opinion of the band, a thing he always did when checking out new talents, Grant found himself listening to her rather than the band's current agent sitting next to him. The voice almost didn't match. It was low, husky, and almost gruff. Incredibly sexy.

Upon Hodge's signal to leave, he escorted his boss and one of their clients from the concert. They weren't interested in the main show. Since the band was already a client, they'd seen this performance more times than could be counted. As they slipped behind the curtain and headed for the back gate, he glanced back to see if she was still there. She was, but the seat next to her was no longer empty. He shrugged. No matter. He had no desire to strike up a conversation with a fame-seeking fan anyway. Been there. Done that. Had the bruised wallet and empty apartment to prove it.

Also check out these titles by Shelley K. Wall:

Numbers Never Lie

Praise for *Numbers Never Lie:*

"Shelley K. Wall calculates a successfully suspenseful romantic tale with this digital page-turner. I loved the supporting characters as they added a fantastic depth to the story. I'm looking forward to seeing what else this author has to offer, and if it is half as interesting as this story it will be well worth picking up."—Night Owl Reviews

"This was one of those reads that had it all: a heavy dose of suspense that kept me glued to the edge of my seat, enough action to make me want to scream out loud, and a lovely touch of mystery and romance. I recommend this one for everyone and anyone; you will not be disappointed. Think John Grisham meets romance … with a touch of *Mission Impossible!*"—Harlequin Junkie

"Corporate shenanigans, betrayal, and a happy ever after are all highlighted in this exciting thriller by Wall. Additionally, there's enough technical jargon to give credence to the story without overwhelming the reader."—RT Book Reviews

Bring It On

Praise for *Bring It On:*

"…a romance full of excitement and intrigue that will keep you turning the pages … If you want a fun, sexy and intriguing read, then this book is for you."—Harlequin Junkies

In the mood for more Crimson Romance?
Check out *Drive Me Sane* by Dena Rogers
at *CrimsonRomance.com.*

Made in the USA
San Bernardino, CA
01 December 2014